Line of Sight

Sasha Thibodaux Series
Book Three

Ali Spooner

Line of Sight

Sasha Thibodaux Series

Book Three

Ali Spooner

Affinity
eBook Press
NZ
2016

Line of Sight

Affinity E-Book Press NZ LTD.
Canterbury, New Zealand

1st Edition

ISBN: 978-0-908351-12-1

This is a work of fiction. Names, character, places, and incidents are the product of the author's imagination or are used fictitiously and any resemblance to actual persons living or dead, businesses, companies, events, or locales is entirely coincidental.

Editor: Ruth Stanley
Proof Editor: Alexis Smith
Cover Design: Irish Dragon Designs

Acknowledgments

I would like to thank my fans for following my stories, providing great feedback and encouragement. Writing wouldn't be so much fun without you. Thanks to Affinity, Irish Dragon for the cover art and the team of editors, readers, and publishers who continue to help me grow as a writer.

Dedication

To Mom, wish you were here to share these stories.

Also by Ali Spooner

Shotgun Rider
The Settlement
Ruined
Terminal Event
Love's Playlist
Cowgirl Up
Twisted Lives
The Epitaph
Bailey's Run
Sugarland
Bayou Justice

Table of Contents

Chapter One

Sasha's eyes stared at her television set. She watched the approach of Hurricane Katrina, the storm taking aim on the Mississippi Gulf Coast. The forecasts of the storm would bring her on land for the second time near Gulfport, but she knew the close proximity of the storm would bring devastation to New Orleans. The city's levee systems and storm pumps were antiquated, stressed beyond their performance limits even during heavy thunderstorms. Sasha knew the city of her childhood well and shuddered when she thought about how unprepared the residents of the city were for what they were about to be challenged with. Her heart ached for the loss that was to strike her beloved hometown, but Sasha knew there was little to be done. The time for action had rapidly slipped away.

†

Kara entered the parlor to find her love in the same position she had been sitting in for the last four hours.

"You, my dear, must take a break from that television set," Kara said as she sat in Sasha's lap, blocking her view of the television.

Sasha moved her head around Kara to gaze at the screen. "This is going to be horrific," Sasha said. "We aren't prepared for a storm of this magnitude and the officials are dragging their feet on evacuation orders."

"So many of the people won't heed them anyway," Kara said, further darkening Sasha's mood.

"Unfortunately, that's true. So many of the residents have lived in their small neighborhoods for their entire life and feel like they are safely tucked away in their homes." She shook her head. "Still, I can't believe they are so blind to the forecasters' warnings to evacuate to higher land."

"For years they've lived with the predictions that a super storm would hit New Orleans and when years pass with no storm, they grow increasingly complacent in their preparations and plans to evacuate." Kara sighed deeply as she ran her fingers through Sasha's hair. "Now that they're facing the very storm they've been warned of for years, they've frozen in their shoes like a deer in headlights."

"I just wish there were something I could do to prevent the devastation that's going to occur," Sasha said.

"I know you do, my love, but there's little that can be done now. You've evacuated my office staff and our closest friends to Baton Rouge where they'll be safe from harm." Kara could see the distress written across Sasha's face as the newest reports were broadcast stating Katrina had been upgraded to a Category Five storm. "The city is in God's hands now," Kara said.

Kara saw the tears glistening in Sasha's eyes as she finally looked directly at her. "I know you're right, but my heart still aches for the families who won't survive this storm."

"Come with me, so I can get a hot meal into you. When the time comes and it's safe, we'll go into town and help those we can," Kara said.

Sasha nodded her head, still saddened by what was about to occur, and followed Kara into the kitchen. Kara had made fresh biscuits with chicken and dumplings. The food was on the table waiting for them. Sasha smiled softly when she saw the meal. It had been Milly's favorite meal, her comfort food if you will, and Sasha sat down to eat with the memory of her lost love still weighing on her mind.

"Will we be safe here?" Kara asked nervously.

"We may experience some flooding from the heavy rains, but we are well protected otherwise. The standby generator has plenty of fuel, and we have food and serum to last several weeks."

"Will the animals be safe?"

"I've secured the stall doors open in the barn for the horses," Sasha said. "They will more than likely stay out in the open as the rains begin, but have the option of moving to cover if they'd feel more secure."

"I'm so happy you are with me, Sasha. I would have no clue how to prepare for a storm like this,"

"There is not much more we can do," Sasha said. "We could have evacuated with the others, but I'm certain we are safe this far from the city."

"I know I'll be safe with you," Kara said, trying to lift Sasha's spirits.

"We'll be just fine." Sasha broke a biscuit in half and sopped up the gravy from the dumplings. "This was a terrific meal," she said as she finished and drank the remainder of her tea.

"I'm glad you enjoyed it," Kara said, smiling from her lover's compliment. "Would you like to join me out on the porch for a while?"

"Yes, I'd like that." Sasha mustered a smile for Kara.

"I'll take care of these dishes later," Kara said as she rose and reached for Sasha's hand.

†

Kara and Sasha sat together in the swing. Sasha's eyes went up to the sky and she watched the clouds as they began to swirl against the deep orange and purple of the coming sunset. "Such a beautiful sight, to be such an omen of bad things to come," Sasha said, her mood turning gloomy once more.

"New Orleans will survive and rebuild better and stronger if necessary," Kara said.

"But at what cost?" Sasha quickly answered. "How many lives will be lost to prove that parts of the city should have never been built upon?" she asked, louder than she intended.

"Hey, I'm on your side."

"I know, baby, I'm sorry, this is all just so senseless."

"I understand, but you must not torment yourself so, my love."

Sasha leaned forward and kissed Kara as the rain began to fall onto the tin roof of the porch and a warm wind blew across their faces. They listened to the symphony of the rainfall until after sunset, and when the creatures of the night began their chorus, Sasha suggested they move inside. "The winds will be picking up soon, and if we stay out here, we will get soaked," she said.

"I can think of so much nicer ways to get soaked," Kara said with a devilish grin.

"Oh, can you now?" Sasha asked and cocked an eyebrow.

"Why don't we go upstairs and I'll show you?" Kara said.

"I'm right behind you," Sasha answered.

Kara took her hand and led her quickly inside. Sasha could not prevent her eyes from looking at the television screen at the size of the storm and slowed almost to a stop before Kara pulled her forward.

"Oh, no you don't. Enough television for you for a while," she said as she pulled Sasha toward the stairs.

Once Sasha could no longer see the television, she laughed and grabbed Kara, lifting her into her arms, carrying her to their bedroom. She placed Kara gently on their bed and began removing her clothing. Lightning flashed outside as Kara reached for Sasha's belt to remove her jeans. She looked up to see the excitement glowing in her lover's eyes. Sasha kicked off her shoes and pressed Kara onto the bed with her naked body. Their mouths came together with a slow, sensual kiss and their moans were lost in the pounding of the rain. Sasha's hands softly caressed Kara's face, their arousal strengthening as their bodies melded together in a lustful dance. Sasha kissed Kara breathless, her hips grinding into Kara's, sending shivers of pleasure through her.

"You feel so good," Kara managed to whisper as Sasha's mouth moved down her neck, licking and teasing her lover into a swirling sensation of ecstasy. Sasha's teeth nipped at Kara's soft skin, each time causing her to shudder with pleasure as her groans of delight grew louder. Kara wrapped her legs around Sasha's waist, driving her hips upward to meet Sasha's hand as she thrust her fingers deep inside Kara. Both lovers released an intense climax and collapsed together on the bed.

Kara sighed and whispered to Sasha, "Now wasn't that more fun than getting soaked in the rain?"

"I don't know," Sasha said. "Let's go check and see for sure."

"What?" Kara stammered.

"I said, let's go check and see." Sasha took Kara's hand and they returned downstairs.

"Sasha, we are butt naked," she said when she realized Sasha was serious.

"So? We're all alone here and no one will see us dancing naked in the rain," Sasha said as she threw open the front door.

"Woman, you are crazy," Kara said, but followed Sasha into the pouring rain.

"Dance with me," she said. Sasha took Kara in her arms and they kissed as the raindrops trailed down their skin. They danced in the rain until a clap of thunder nearby sent the soaking wet lovers racing back to the porch, laughing wildly as they ran into the house.

"So what do you think?" Sasha asked.

"I think they are both very enjoyable ways of getting soaked," Kara said with a grin as she tossed a towel to Sasha.

Sasha noted a trembling in Kara's lower lip and saw that her lover had gotten a chill in the cool rain. "Let's take a shower to warm up and rinse off," she said.

†

They showered and dried before they stretched out on the bed to watch the storm raging outside. Lightning flashed brightly through the windows and periodically they could hear the hail hit before bouncing off the roof and windows when an exceptionally strong storm cell moved through.

"How can something this beautiful be so terrible?" Kara asked.

"I don't know, my love," Sasha said kissing the top of Kara's head, her eyes staring out the window at the raging storm. She held Kara in her arms until her lover fell asleep and then slipped from the bed to dress and go downstairs.

†

Sasha sat in front of the television all night and watched Katrina make landfall early the next morning. She cringed every time a news report broke in, and she watched in horror as the footage and photographs began to broadcast, showing the utter destruction of the Mississippi Gulf Coast. Buildings, homes, and trees tossed about like matchsticks, scattered or in mounds, representing lives that were ruined or worse yet, lives that had been lost in all the destruction.

Tears were running down Sasha's cheeks as the first images of New Orleans made it on the air. A local news channel had managed a live feed and Sasha watched water from swollen Lake Pontchartrain rush across its northeast banks to flood Slidell and adjoining areas in horror. Even more horrendous was the levee she watched give way letting thousands of gallons of water rush into St. Bernard Parish from the mighty Mississippi River Gulf Outlet. The video crew realized all too late the precarious position they were in and rushed to flee the danger zone, but they were caught up in the swift moving water and while Sasha watched in shock, the camera image suddenly went blank.

†

Kara woke to find that Sasha had left the bed and she pulled a robe around her shoulders before starting for the stairs. She found Sasha in the parlor with tears rolling down her cheeks as she watched, in disbelief, the horror and devastation filling the television screen. Kara sat behind Sasha and wrapped her arms around her lover, providing what comfort she could.

They watched homes swept off their foundations, the powerful water ripping them apart. Sasha's tears returned with a vengeance when sunrise revealed people stranded on their roofs, begging for help as helicopters filled with news cameras flew helplessly across the city. Film clips showed bodies floating facedown in the muddy waters and people fleeing from neighborhoods, desperately searching for higher land to wait out the rising waters. The most disturbing footage, from the Mississippi Gulf Coast area, showed entire city blocks swept clean of homes and businesses. One of the barge casinos normally moored in the Gulf of Mexico, near Biloxi, forced onto land by the raging waters, was now sitting at the front steps of the civic center. Even a structure of that immense weight could not be spared from Katrina's wrath. The casino had been pushed several miles down the coast and then a few hundred yards inland before coming to rest.

The mayor announced that the Superdome was a shelter for the many unfortunate souls who chose not to or could not evacuate the city. The I-10 bridge to the east of the city had collapsed like an accordion, so relief from the east would have a long detour before it could reach the city. The worn concrete of the remaining interstate sections loomed above the city like an apparition as residents made their haggard journey to the Superdome. The faces of the people wore the shocked expressions of disbelief and anger that they were going through a personal hell, either unsure of the whereabouts of their families or certain of their tragic deaths.

"These people look like refugees from a war," Kara said as she pulled Sasha closer.

"A war that has just begun," Sasha said.

†

As with most human tragedies, the worst elements of mankind erupted in New Orleans. Television screens were jammed with video footage of looters pushing carts and lugging electronics through waist-deep water back to destroyed homes with no signs of power. People trying to find food to survive were being attacked by fellow looters, and the flooded streets of New Orleans became a war zone.

The afternoon wore on and the rains began to subside, however, as much as fifteen inches of rain had fallen in some areas. The torrential rain swelling the banks of Lake Ponchartrain, and a storm surge estimated at fourteen feet, caused a catastrophic failure to the city's levee system with more than fifty breaches resulting in over eighty percent of the city submerged in floodwaters.

"That's incredible," Kara said as a view from a helicopter showed the flooded city.

"The coast guard is already at work searching for survivors," Sasha said with a glint of hope in her voice.

The death tolls in Mississippi and New Orleans were rapidly rising and estimates of the number of missing individuals was initially in the thousands. The coast guard and other disaster crews worked endlessly in their search for survivors. The national guard was deployed to assist a depleted police force in regaining control of the city's streets and to assist with search and recovery efforts. Most of the streets were under water and traveled only by watercraft or large military vehicles without the threat of being flooded out. Nonmilitary personnel were urging residents to stay off the streets as carjacking and looting was still a major problem. Shots rang out from rival gangs and rebellious citizens who were taking advantage of the misfortune of the city.

News clips aired documenting people rescued from their homes, atop tall buildings, or struggling in the chest-deep water. Their faces were blank slates of shock as rescue workers provided transportation to the Superdome for food, water, and shelter. Sasha felt thankful that at least some portion of the residents survived and were brought safely to shelter.

Other clips showed mothers pleading with police and military staff to find their children or their husbands that had become separated during the storm. "I wish I could do something," Sasha said again, after one such video report.

"The waters should begin receding soon," Kara said. "Once it's safe for us to travel, we will go to provide whatever assistance we can."

"Marcus has an airboat, so maybe we can use that to help with the rescues," Sasha said.

"That's a good idea," Kara said. "Why don't you try to call him and set that up?"

†

Sasha went into the kitchen and was surprised to find that she had a dial tone on her line. But when she dialed Marcus's number she received a recording that all circuits were busy. That didn't surprise her, as she knew that most of the working telephone circuits would be busy securing supplies and assistance to the storms' victims. She walked into her office and picked up her cell phone, but received the same monotone message.

"All circuits are busy on landlines and cell lines," she said when she returned to the parlor. "I'm going to go out and check on the animals." Sasha went to the closet to pull out her rain slicker.

"Would you like me to warm up some food?"

"That would be great." She kissed Kara saying, "I'll be back in just a few minutes."

"Hurry back and try to stay dry," Kara said as she watched Sasha leave.

†

Sasha walked quickly across the yard to the barn and found her two faithful companions, Aries and Hera, standing in their stalls calmly munching hay. "I'm glad to see you two have survived this terrible weather," Sasha said as she stroked the large stallion's neck. Aries turned his head to face Sasha and nuzzled her softly. She refilled their feed bins and dropped more hay into the stalls before pulling her hood above her head and making a dash for the house.

†

Two days later, Sasha and Kara were able to take Marcus's airboat and assist in the rescue effort. They ran the craft down to the Lower Ninth Ward and were able to take two families from their rooftops. The people, exhausted and dehydrated, allowed Sasha to lower them down into Kara's arms. They were able to transport them within two blocks of the Superdome, where national guardsmen transported them the remainder of the distance to the shelter. When darkness approached, the national guard asked Sasha to halt their search for the evening, claiming it was too dangerous to attempt rescues in the thick darkness. Reluctantly, Sasha and Kara returned home, tired, but relieved that they could finally do something productive.

For the next week, they participated in the rescue of New Orleans' residents, assisting some forty people in the process. When the effort turned to recovery, Sasha agreed that it would be too dangerous for them to participate, so they watched the efforts from their home.

A month passed as the cleanup efforts continued and the residents who had evacuated began to move home. It would never be the same town, but New Orleans was alive once more.

Chapter Two

Sasha sat on the front porch reading the newspaper as Kara approached with a cup of coffee.

"They found another," she said with disgust in her voice.

"How many does that make?" Kara asked.

"Four, that the authorities know of," Sasha answered. "Who knows for sure, it could be twice that many in all this mayhem."

Hurricane Katrina had devastated New Orleans only months before and the city crawled with the worst elements of mankind. In the past, the nights were the worst, when addicts, thieves, and murderers stalked the night, but with the confusion and turmoil, the days were just as dangerous.

"I wonder if the police have a clue what his motivation is."

"The paper makes them look clueless," Sasha said. "They have their hands full just dealing with the day-to-day murders and crimes from warring gangs, and the force is still critically under manned."

"The perfect time for a serial killer to move in."

"What makes you think he is new to the area?" Sasha asked curiously.

"Good question. I just assumed whoever he is could not be a native of the area," Kara said.

"And you assume it is a male," Sasha teased.

"Well, data suggests that most serial killers are white males, between the ages of twenty-five and thirty-five, so I was taking a stab in the dark," Kara said with a grin as she handed Sasha a cup of coffee.

"You're probably correct in your assumptions, my dear. I'm merely teasing you this morning."

"I know, my love, I just don't understand a mind that kills so much for pleasure. Do you think he could be immortal?" Kara asked.

"He would probably not fit into your age profile, if he is," Sasha teased.

"Very funny," Kara said with a grin.

"I would like to think that an immortal cherished life too much to waste a human life so needlessly and ruthlessly," Sasha said. "If you read between the lines of the newspaper reports he brutalizes his victims while they are alive."

Kara sighed. "Will the city ever return to normal?"

Sasha chuckled. "My love, there is nothing normal about New Orleans. The hurricane just uncovered another layer of evil when the waters from the lake and river flooded the area."

Sasha returned to the article as Kara walked into the house to prepare for work. When Kara was dressed she returned to the porch and kissed Sasha goodbye.

"I'll see you later today," she said.

"I'll be ready and waiting for your return," Sasha said as she smiled at her lover. They had made plans to go into town for dinner and Sasha was excited about their date.

†

The dark figure watched the woman stroll down the sidewalk. “Welcome back,” he whispered as she climbed the steps to her apartment.

The way her body swayed when she walked made him hunger, and he strained to quell his excitement. She had succumbed to the last man’s charms so easily. He had watched her the previous weekend when she danced wildly and drank more than her share of free drinks. She left the club with the provider of the drinks and the dark one had followed them back to her tiny apartment near the campus. She put up no resistance to the young man’s advances and he watched from the balcony while the man took her roughly, her moans of pleasure ringing throughout the night. He felt his body stiffen as she turned her face toward the window. If her eyes were not glazed with desire, she possibly would have seen the red glow of his eyes peering through the light sheers covering the window. He watched until the man had finished his brutal rutting and then turned away into the night.

“Soon you will be mine,” he whispered his promise to her unhearing ears.

†

When Kara drove them into town for dinner they passed a dark figure walking down the sidewalk. Kara instinctively took her foot from the gas slowing to get a better glimpse of the man stalking through the night. His dark clothing, and the lack of repaired streetlights in the area, made it impossible to see his face, but the man reeked of evil. Kara looked at Sasha who was also staring after the figure.

"Do you feel that?"

"An overwhelming sense of evil," Sasha said. "Yes, I feel it too."

"Should we intervene?"

"We don't know that he has done anything, but he definitely has wicked thoughts running through his mind."

Kara turned the car around as they went back in search of the man but he had disappeared. Even Sasha's powers to track him with her mind came up blank.

"Nothing," Sasha said. "Let's go on to the restaurant and we will take a spin through the Quarter later."

Kara made a U-turn and resumed her route to the restaurant. They shared a romantic candlelit meal and then, as promised, made a pass through the Quarter, but neither of them could pick up any signs of the evil they had both felt earlier. "Let's head home, sweetie," Sasha said as she placed her hand on Kara's thigh.

†

Later that week, the dark one waited outside her apartment and watched as the woman dressed for a date. She took great pains selecting the tight jeans and blouse she would wear, then after spraying perfume she disappeared from the bedroom. Moments later, the front door opened and the woman slipped into the darkness of the night. He stepped from the shadows and followed her until she entered a bar and walked to a table where a young man waited for her. Satisfied that she would be out for several hours, he walked past the bar where he had first seen the young woman and traced the path back to her apartment. He suspected that she lived alone, but wanted to make sure before he initiated the final phase of his plan He easily picked the lock and pushed the door open to a dark room. His vision adjusted quickly and he closed the door behind him and climbed the stairs that would lead him to the bedroom. There were no signs of anyone else living in the apartment, one toothbrush and comb in the small bathroom. He looked into the mirror and smiled, knowing his plan was falling into place.

"So you live all alone," he said. "It couldn't be more perfect."

†

Number Eight was a college student, just as the six before had been, and no one would miss her before Monday morning classes. Only the first varied from this pattern, a business traveler to the city. His smile increased, as he knew he would have plenty time to enjoy the coming weekend. He stepped into the bedroom and took in the bareness of the room. Her room was only dimly lit by a small nightlight near the bed. He walked around, his eyes taking in every inch. There were no pictures of family or friends hanging on the walls or on the one small dresser.

"You must really be all alone," he said. "No family, no friends, just the men you seduce and bring back here. No pictures of them either, but each one leaves their mark on you."

He stopped and opened a drawer to find silky underwear, soft to his touch and he raised a pair of them to his face. They smelled of the same perfume the woman wore, and he breathed in the scent, filling his lungs. He rummaged through the drawer and found several large dildos and some black silk stockings. He took the stockings and walked to the bed. It was a queen-size bed on a sturdy iron frame. Attached to each corner of the headboard were soft leather restraints. Almost too convenient he thought as he searched the room with his eyes.

Curious, his heart pounding like a child opening a treasure chest, he dropped the stockings on the bedside table and opened the single drawer of the nightstand. Inside he found several packs of condoms, lubricant, and a set of nipple clamps. Number Eight really enjoyed her sex and liked it rough and in large proportions. He knew from her mailbox that her name was Susan Miller, but he would not allow himself to think of her as anything but Number eight. He could not allow himself to feel for her as another human, and would treat her as merely an object to satisfy his needs.

He stretched out across her bed and chuckled at the mirrors she had installed on the ceiling. *Such a wanton little freak.* He reached over to pick up the silk stockings. *I will be more than happy to play your little games.* In the dim light of the room, his image distorted in the mirrors as he dangled the silk stockings to stroke his cheeks like a lover's soft lips. He closed his eyes and allowed his thoughts to wander back to a time when his lover kissed him tenderly and cared for his every need.

"Anastasia," he moaned as the silk fabric kissed his skin…

Anastasia had seduced him nearly three years ago. She was a tall beautiful woman with a thick Russian accent and long, flowing hair. They had met in the Quarter during a study break for him. He had been a medical student at the time and was four years into his studies when he met the alluring Anastasia. Stunned by her beauty and her sexual appetite, he was lost to her immediately. After their first night together, nothing else mattered to him. He dropped out of medical school and spent his days and nights entertaining his beautiful lover. She had a flat on Bourbon Street, a perfect location to satisfy their every desire.

They were a perfectly matched couple, she a beautiful temptress and he a darkly handsome charmer to both sexes. Anastasia took advantage of his charms when her desire hungered for more than one partner and he could easily entice another male or female to join in their debauchery. She took great pleasure from the attentions of two males or feasting on a female while he drove her to new heights with his deep, powerful thrusts.

As their years together passed, Anastasia's needs grew darker and he felt himself falling deeper into her world of perversion. She was his obsession and he allowed his need for her to force him into much more brutal acts. Anastasia nearly fainted from pleasure while she watched him thrust deeply into a tight rectum or vagina of one of her bound victims. She would grind their faces into her sex to muffle their whimpers of pain. He took no pleasure from them, but Anastasia would ride him into utter exhaustion once she tired of her game…

"Why did you leave me?" he cried softly as he felt his loins burning intensely.

Removing that visual from his mind, he turned his attention back to the woman who slept in this bed. Soon she would be the subject of his will and desires and he felt himself stiffen with the thought. He was in no rush. He would make Number Eight suffer with anticipation before he would take her for his own.

In the silence of the room, he stood and smoothed out the bedspread, then laid the black stockings across her pillow. He doubted that she would realize someone had been in her apartment later that night when she returned, but he could not resist the temptation of leaving her a clue.

"I will see you soon," he whispered, then turned to walk from the room.

He went quietly down the stairs and checked to ensure the door locked behind him as he blended into the night. He casually strolled back to the bar and took a seat on a stool. He drank an icy beer as he watched the woman grind into the crotch of the man she had met as they danced in the small crowd.

From the provocative way she danced with him, he was certain the man would be invited back to her apartment after a few more drinks. He would not wait in the darkness to witness the event and left the bar to make the short walk home. Very soon now, he would have her for his own.

Once inside the flat, he stripped out of his clothes and slipped naked between the cool sheets. The air conditioner was working full speed, but it did little to soothe the fire burning in him as he visualized Number Eight on the dance floor. Her long hair shimmered in the lights just as Anastasia's had when she danced. He forced his eyes to close and he dreamed of Anastasia, his body aching for her touch as he thrashed in the bed.

Chapter Three

Anastasia had woken him one morning nearly six months ago as she packed an open suitcase on the end of the bed. Startled by her movements, he wiped the sleep from his eyes as he sat up. "What is going on?" he asked. "Where are we going?"

"My dear Talis, I am going back home to Russia," she purred in her thick accent.

"But, what about us?" he asked.

"You've been a terrific lover, but I feel it's time for me to go home," she answered.

"So let me go with you," he pleaded.

"There's no room for you in my life in Russia," Anastasia said cruelly. "I have signed the deed to the flat over to you and there should be ample funds in the account to keep you comfortable for some time yet," she added as she zipped the suitcase shut.

"That's all there is, you can just leave like this?" Talis asked with tears threatening to break through.

"You really didn't think I would stay here forever, now did you, Talis?" she said as she taunted his feelings for her.

"You said you loved me," he said.

"Yes, I do love you, Talis, but my needs have grown beyond what you can provide, my lovely boy."

"Tell me what it is, Anastasia, and I swear I will learn," Talis pleaded.

"It is never that easy, Talis," Anastasia said. She then bent to kiss him on the cheek, spun on her heels and in seconds was gone from his life.

Shattered by her betrayal he did his best to drown his sorrow. He could not understand why Anastasia would leave him with no warning signs whatsoever. Dark thoughts started to grow in his mind.

When liquor failed to erase her from his memory, Talis began to hunt for a replacement.

The first woman he met had a striking resemblance to Anastasia, and she was fiercely attracted to his good looks. A successful businesswoman, she came to New Orleans to attend a conference, but after meeting Talis, they spent the better part of the week in bed. She was aggressive and rebellious in bed, taunting Talis to make her scream, which he frequently accomplished as he took her ferociously in every manner possible.

On their last night together the woman had snorted several lines of premium cocaine before performing oral sex on him. Talis assumed she had passed out from the drugs and did not realize until hours later, when he attempted to wake her the next morning, that the woman was dead. His initial reaction was to panic and leave the room as quickly as he could, but he managed to calm himself. Covered in a cold sweat, he was able to dress and leave the room and hotel without detection. He had certainly left plenty of DNA evidence and fingerprints in the room and for the first few days after her death, Talis waited for the police to rush into the flat to arrest him.

He watched the newspaper for evidence of his crime, which finally appeared three days later in an obscure section as the police reported a random death of a business traveler in a local hotel. An autopsy was necessary to determine the exact cause of death, however the article stated there was no immediate evidence of foul play.

As the days wore on and there were no SWAT teams crashing through his door, Talis's confidence grew knowing that he had eluded detection. There would be no record of his fingerprints or DNA on file with the authorities. He continued to monitor the paper and in a small follow-up article, the paper reported her death as an accidental overdose of cocaine. Talis knew there was enough evidence to show that the woman had company on the night of her death, but the local authorities were so overworked already they accepted an overdose without question. After all, she wasn't local and unless someone came forward to question the autopsy results, the case would remain closed.

†

An evil seed had been planted that night when by accident he had asphyxiated the woman during his pleasure. As the days continued and there was no news of an imminent arrest, Talis grew to believe that he could not be captured and the evil seed began to blossom. Soaring with self-assurance, he began his hunt again that evening and within hours had his next prey targeted.

Number Two had been selected in a rush. She was not as beautiful as the first, but the sexual excitement Talis felt made her looks insignificant. Instead of taking pleasure from her for days, he took what he wanted from the woman and toyed with her for several hours before encircling her throat and strangling her as he released deep inside her torn and bruised body.

Talis raced to the newspaper stand the next morning. His anger flared and his disappointment grew when her death failed to be the highlight of the local paper. He would have to wait another three days before one of her classmates found her just as he had left her in her small home. As he read the article, he swelled with an erection and he knew then he could not stop.

He cut out the article with hands shaking from excitement and pinned it to the wall of his bedroom. He regretted that he had not saved the article from his first, but he would go into the newspaper's archives to retrieve a copy, and would post it with the others that were yet to come. He sat on the edge of the bed and masturbated as he read the article again, and then closed his eyes to see the woman struggling underneath him as he took the life from her. He shook with violent spasms as his orgasm raced through him, then fell backward, sweaty and exhausted, on the once crisp sheets.

†

When Katrina came and the rains began to fall, he prayed he would drown or be washed away from the horror his life was becoming.

"Take me," he railed against the storm. "Take me and wash me clean," he shouted as the floodwaters began to rise as he walked through the Quarter. Talis knew he had become a vile creature, but the pleasure he received from his victims far outweighed his momentary remorse.

Hurricane Katrina disrupted his hunting for several weeks. The streets were crawling with police and national guard who tried desperately to return some sense of order to the city, with no clue of the evil hunter that followed their movements carefully in person and through newspaper articles.

As the months passed, residents and students began to return to the city, much to his delight. He ached to hunt and take what so easily would be his. Talis had spent night after night pleasuring himself as he handled the objects in his growing collection, the souvenirs he had taken from his victims to place in his shrine. But, even the excitement he experienced from them waned quickly and he was compelled to return to the hunt.

†

It took the police two more victims to begin to recognize the pattern that was developing. Even then, they were not certain they were all connected. Talis had thrown them a curve with Number Five. Not only did he commit the crime during the week, he also chose a male instead of female. It had been nearly a month since the last victim and he craved to physically dominate his next victim. He knew a woman would be no challenge for him so he began trawling the gay bars just a few blocks from his flat.

The tight jeans he wore highlighted the large bulge on the inside of his right thigh and it drew immediate attention as soon as he walked into the bar. It didn't take long before he found himself surrounded by young, enthusiastic men. He pulled the tight, black shirt over his head and looped it through his belt as he gyrated on the dance floor in a small group; several pairs of hands caressed his muscled body in a blur of heated desire.

He selected a dark-haired young man from the group and took his hand to lead him from the dance floor. He sent the man to the bar for beers as he slipped his shirt back on. When he returned to the dark booth and slid in beside Talis, the young man's hand covered the bulge swelling between his thighs.

"My name is Terry."

"Do you have a place close by?" Talis whispered in the man's ear.

"About a twenty-minute walk from here."

"Do you live alone?"

"Yes," Terry said with a warm smile.

"Perfect," Talis returned the man's smile.

Terry continued to stroke him as they watched the crowd and finished their beers. Without speaking, the young man stood and followed Talis out of the bar as they began the short walk to his home.

Talis could feel himself quivering with excitement as they strolled down the street. As they approached an area where a corner streetlight was not working, Talis grabbed Terry by the shoulders and pressed him hard against the wall of a small alley. His eyes were glowing with lust as he pinned him against the wall with a rough, full-mouth kiss. When they broke off the kiss, Terry took his hand and led him back onto the sidewalk, walking quickly to a small house.

Once inside, Terry took them directly into a bedroom. Talis spun the man on his heels to face him, ripping the shirt from his chest and pushing him back on the bed. He tossed Terry's shoes into a corner and pulled the jeans from his body quickly. The young man leaned back on his elbows and eagerly enjoyed the show as Talis slowly stripped out of his clothes before sitting next to him on the bed. There was a flash of fear or maybe it was anger that Talis saw in the man's eyes as he roughly rolled him onto his back and buried his right hand in Terry's curly hair.

For several hours, Talis took and gave pleasure to the young man. When he grew tired Talis rolled onto his back on the bed. He closed his eyes and allowed the man to caress him until he fell asleep. Rest came easily, as Talis had expended a large amount of energy. When he woke a couple hours later, Terry had fallen asleep on his shoulder, and for a brief moment Talis regretted that he would kill the man. Terry had proved himself as a willing fuck partner, who would take any abuse Talis chose to inflict upon him. Talis smiled a wicked smile. He would give him the fuck of his life before he died, however. He gently shook the man awake.

"Do you have restraints?" he asked.

Terry nodded his head and got off the bed to retrieve them. He handed Talis four leather cuffs with long straps and waited his instruction.

"Lie on your back."

Terry lay down on the bed as Talis commanded and Talis moved to straddle his chest. He placed a cuff around his right wrist then looped the strap through the restraint. Talis raised the man's arm above his head, restrained him securely against the headboard, and repeated the process with his left wrist.

Talis had grown hard as he restrained the man and Terry eagerly licked his lips as Talis sat on his chest. "Do you want to get high?" he asked.

"What do you have?"

"In the top dresser drawer there are a few joints that have been laced with ecstasy that will blow your mind."

Talis had never experimented with ecstasy. Now though, he was eager to try anything that would increase his pleasure. Finding the joints and a small lighter, Talis sat on the edge of the bed and lit the joint, drawing in a lungful of the pungent smoke. When he slowly exhaled, he felt a weird buzzing in his brain and turned to grin at the young man tied to the bed.

"This is good stuff," he said as he took another draw and offered the joint to the man's lips.

Terry pulled hard on the joint, holding it inside his lungs as long as he could before exhaling and then returned Talis's grin. "I knew you would like it," he said. "It makes you hard as a rock." He snickered as he took a second draw. Talis took one last draw from the joint and crushed it out in the ashtray. When he exhaled the breath, Talis felt stronger than he ever had before.

Talis's senses soared with excitement as he drove his cock into the young man and his hands encircled the man's throat. As his fingers dug into the soft flesh of his neck, the man began to struggle against Talis. Tightening his grip, Talis's weight held the man in place as the life began to drain out of his body. He came violently inside the man as the struggle ended and Terry's eyes, wide with terror, fixed on the ceiling.

Talis withdrew and allowed the man's legs to fall back as he sat on the edge of the bed and wiped himself clean. He then placed the dirty towel over the man's face to cover his lifeless eyes.

Talis pulled the shirt over his head, lit another of the fantastic joints and smoked it, breathing deeply of the strong smoke as he continued to dress. He picked up the jeans Terry had been wearing, pulled the wallet from his back pocket and flipped it open. He thumbed through the few bills tucked inside and reached for the driver's license. Staring at him from the picture was Terry Mahoney, who was nothing more to Talis than number five. He took a final drag from the joint and dropped it into the ashtray. He slipped the driver's license into his pocket and turned to face the dead man on the bed.

"I had a marvelous time, Terry." Picking up the last of the joints, Talis walked back into the night. The sky was beginning to brighten as he reached the Quarter and Talis decided he would stop in at an all-night diner for breakfast before going home. He ate his fill of fried eggs, grilled pork chops, fried potatoes, and toast. After leaving a healthy tip for the handsome waiter Talis walked the short distance home as the sun began to crest the horizon. Talis pinned the driver's license to the wall of his growing shrine. His fingers caressed the souvenirs he had collected with loving strokes. Talis walked from the room to shower and then fell into bed to sleep the day away.

Chapter Four

As the months passed, he collected the newspaper clippings, posting them to the wall as his collection of driver's licenses and other tokens grew. The game had grown easy for Talis, and the incompetent police were making no progress linking him to the murders. He began to imagine himself as a specter, able to walk unobserved through life, taking whatever he wanted, whenever he chose, without risk of consequence. His behavior grew bolder.

With Number Eight he began to openly stalk his victims. Entering her apartment had given him a needed rush of excitement and he planned something very special for her. His contempt for the police had cultivated his confidence to the point he felt they would never capture him, so Talis decided he would taunt them with his cleverly devised clues.

Number Eight was just like him in some ways. She was as much a sexual predator and narcissist as he, in search of the perfect sexual partner to meet her needs, taking from them what she wanted. He would give her that and more than she wanted before he finished with her.

Talis waited at the bar and just as he expected she came walking through the door. He waited until she had ordered a drink and slipped into a dark booth before he made his approach.

"Are you waiting for someone?" he asked.

She had noticed the large bulge in his jeans as he approached and smiled to welcome him. "No one in particular," she said.

"May I join you then?"

"Please do," she said and moved over on the slick booth seat.

"I can't believe a woman as beautiful as you is alone tonight."

"Since the storm, the crowd has really thinned out," she said placing her hand on his thigh.

"Lucky for me then," he said as he felt her hand locate what she was searching for.

"I think I will be the lucky one," she said, her fingers measuring his length.

"Would you care to dance?"

"I hoped you would ask," the woman answered as she took his offered hand.

She groaned in his ear as they danced close to a slow song and her tiny hand crept between his legs. Every chance she got, she rubbed up against him or stroked across his thigh before they sat in a dark corner and talked. When she excused herself to use the ladies' room, he ordered a final round of drinks.

When she returned, her cheeks were flushed with excitement and he could sense her hunger as her hand returned immediately to his crotch. "I must have this and soon," she purred.

"When you're ready, you'll have all you can handle." He encouraged her to finish her drink and they would be off. She gladly reached for the cocktail and downed it in one gulp. He stood, taking her hand, and stepped into the cool evening as they started down the walk. She guided him quickly toward her apartment. She was eager to have this dark stranger in the sack and did not take notice of the blurriness of her vision as they started up the steps to her small apartment. His timing was perfect and the drug started to take effect just as they neared the front door. She swooned and he easily supported her with his left arm as he took the key from her hand and unlocked the door. He lifted her in his arms, and kicked the door open then walked inside. He closed the door, listened to the soft click of the lock and headed for the stairs.

Talis carried her slight form easily up the stairs and laid her on the bed. He sat beside her and allowed his hand to stroke through the softness of her hair. "You're quite beautiful," he whispered as his fingers unfastened the buttons of her blouse. He easily removed her blouse and bra as he held her limply in his arms. Then he worked the tight jeans and panties off her. He allowed his fingertips to run lightly over her skin as he examined her closely. Her breasts were full and firm and her mound was closely shaven, just as he preferred.

Talis removed his shoes and sat on the bed next to her, softly caressing her skin. He had originally planned to have her restrained when she woke from the drug he had given her, but as he watched her, he decided to alter his plan.

He leaned back against the iron frame of the footboard and watched the woman's eyes begin to flutter open. She opened her eyes, and saw him sitting at the end of her bed and smiled at him.

"What happened? I don't remember coming home."

"I think you drank that last drink too fast and it caught up with you," he said with a charming smile.

"And you just had to undress me?" she said when she realized she was naked.

"I thought you would want to be comfortable."

"So, why are you still dressed?" she asked, eyeing the bulge in his jeans.

"I thought I would be a gentleman and wait until you awoke."

"Why don't I see if I can help you out then," she said, crawling down to the end of the bed.

Susan kissed him deeply as her hands tugged his shirt from his jeans and she broke the kiss only long enough to slip the shirt over his head. Her hands ran across his muscular chest and she moaned deep inside his mouth. Her fingertips brushed across his erect nipples and then she raked her nails down his side.

"You feel so good," she breathed against his skin, kissing down his chin.

Talis stretched his arms across the footboard and rested his head back as her mouth licked down across his chest and her teeth made contact with his nipples. Her right hand rubbed his crotch while making her way down his body planting light bites in her wake.

Her hands worked on his belt and the fastener of his jeans. She eagerly manipulated the zipper and cooed her pleasure when she opened his fly to reveal his bare skin. Her fingers easily fleshed out his erection and her mouth greedily covered his tip.

Talis enjoyed her aggression and allowed her to continue giving him oral pleasure. He could feel his erection growing harder as she took more of him into her eager mouth. She was hungry for more and straddled his waist lowering herself onto his swollen cock. Her velvety wetness surrounded him as she took him fully inside her lust-filled body.

Talis groaned when she picked up speed with her thrusts forcing him deep inside her with each of her strokes.

Her wails echoed in the room as she climaxed and fell forward against his chest.

Several minutes later he withdrew from her and rolled onto his back. The woman turned to face him and laid her head on his shoulder. "You are a fucking monster," she said before her hand stroked down his belly.

"That's just the beginning," he promised.

She had several orgasms before he arched his back and thrust deeply inside her filling her with his offering. She passed out in exhaustion and he moved from the bed. Then he used the cuffs attached to her bed to restrain her limbs, with her still facing the foot of the bed. He walked into the kitchen to find a notepad and pen, sat down at the end of the bed, and began to write.

Number Eight is in my sight
Fun and games will fill tonight
Tomorrow starts another day
A game of life we shall play
If you solve the riddle in time
Number Eight will be yours not mine
A final clue you will receive tomorrow
Only you can prevent the sorrow-
TBS

Talis smiled as he read his note, then dressed and picked up Susan's keys. He tucked them and the note into his pocket and then gagged her using her black silk stockings. He would be quick, but he did not want her to wake alone and start screaming in panic. *There will be plenty of time for that later.* A wicked smile played across his face. He left the apartment, walked the short distance to the police station, and slipped the note under the front door. He could hear the clock of a nearby cathedral chiming eleven as he rushed down the sidewalk.

He entered the apartment feeling excited and confident. After checking on the woman and finding her fast asleep, he took a shower to wash her from his body. He wrapped a towel around his waist and walked back to the room. Talis removed the stockings and restraints. He wouldn't need them now that he'd returned. She was more than willing to submit to his desires and he was certain she would do anything he asked. He sat down on the bed to watch her sleep and began thinking of the final clue he would send to the police tomorrow.

†

An off duty officer walked through the front door and picked up the slip of paper from the floor. He opened it, read the note, making no sense of it at all, and took it over to the front desk.

"Take a look at this, Sarge," he said as he handed the note to the officer sitting behind the desk.

"What the fuck is this?" he asked after reading the note.

"I have no idea, but someone slipped it under the front door," he said.

"Detective Brody is on duty tonight, take it to him and see if he can make any sense of it," Sarge said.

The officer handed the note to Brody with an explanation of where he found it. Brody opened up the slip of paper and his eyes flew to a crime board behind his desk. "Holy shit," Brody said. "Ask Sarge to get the chief of detectives in here as fast as he can."

"Yes, Detective," the officer said and left the squad room.

"How can there be eight? Who are we missing?" he asked himself as he studied the board behind him. There on the board were five of his victims and, as Talis had assumed, they had not connected him to the businesswoman's death, or the man's.

"You are one bold son of a bitch," Brody said as he read the note again. He knew exactly where the note had come from and did not bother to preserve the note for fingerprints. They had plenty of fingerprints and other DNA evidence, but no suspect to match it.

Sarge walked into to the room. "The chief is on his way."

"Thanks Sarge. Can you do me one more favor?" he asked.

"Sure, what is it?"

"Can you poll the computer for unsolved murders from the last three months for me and pull the files?"

"It will take a while, but I will get right on it," Sarge said and left the room.

"Thanks," Brody said as he stared at the board, unaware that Sarge had gone.

Thirty minutes later, Brody was poring through the first of the files Sarge had pulled for him and was in deep concentration when Chief of Detectives, Truman Crawford, arrived.

"What do you have, Brody?"

"The bastard is taunting us," he said as he passed the note to his boss.

"Eight," he exclaimed. "Who have we missed?"

"That is what I am trying to figure out," Brody said. "Sarge is pulling files on all unsolved murders over the last three months."

"He doesn't give us much to work with in this note."

"He never intended to. He just wanted to let us know he is active again and smarter than us. Tomorrow's clue will be our only hope of saving her."

"Let's hope we get it in enough time to react," Crawford replied. "How was this one delivered?"

"It was slipped under the front door of the precinct house."

"Even he wouldn't be stupid enough to attempt that again."

"I would hope not, but I think we should rig a camera there just to be sure," Brody said. "What can it hurt, since we don't have anything on this freak yet?"

"TBS, I wonder what this stands for?" Crawford said.

"That's the only easy part. He strangles all his victims, so he has decided to call himself The Bayou Strangler."

"Not very original, is he?" the chief mocked.

"No, but he is clever enough to be ahead in this game so far," Brody said.

"We need to have every available brain here tomorrow night too. The more heads trying to decipher this riddle the better."

"We have feebies in town too," Crawford added, referring to the local FBI investigators.

"I hate to pull them into our case, but we have to stop this man soon."

"I will give them a call and get them over here," the chief said and left the office.

†

As he watched her sleep, Talis thought back to the day he located the crypt. A grin crossed his face, he was a genius in developing his plans. After the storm he had roamed the streets and his curiosity had taken him to the St. Louis Cemetery. The rushing water had damaged several of the crypts. Near the back, he found exactly what he was searching for—a crypt broken open by the floodwaters. Talis crept through the small opening. *This will be perfect.* A plan began to formulate in his mind. He returned to his flat and dug out a pair of bolt cutters. He stopped by a local hardware store and purchased a new padlock, a bucket of plaster, and a large flat blade to spread the plaster. He took a taxi to the cemetery and walked in carrying his goods. If anyone saw him enter, they would think he was a caring family member, come to make repairs from the storm.

He cut the lock from the door and opened it to reveal a lone coffin, still in good condition. He smiled as he opened the bucket of plaster and began repairing the wall from the water breach. As the sun started to go down, he pulled the coffin from the slab and lowered it to the ground. He twisted the seal locks on the coffin until he was able to open it. A blast of foul-smelling air rushed from the coffin when he lifted the lid. He waited for the putrid air to clear and again stepped to the coffin. Talis removed the bones that were resting within. He tossed them inside the crypt with a brief apology. "Sorry for disturbing your rest. I will return your remains after I'm done."

Talis closed the lid and lifted it back into place. He shut the door, slipped the new lock into place, and dropped the keys into his pocket. He inspected the plaster repair and confident of his work, retired back to his flat to shower and roam the streets of the Quarter.

Now, with his plan in place, he crouched on top of a nearby crypt and reviewed his surroundings. The full moon had risen overhead as he waited. He watched the traffic on the streets pass by, as people flocked toward downtown in the early hours of the morning. Ironically, from his position, Talis could easily view the front door of the precinct house. He could witness the comings and goings of the department and would watch from this viewpoint, as his message arrived later the next evening.

†

The woman awoke in the late morning and again saw Talis sitting on the end of the bed, watching her sleep.

"You're still here," she said with a smile.

"Yes, I had such a lovely time last night, I thought maybe we could go to dinner tonight and come back for some more fun," he said.

None of her previous "dates" had ever offered to feed her dinner after they had gotten what they wanted from her. She always woke up alone the next morning with not even a note of thanks.

"Dinner would be great," she said. She could imagine the envious glares she would receive as she walked in on his arm. He was a handsome man. "You were such a naughty boy," she said again as Talis watched her with a wicked smile.

"You didn't seem to mind."

"You were fucking incredible."

Talis climbed from the bed.

"Where are you going?" she asked.

"Back to my place for a short nap, shower, and some clean clothes," he said. "I will make reservations and be back here at seven."

"I'll be ready," she purred from the bed. "How should I dress?"

"Do you have a slinky, short, black dress?"

"Of course I do."

"That should do fine then," he said as he dressed. He leaned over and kissed her. "See you at seven."

She watched him leave and then fell back onto the bed. Had her knight in shining armor finally arrived, she wondered. Wearing a smile, she crept from the bed and went to her closet to pull out her black dress. "You want slinky?" she said as she hung the dress on the closet door.

She then went to shower and shave, even though she was still relatively smooth. She would put on her best performance for this date, she promised herself. This man may really be the one.

†

Talis collapsed onto his bed and slept for three hours after calling to make reservations for dinner. He was exhausted from all the recent exertion, but his mind whirled with excitement as he lay on the bed and willed himself to sleep. It would be a long, exciting night ahead and he wanted to be sharp. He dreamed of Anastasia and when he woke up, he found he had grown painfully hard. He masturbated in the shower, coming intensely, as he thought of how the woman rode him hard, just as Anastasia had done in the past.

Talis took great care in preparing for the date, grooming himself meticulously. He would be parading his victim right under the nose of the authorities and they would still be clueless to his real identity. He dressed in black slacks and a form-fitting black shirt, which enhanced his dark brooding looks. He smiled back at his image in the mirror.

"The Bayou Strangler," he said. "Such a handsome devil you are too."

Talis packed a small bag with black jeans, a black T-shirt, and black sneakers for later that evening and then sat down at his desk to write his next note. He tucked the note into an envelope and on the outside he wrote, "Detective Brody."

He knew Brody was New Orleans's finest detective and he was certain Brody would be the one to unravel his clues. The rest of the force were mere dullards compared to him. Talis had become aware of Brody through his perusal of the crime section of the newspaper. Every large case that had been broken was due to the cleverness and good investigative abilities of Brody, and in his own demented way, he respected the detective. "Time to play, Detective Brody," he said as he slipped the envelope into the bag.

He sprayed his body with the rich-smelling cologne that Anastasia had given him. He had used it sparingly to conserve her gift, but tonight was a special occasion. He picked up his bag and left the flat, his heart racing with anticipation.

When she opened the door, he smiled warmly at her. "You look ravishing," he said.

"You look incredible yourself," she said as she led him inside. "Planning to make a night of it?" she asked, when she saw the bag he was carrying.

"I was hoping to," he said confidently.

"I hope to have a repeat performance," she said, her eyes glowing with excitement.

"Oh, you will be screaming before you know it," he said with a wicked grin.

"Are you going to try and fuck me to death tonight with this monster?" she teased as she reached between his legs.

He felt his body twitch with excitement when she asked the question and saw her smile when she felt his firmness. "I will give you exactly what you wish for," he said with a soft smile.

He then offered her his arm. "Are you ready?"

She draped her arm over his and allowed him to lead her into the night. They walked a short distance to the restaurant and were quickly seated by a handsome host. She slid into the intimate booth and he sat down beside her. Her hand went directly to his lap as they perused the menu.

They ordered drinks and an appetizer as her hand worked slowly across his thigh. *Two can play this game.* His hand slowly worked underneath her dress. His fingers softly caressed the inside of her thigh, and she gasped when his fingers brushed across her clean-shaven mound. He could feel her wetness pushing past her lips and he slowly stroked a finger through it up to her swollen clit. He removed his hand and stuck the tip of that finger in his mouth, sucking her juices from his finger.

"I know what I am having for dessert," he said, eyes shining brightly with excitement.

She nearly swooned when he touched her and she knew that tonight would be even more enjoyable.

They ate the meal in relative silence, the touches of their hands and eyes communicating the raw sensuality that they would soon be sharing. When the waiter asked if they would like to order dessert, she giggled and they declined his offer. He paid their check and, after leaving a generous tip, Talis took her hand and they began the walk back to her home.

Along the way, they passed a park, completely dark and hidden from view. He led her inside and took her in his arms for a heated kiss. While their tongues danced, she reached down between them, caressing his erection.

"My place, now," she panted.

He followed her inside, unzipping her dress as they walked up the stairs to her bedroom. He spun her around on her feet as they reached the bed and lowered the dress from her. She kicked off her shoes as her fingers worked the buttons of his shirt. She pushed the shirt off his shoulders and it fell into a pile at his feet, his trousers quickly following.

Talis fucked her for an hour, watching himself perform perfectly in the overhead mirrors, until she collapsed on the bed in complete exhaustion. "I'll go fix us a drink," he said as he left the bed and walked naked to her kitchen.

With eyes glazed with arousal she watched him walk, amazed by his beautiful body. She could barely sit up when he returned carrying two drinks. He handed her the drink as he sipped his and watched as she greedily gulped hers down.

"A bit thirsty?" he asked.

"You have made me so wet I am dehydrated," she said as she placed the glass on the bedside table.

"I take full responsibility," he said as he offered her his drink.

She took the glass and took a deep drink from his as well, before handing it back to him. "I feel funny," she said.

"What do you mean funny?" he asked innocently.

"I have a strange buzzing in my head and I am suddenly sleepy," she said.

"We have all night, so take a nap and when you are refreshed we will continue," he promised.

He no sooner spoke the words before she collapsed onto the bed. Talis quickly retrieved his bag and dressed, slipping the note in his pocket. He slipped the black dress back over her and lifted her into his arms. He crept from her house, leaving the door unlocked and took back alleys and dark streets until he reached the cemetery and laid her softly on the ground. He took the keys from his pocket and opened the crypt.

He pulled out the coffin and opened the lid. Talis picked her up and placed her into the velvet-lined container. He leaned down and kissed her soft lips then lowered the lid, securely tightening the seals. He rolled the casket inside a slot barely big enough to hold it and then locked the door behind him. Talis walked several blocks and flagged down a taxi on a darkened corner. He paid the man twenty dollars to drive around for ten minutes before delivering his note to the precinct house. Talis rushed back to the cemetery. He sat on top of the next crypt to wait for her to awaken.

Talis smiled as he watched the taxi pull in front of the precinct house and the driver disappear inside to deliver his message.

There was never a shortage of people flooding the streets looking for the hottest party spot and the best place to pick up a date for the evening. Anastasia once told him anything goes in the Big Easy, and that mindset made his hunt easy. He grinned as a car full of college-aged kids pulled up to a traffic light just outside the cemetery. Obviously drunk, one of the young men hung half out of the window and shouted a string of obscenities into the night.

"Enjoy your youth while you can," he whispered.

Talis remembered being that age and having the same arrogant confidence in his own immortality, and a wicked smile crossed his face. He watched as the car sped away when the light turned green then a muffled sound caught his attention. Number Eight was coming awake. He turned toward the recently renovated crypt and cocked his head, waiting for the next sound.

†

The young woman had regained consciousness and was slowly becoming aware of her surroundings. The drug he had slipped into her drink was beginning to wear off and she opened her eyes to pitch-blackness. She struggled to lift her drug-weighted hands and her fingers felt the smooth, coolness of wood. Every place she touched above her she felt wood, and when she attempted to lift her feet, she felt the same restraint. Her eyes grew wide with fright as the realization that she was inside a coffin sunk into her sluggish brain. She cried out as panic raced through her as she pushed with all her might. The lid raised several inches and then struck a solid force. Her arms rapidly lost strength and she could no longer hold the lid. When the lid snapped shut, she heard a soft click as the latches he had triggered snapped in place. Horror overtook her when she realized she would never open the coffin again.

The woman had no memory of how she had come to this location. She remembered the handsome, charming man who had taken her to dinner and bought her drinks, but after that, her memory went blank. She had no clue where she was and her body was slick with nervous perspiration as she tried with desperation to free herself from the coffin. After nearly an hour of struggling, she collapsed in exhaustion. She listened for the sound of anyone near in hope she could yell out and get their attention, but all she could hear was a soft voice whispering.

"There is no need to struggle, you are perfectly safe," the voice said.

The woman shivered from the coolness in the voice. “Who are you and why are you doing this? And where am I?” she demanded.

“Who I am is none of your concern and it doesn’t matter where you are,” the voice answered. “No one could hear you should you yell out and you are quite safe for the moment,” he assured her.

“What do you want from me?” the woman asked, her voice trembling in fear. “If this is your idea of foreplay, you are seriously screwed up.”

“I plan to give you exactly what you want,” the soft voice answered. With a deep laugh he continued to taunt her. “Precisely what you asked for earlier tonight,” he whispered.

The woman’s brain was still cloudy from the effects of the drug he had slipped her and she found it difficult to understand. “What are you saying? I can’t remember much from tonight,” she cried through her tears.

“I will leave you for now to think about it and I will return to you very soon,” the voice promised and went silent.

“No, please don’t leave me here,” she begged, but her words fell silent against the cold walls.

Chapter Five

Sasha took the paper from the box and walked back to the house. She sat out on the porch sipping her coffee as she opened the paper and read the headline.

The Bayou Strangler taunts police with victim Number Eight it read in bold print.

"Son of a bitch," she said just as Kara stepped out the front door.

"I beg your pardon."

"This," Sasha said as she lifted the paper for Kara to read the headline. Sasha read the article to her describing how the serial killer, who named himself TBS for The Bayou Strangler, had sent a note to the police telling them of his latest victim, number eight according to his count.

"He is growing bolder and more arrogant," Kara said. "I can't believe the police would allow this information to leak to the newspaper either."

"I am sure they had no intention of this information getting out to the public."

"Is there anything we can do?"

"Formally no, not without drawing attention to ourselves, but I think we can keep our senses open while we are in town and maybe do more patrolling of the Quarter," Sasha said.

"Why patrol the French Quarter?"

"All of his victims so far have been college students and where do college students hang out at night?"

"In the French Quarter," Kara answered. "I see where you are heading now."

"Right now that's the only thing I can think of," Sasha said. "It would be great to have a copy of the police case files, but that isn't going to happen."

"No, I don't think so either."

"So, we start tonight then?"

"Yes, tonight."

"You have to promise me one thing," Sasha said.

"What is that?"

"That you'll never hunt for him alone, that you'll always be with me," Sasha said.

"I promise," Kara said.

†

The chief of detectives slammed the paper down on Brody's desk and asked, "What the fuck is this?"

The paper flopped open and Brody read the headline. "Jesus Christ! How did that get out?"

"I think it is obvious we have a leak somewhere on the force," the chief said.

"So now on top of everything else, we have to deal with a leak inside the department

"We'll deal with that later, if we can. Right now, we need to focus on the case." Brody looked worn out and Crawford knew he had studied the files all night without a break. "Have you learned anything more?"

"I think I have uncovered another of his victims, but I can't be positive," Brody said. "It is not his typical victim."

"How so?"

"This one was male. A young gay man found restrained and dead from asphyxiation in his home."

"A male, when all the others were female? That is a twist."

"According to the timelines he would have been victim number five, just weeks after the storm," Brody said.

"What leads you to a connection?" Crawford asked.

"Several things, death by strangulation, sexual activity, physical domination by use of restraints, it all points to our boy escalating. If he was unable to play his nasty little games right after the storm due to the increased visible presence by the police and national guard, I think he built up a terrible desire for action and chose a male as more of a physical challenge."

"That makes sense, so let's add him to the board."

"There is one other thing that worries me," Brody said.

"Which is?"

"Laboratory results revealed the victim had smoked a joint laced with ecstasy prior to his death, and if TBS is now addicted to the drug his sexual needs will double."

"I think his addiction is stronger than the drug, and he won't do anything that detracts from that, but it won't hurt to bring in vice to see who is marketing E on the streets."

"What time are we meeting today?"

"The Feebies and all detectives will be here at ten," Crawford said. "Why don't you hit the crib for a few hours of sleep before they arrive," he suggested.

"That's probably a good idea. Please make sure someone wakes me by nine forty-five," he said as he left the desk.

"Will do," the chief said as he turned to study the board.

†

The time for sleep faded all too quickly for Brody. When he was shaken awake, he felt as if he had just laid down. "I'm going to take a quick shower and then I will be out," he told the officer who had woken him.

The shower did little to lift his spirits, but it did help him wash the sleepiness from his body. After he dressed in fresh clothes and stepped back into the squad room, he felt the energy from the group massed there.

Brody briefed the group on what they knew so far of the victims, the killer, and his modus operandi. Crawford took over from there and assigned work groups to review each case file to see if they could glean more clues from the evidence he left behind.

The day wore on and Brody felt they had made very little progress on the case. There had been no reports of missing persons, not that he had expected any. All of his victims thus far had lived alone, and wouldn't be thought missing until they didn't show up for class or work. The tension grew thicker in the air with every passing hour as they waited for their next clue.

Brody was staring at the pictures of victim number five when the on duty sergeant brought a man holding an envelope with Brody's name on the outside to his desk. He took the envelope carefully by one corner. "Who are you and where did you get this?" he asked the man.

"My name is George McKenzie, and I am a taxi driver for White taxi. I was flagged down by a man on the corner of Bourbon and Barracks street who paid me twenty dollars to drive around for ten minutes and then bring this envelope here."

"What did he look like?"

"He was dark," George said. "I mean it was dark. The light was out on the street corner."

"Was he white, black, young, old?" Brody prompted.

"He was white, tall, well over six feet and well-built from the size of him. I think he had dark hair and eyes, but it was hard to tell. He was wearing dark clothes too, which didn't help."

"Do you think you could describe his face to a sketch artist?"

"No man, I didn't see him good enough," George said.

"Okay, George, I want you to take this officer back to the spot where you were flagged," the chief said as he pointed to a young uniformed officer. "Walk the path well and look for anything that might be a clue," Crawford said. "I will send the crime scene techs out, but I want you there now. You can catch a ride back here with one of the units after you've finished your search."

"Yes sir," the officer said and followed George back to his taxi.

Brody turned the envelope over in his hands and carefully peeled it open. A crowd had gathered around his desk as he pulled the single sheet of paper from the envelope, opened it, and laid it on his desk. Everyone bent closer to read the words scrawled boldly on the paper.

The time has come for us to play
Only you can save the day
My favorite toy as of yet
I give her up with huge regret

Number Eight is praying for you
To use your head and pull her through
She's resting now, dressed in her best
Hoping you can pass the test
Her time is near and so are you
If she calms her fear, she will make it through
If she panics she will quickly fade
A premature ending to your crusade
Look to the north and look to the west
Past where the oldest rest
Once was damaged but now repaired
Look for the clues I left them there
Hurry now her time is dear
I will write again, you need not fear
TBS

Talis smiled from atop the crypt. "Message delivered and now the hunt begins," he said as the taxi driver and a uniformed officer climbed into the taxi and sped off.

He jumped down from the crypt and listened closely for any sounds coming from the crypt. Hearing none, he walked quickly from the cemetery. Boldly walking past the precinct house, back to Number Eight's home, where he went inside to retrieve the bag with his clothing, then stopped to rummage through her purse. He smiled when he saw several hundred dollars that he slipped into his pocket. He wasn't sure how much longer his money would hold out, so he helped himself to the cash. *She won't have a need for this anymore.* Then he took out her driver's license and slipped it into his bag, before closing the door behind him, careful to make sure it locked. Soon the streets would be swarming with police, so he quietly slipped into the night.

After an hour, the woman in the coffin lost the energy to pound against the coffin lid and she found it harder and harder to breathe. Her hands fell back to her sides as her lungs began to burn from the lack of oxygen. She felt the cold approach and she closed her eyes surrendering herself to the darkness.

†

Kara and Sasha drove around the city until nearly two a.m. They covered the Quarter from every direction several times, finding nothing that set off any triggers for either of them. Kara turned north one final time and when they reached the St. Louis Cemetery, a uniformed officer directed them down a side street. Blue lights were flashing everywhere. As they watched a stretcher was loaded into a waiting ambulance, the body covered with a pristine sheet.

"I don't know what happened here, but it doesn't feel good," Sasha said. "I think they found number eight." She sighed.

"Should we circle around and see what we can find out?"

"No, if that is truly her, and I think it is, we don't need to be seen in the area," Sasha said. "Head for home and we'll see what is in tomorrow's paper."

Kara followed the river and crossed the bridge as she drove for home. She held Sasha in her arms after they climbed between the covers. "He will make a mistake," Kara said. "They always do."

"I pray that it is soon. First the storm and now a serial killer, how much more can the city take?"

"I don't know, my love," Kara said as she stroked her lover's hair.

†

Brody had rushed to the copier and made twenty copies of the note so everyone could study the clues. He passed them out and listened as the collective brainpower went to work.

"He has her confined somewhere where her air is limited," Crawford said.

"Look to the north and to the west…past where the oldest rest," Brody rambled. A light bulb went off in Brody's head as he jumped from his chair. "She is in the cemetery," he shouted. "North and west would be the St. Louis, one of the oldest and right under our damned noses. That bastard!"

"Holy shit, I think you are right," Crawford said. "Okay, everyone, get to the cemetery and spread out."

"Wait. Look for a crypt that has been recently repaired, he says he has left evidence there, so we need to fan out and cover the cemetery as quickly as we can," Brody said.

Twenty-five men grabbed flashlights and rushed to the front door. They turned north and crossed the intersection to enter the cemetery. Even in daylight, the cemetery was like a maze, and it took nearly twenty minutes for one of the detectives to stumble across the bucket of plaster the killer had left behind. He got on the radio and announced he had found a recently repaired crypt in the far right-hand corner of the cemetery. He watched as flashlights bounced as the others came running in his direction.

"Dispatch, we need a cruiser with bolt cutters at the St. Louis Cemetery," he called into the radio when he checked the door and found a new lock installed. "Send a bus as well," he requested. The doors to the crypts opened outward with the coffins inches away on the inside, so there would be no kicking the door in. The detective grabbed the handle and gave a good jerk, but the solid door remained in place.

Brody heard the approach of a siren as he reached the crypt and the detective who had found it radioed where they needed the bolt cutters. An eternity seemed to pass before they heard tires screech to a halt and footsteps running toward them. Brody grabbed the bolt cutters and snapped off the lock as two other detectives opened the door and grabbed the coffin, tugging it from the slab.

They lowered the coffin to the ground and the men quickly worked to loosen the locks on the seals. When the last seal was broken free, they yanked the lid to the coffin open. Light shone across the purple-tinged skin of Number Eight's face as Brody bent down to check for breathing and a pulse. She was already turning cold and he knew they had arrived too late. He stepped back to allow the paramedics approaching to tend to her. They confirmed what he already knew. Deprived of oxygen for too long, there was no chance of reviving her.

"We have to get that bastard," Brody said to the chief. "We pieced together his riddle quickly, but he did not leave us enough time to reach her before it was too late," he said with emotion crackling in his voice.

"You did all that you could, Brody," the chief said as he wrapped an arm around Brody's shoulders and led him away from the crypt. "Let's meet back at the precinct house," he said to the rest of the group.

Brody walked sullenly from the cemetery to the precinct and sat heavily behind his desk. When everyone had reassembled, Crawford took over.

"There is nothing we can do for number eight," he said. "We must now focus on her and find out everything we can about her, starting with her identity." He looked around the room. "Martinez and Thomas, I want you to hotfoot it down to the morgue and get some pictures of the victim and bring them back here. Then we will send out teams to begin hitting the bars on Bourbon to see if we can locate anyone who knows her."

"Yes sir," they said and left the room.

"Green and Johnson," Crawford said, "I want you to take the plaster bucket and lock to crime scene for testing and fingerprints. I know we don't have a hit on him yet, but we need comparisons so we know this is the real deal and not a copycat.

"I know it is a shot in the dark, but I want you three to start canvassing hardware stores at first light to see if you can track down who bought plaster of this type. With all the repairs and construction going on it will probably be impossible, but we must follow every trail. Hell, we have to get lucky somewhere.

"The rest of you head home and plan on being back here tomorrow to continue on the task force. Hopefully by then, we will have something to work with." The men started filtering out of the room but Brody remained seated, staring at the note.

"That means you too, Brody," he said.

Brody started to protest but Crawford cut him off.

"I need you fresh tomorrow, and there's nothing you can do tonight. Our boy has an attraction to you, so he will be contacting you again soon. I want you sharp. Understood?"

"Yes, Chief," Brody said. He walked through the back door and climbed into his sedan for the twenty-minute drive home.

Chapter Six

There was nothing on the news channel regarding the events at the cemetery, but the front page of the newspaper boldly stated: *"TBS Claims Eighth Victim"*

The article had very little information on the victim, as the identity had not been determined. It stated that the eighth victim of the TBS serial killer was discovered at the St. Louis Cemetery, right under the noses of the New Orleans Police Department. The reporter cited an anonymous witness who claimed the killer had sent a riddled message to the police, but they were unable to solve the riddle to rescue the victim in time. The article went on to state that Detective Kyle Brody was heading up the task force and the note received was addressed specifically to him.

"I bet Detective Brody is fit to be tied, if he has read this article," Kara said as she read over Sasha's shoulder. They had met the detective when the Bellfontaine brothers kidnapped Kara, several years ago.

"You know he has to be, first he taunts the entire force, and now he seems to be targeting Brody. I know it had to crush him to find the woman too late for a rescue."

"I wish we knew more of the details. I may send Ted down to the DA's office tomorrow to visit some old friends and see if he can learn anything new."

"You are so clever, my love," Sasha said as she tilted her head back and kissed Kara.

"The more we can learn about him, the better chance we have of tracking him down," Kara said. "I don't guess I need to tell you that though."

Sasha knew Kara was still prodding for information on her involvement with the disappearance and deaths of the Bellfontaine brothers who had kidnapped and held Kara captive while they had hunted down the state's primary witness against them. Sasha did not respond outwardly to Kara's comment, but she had to work hard to restrain her laughter. Sasha knew Kara was dying to know the details, but she remained firm, choosing to prevent Kara from being knowledgeable in the event she was ever interviewed regarding their disappearance.

"He is very clever and unlike the Bellfontaines who flaunted their power openly, he will hide his in riddles and taunts to Brody," Sasha said.

"He is such a nice man. I just hate that he is being put through this."

"I do too, but I know if anyone can catch this killer, it will be Brody."

"He is a good detective," Kara agreed.

†

Talis woke up late the following afternoon and showered before preparing a meal to feed his ravenous appetite. After he had filled his belly, he took out a notepad and pen and began to write.

Dear Detective Brody,

I was very disappointed to read that your efforts to save Number Eight were not successful. She was a beautiful woman and we shared some similar appetites. In a small way, I feel like you caused me to lie to her, because I assured her that you would be coming soon to her rescue. We both let her down on that aspect. I was certain you would quickly unravel the clues and pull her out in the nick of time. I had been so impressed with your skills in the past. Alas, I guess next time I will have to give you a head start.

I will take a rest now and give you time to sort your evidence and I know you have plenty to go through. By the way, have you uncovered the other two yet? Think hard on that one, my man. I will let you know that Number One was swept under the rug by your own department, so look deep inside yourself to find her.

When I have Number Nine in my line of sight, I will write you again to start our next game.

Happy hunting.

TBS

Talis read over the note. He intended to taunt Brody, but not to the point the man would lose confidence in his abilities. Brody did have an excellent reputation for solving crimes and Talis knew his hunting would eventually end and he wanted Brody to be the one who captured him. He would tell them of his spiraling debauchery, all to please Anastasia. How her betrayal had given birth to the evil inside him when she returned to Russia and abandoned him.

He placed the note in the envelope and licked the bitter glue to seal it, before turning it over and scrawling the address to the police department. He took great pleasure in writing on the bottom left corner, Attention Detective Brody, in his bold writing. He fumbled through his desk and found a stamp, which he placed on the envelope, and dropped it off at a nearby post office. Brody would probably receive his note by tomorrow at the latest. He smiled to himself as he walked home. He stopped at a local market, picked up the newspaper, and then rushed home to read the story of his latest escapade.

He read the article several times before cutting it carefully from the front page. He took a pushpin and pinned it up on the wall next to Number Eight's driver's license. "Not a large piece, but I am sure there will be much more in the coming days," he said as he straightened the edge of the license.

†

Brody slept fitfully, tossing and turning throughout the night. His mind kept playing what-if. What if he had done this or that, until he finally came to the resolution that nothing he did would have mattered. TBS had simply not left him enough time to rescue the woman and that was that. He made himself breakfast and was drinking his coffee when he heard the familiar thump of the newspaper striking his front door. The man who made his delivery wasn't always consistent with the time of delivery, but he certainly had an accurate throwing arm. Brody opened the door and the paper was resting on the welcome mat.

He kicked the door closed behind him and opened the paper as he walked to the kitchen. "God Almighty," he said when he read the headline and the ensuing article. The paper made them look like a bunch of morons by providing the scant information they had in the article. He knew the autopsy report would reveal that the victim was already dead minutes after he received the note, but those were details that couldn't been leaked as there were very few that were privy to that information. Still the obvious leak from his department infuriated him to no end. He quickly reread the article and, after dumping his dishes into the sink, went to dress for work. It was bad enough the killer was taunting him. *I sure don't need the local press to start hounding me too.*

He pulled into the parking lot at the precinct house and went directly to the chief's office.

"Welcome back," Crawford said. "I hope you were able to get some rest."

"A little bit," Brody said. "What is the latest?"

"We know who Number Eight is. Her name was Susan Miller and she lived only a few blocks from here. Crime Scene is finishing up at her apartment as we speak."

"Did he leave more than his usual fingerprints and DNA behind?"

"Not that we can tell so far. From the semen stains and tousled bed it looks like they had been very busy over the weekend. We were able to get a hit at one of the local bars where she was a regular when a bartender recognized the photograph." The chief shook his head. "He also said she came in frequently on the weekends and usually left with a different man each time."

"Did he remember her coming in this weekend?"

"As a matter of fact, he did, but did not know the identity of the man she left with. He gave the same broad description as the taxi driver. Tall, dark, well built, but rather ambiguous on a facial description. We have run across one other piece of information," Crawford continued. "Several of his victims were missing their driver's licenses and when the

CSI boys checked her purse they found credit cards, but no cash or license."

"So he is taking them for trophies," Brody stated.

"That's what it looks like. Other than that, Miller was a third-year nursing student at Tulane, no known family and the university is helping the examiner's office track down the next of kin."

"What are we going to share with the media?"

"I think we should give a full disclosure of her identity once notifications have been made and see if we can get a few more leads," Crawford said.

"I agree. He has varied from his routine with this one. His hands did not choke the life from her, and I bet my last paycheck that he took her out on the town for dinner or drinks or something to flaunt her in the public's eye, before placing her in the coffin," Brody added. "His arrogance is growing with each day that passes without being captured."

"I have only worked one other serial case in all my years," the chief said.

"How did it turn out?"

"He killed six young women before his guilt overwhelmed him and he swallowed the barrel of a thirty-eight," he said. "I think it is very rare for one to take his life, but after a while, some of them begin to feel remorse for their victims or they get tired of the game and wish to be caught." The chief looked up at Brody, "I hope our boy gets tired soon."

"Me too, the ethos of the Big Easy would make it easy for him to hunt for years," Brody said with a solemn tone.

A uniformed officer knocked on the door. "Excuse me, Chief, but I think you will want to see this," the man said as he handed him the envelope he had been carrying.

"Where did you get this?"

"My brother works in the sorting department of the post office, so I asked him to keep an eye open for mail addressed to Detective Brody," the officer said.

"Officer Williams, correct?" Crawford asked.

"Yes, sir," the man said with a proud smile for being recognized by the chief of detectives.

"Excellent work. That was brilliant thinking."

"So brilliant, Chief, I think we could use him on the task force," Brody said.

"How about it, Williams, would you care to join us?"

"Oh hell yes, I mean yes, Chief, I would."

"Go tell the duty office you have been reassigned and get back in street clothes, preferably something casual," Crawford said. "By the way, Williams, how old are you?"

"Twenty-six, sir."

"Good age. Where would you take a woman out to dinner if you really wanted to show her off in the Quarter?"

"There are several places I could think of," Williams said.

"Great, I want you to take this DMV picture of our latest victim to the streets and find out where she had dinner last night, something Cajun and spicy according to the ME," the chief said.

"Here, take my sedan, it's the ugly blue one," Brody said as he tossed the keys to Williams.

"I'm on it," Williams said.

Crawford looked at Brody and handed him the envelope. "We might as well see what our boy has to say."

Brody carefully opened the envelope and took out the short note, placing it on the desk so he and the chief could read it at the same time.

"So he knows we haven't found his first yet," Brody said. "I feel confident that the young man was the other we hadn't uncovered. I will get Sarge to go deeper into the archives. Someone who had been swept under the rug by my own department," he read. "Any ideas what he is referring to here?"

"Maybe a case that was closed when there was obvious evidence there was more to it," Crawford said. "If it is older than the ones we have on record, then it probably happened before the storm. Maybe just maybe, close enough that evidence was overlooked during all the approaching mayhem from the storm."

"So we need to check all female deaths back to July?"

"I think you would be safe with that timeline."

"I hope he needs a long rest," Brody said. "We are nowhere close to being ready for his next victim."

"Maybe a few weeks, a month tops," Crawford predicted. "He knows he has stirred up a hornet's nest and will want the streets to calm down, but he will need to feed his ego before we are ready," Crawford predicted.

"If he is taking souvenirs, you can bet he is watching the papers and news closely as he builds his shrine to his victims. Maybe if we keep the story alive by reporting bits and pieces of what we have determined, it will be enough to satisfy him for a while," Brody suggested.

"It is worth a shot. I think we should brief the university presidents to beef up their security patrols also," the chief said.

"I will leave that in your hands. You hobnob much better than me," he teased.

"Thanks," Crawford said. "Maybe I can convince the mayor into doing it for me." Brody roared with laughter.

"God only knows what would happen then. By the way, shouldn't you bring him up to date?"

"He has been ringing my phone off the hook," the chief said. "I hate dealing with the bastard. I might as well get it over with."

"Chief, I would be cautious of what information you disclose to him," Brody said. "If ever there was a man who needed some positive publicity, it would be our dear friend the mayor."

"I agree and will give him only the basics," Crawford said. "Wish me luck."

"Good luck, boss," Brody followed him out in search of Sarge to request he pull some additional records. He also made a copy of the latest note and pinned it up on the crime board. Brody looked at his own growing shrine and studied the faces and pictures closely, searching for anything he had missed.

Williams came bouncing back in thirty minutes later, wearing a huge smile on his face. He sat down next to Brody and flipped open a notepad. "She had sautéed crab fingers for an appetizer then a Cajun grilled grouper for her meal," he said. "She skipped dessert as she and her companion had more urgent plans."

"Did you get a description of the companion?" Brody asked.

"He was a beautiful hunk of eye candy, according to the waiter who served them." He chuckled and continued to read. "Dark brown short cropped hair, bedroom eyes, broad shoulders, and hung like a horse."

"Is that a direct quote as well?"

"I believe the man said he had a cock to die for," Williams said.

"Remind me to request that all future eyewitnesses be gay," Brody said. "Can he describe the man to a sketch artist?"

"Down to a minute scar on the man's temple. He is working with the artist as we speak."

"Excellent job, Williams," Brody said as he slapped the man on the back. "Go back and bring me the sketch as soon as they finish."

Williams stood to leave the room. "You did good work."

"Thank you, Detective."

"Just call me Brody, like everyone else."

"Thank you, sir," Williams said and left the room.

With that news, Brody felt better than he had for several weeks. The arrogance of TBS may turn out to be his undoing. Brody almost felt disappointed that he would make such a mistake and felt that there must be something else. Identifying him like that would be too simple.

He stopped by the front desk to speak to Sarge. "I am going over to the woman's apartment, but if Williams comes back before me, send him over please."

"Will do, Brody," Sarge said.

Brody stepped out of the precinct house and turned left. He walked four blocks, took another left, and followed the trail of yellow crime scene tape to the location where the Miller woman lived. He stooped under the tape and, putting on gloves, stepped through the front door. He could hear the crime scene techs at work upstairs and followed the sound of their voices.

The room was filled with the musty scent of sex, but something else hung in the air and Brody followed the scent into the kitchen. "Can you guys smell cologne?" Brody asked.

"Something rich and sensual," a female tech said. "This is the first time we have noticed that."

"It could have been there, but masked from the smell of decomposition of his victims," another tech said. "She wasn't killed here and left to be discovered for several days. We are lucky to have such a fresh scene."

"Anything other than the cologne that is new?"

"Sex toys," the female said.

"What kind?"

"A large dildo and nipple clamps were beside the bed, and several other toys were found in her drawers."

"So that's what he meant by appetites."

"Excuse me?" the woman said.

"Nothing, just thinking out loud," Brody said. He sat at the small kitchen table and noticed the notepad and pen that were resting there. He picked up the notepad and looked at it closely. He could see the imprint of the handwriting from the page that had once rested on top and Brody realized the killer had sat in that very spot as he penned the note to him. Brody told the techs to add the notepad and pen to their evidence and walked back to the precinct.

†

Talis knew that if the police moved quickly, they would be able to have a good idea of what his face looked like. He was certain the waiter at the restaurant had stared at him long enough to memorize every pore in his skin.

He had planned to lay low for the next few weeks, but now he may need to take some drastic measures. He had always heard blonds have more fun, so maybe it was time for him to find out or maybe he would just buy a hairpiece. He would think of something, he always had. Or, maybe it was time to head out of town to visit some friends out in the bayou and catch up on some fishing. He needed to think, so he lay down on his bed and looked up at his shrine.

†

Kara walked up behind Sasha as she cooked dinner for them. “You know it is almost that time?” she said.

“What time is that, my love?” Sasha knew she was referring to Milly’s birthday. Milly was the daughter of James and his wife, a second generation of caretakers who had worked for her for many years. Their daughter Milly, named after Sasha’s deceased lover, even held a striking resemblance to her.

“Time for Milly’s birthday. In a few more weeks she will be eighteen, and in a few more months she will leave for college,” Kara reminded her. “Have you given any thought to a present?”

“Well, she has signed up to get a head start on college by taking a few night classes at Tulane in the spring, so I thought we might get her a car.”

“That would be very practical and she wouldn’t have to be seen in her dad’s beat-up truck,” Kara said with a grin. “Have you talked to them about it yet?”

“No, I wanted to discuss it with you first. I was thinking something small like a Civic or Sentra that would be easy on gas and safe to maneuver on the narrow streets of Nawlins.”

“The Civic is a little more stylish, baby.”

“Yeah, I was leaning toward that as well and the price is not bad.”

“So what color?”

“Blue of course, it’s Milly’s favorite color.”

“Why don’t you have a chat with James tonight and we will do some shopping tomorrow.”

“I will,” Sasha said as she scooped out two bowls of gumbo. “Will you take these to the table while I get the corn bread?”

“Of course I will, darling,” Kara said as she took the bowls from Sasha.

Chapter Seven

Kara and Sasha drove to Baton Rouge the next day to buy Milly's birthday gift. The dealer in New Orleans had not reopened his dealership yet after Katrina, so they were off on a road trip. It had been quite some time since they had traveled from New Orleans together and they decided to stay overnight in Baton Rouge. They arrived early and went directly to the dealership and by midafternoon had made their purchase and left with an agreement to return the following morning to pick up the car.

They drove to the hotel, checked in, and showered before dressing for a night on the town. Sasha had made reservations at a nice restaurant and then had plans to take Kara to a Broadway show hosted by LSU. It had been quite some time since they had shared a romantic evening together and Sasha made the best of the opportunity. After the final curtain fell on the show, Sasha asked, "Would you would like to find a cozy spot for a few drinks?"

"I would rather take you back to the hotel, stretch out on that king-sized bed and make love until the sun comes up," Kara said.

"I really like that idea," Sasha said as she turned the car into the traffic and started back toward the hotel.

The full moon was shining on the bed when they entered the room. Sasha took Kara in her arms and danced her across the room to an imaginary tune. When they reached the bed, Sasha leaned down and covered Kara's lips with a tender kiss. "I love you so," she whispered as her hands slid beneath Kara's blouse and lifted it above her head.

"I love you too," Kara said as Sasha slowly undressed her, planting loving kisses over her skin.

When she had Kara undressed she gently pushed her back onto the bed then slowly removed her clothing. She loved the way Kara's eyes shone as she watched her undress and tonight they were exceptionally bright in the moonlight. She approached the bed and pressed her body into Kara's. Kara's hands encircled her, pulling her close.

Kara whispered sweet words to Sasha as she used her hands and mouth to stoke Kara's passion. "That feels so good, baby," Kara purred as Sasha's lips caressed the soft skin of her breasts, nuzzling into them with her cheeks as she slowly made love to Kara.

"Oh, yes, Sasha," Kara crooned as Sasha's tongue parted her lower lips for a sensual kiss, swirling inside Kara as her hips rolled up to meet Sasha's tongue.

The sounds of their lovemaking lasted deep into the night and when their passions were sated, Sasha held Kara in her arms. She concentrated on their heartbeat and felt the single pulse that ran between them. One love, one pulse, she had remembered Milly telling her so many years ago when she first transformed Sasha. She closed her eyes and drifted into sleep.

"I love you too, Sasha," Kara said before she realized Sasha had fallen asleep. Had she heard Sasha's thoughts or was she picking up a projection from another immortal, she wondered. She was still contemplating the answer when her eyes fell closed and she joined Sasha in sleep.

†

Talis packed the largest suitcase he owned and stepped out into the darkness. He walked the short distance to the garage where he stored his car and tossed the suitcase in the trunk. He slipped in behind the wheel and prayed the car would still start. It had been months since he had driven and he breathed a sigh of relief when he turned the key and the engine roared to life. He turned on his headlights and pulled from the garage, parking at the curb as he returned to close and lock the door.

Sleep had done wonders for his need to think clearly. He confirmed his decision when he opened the newspaper that morning and saw a sketch of TBS that resembled him enough to bring him under suspicion if someone were to recognize him. He drove carefully down the dark avenues until he reached the bridge. He turned south, crossing the Mississippi and drove deep into the night.

†

The chief of detectives shouted for joy when Brody told him they had a sketch of TBS and rushed back to the precinct house to see it with his own eyes.

"If this is accurate, I can see why young women fall easy prey to him," Crawford said. "He is a handsome devil."

"Devil being the key word," Brody said.

"So, what are we going to do with this?"

"I think we need to send it out through the media and set up a tip line. I also think we need to continue our canvass, while our luck is still with us. Williams did such a great job of getting us this far, I think he should continue to snoop around the Quarter to see what he can uncover."

"It will drive him into hiding," Crawford warned.

"He already told us he is taking a rest, so passing him on the sidewalk can be ruled out," Brody said. "The more eyes we have searching for him the better."

"Let's run with it then," the chief said. "I am going to call the mayor to give him an update."

"Consider it done," Brody took a copy of the artist's rendering and placed it upon the crime board. "Now you are in my line of sight," Brody said to the dark image staring back at him. "Williams," Brody shouted.

"Yes, sir," Williams said as he stepped into the large office.

"I want you to take this sketch into the Quarter and see what you can find out about our boy. Take your time, going door to door if you need to, but find out what you can."

Williams took the copy of the sketch from Brody and headed for the door. "Happy hunting," Brody said, not realizing he had used the same line as TBS.

"I will do my best, sir."

"I know you will, that is why I chose you," Brody said with a smile.

Williams left and Brody thought about how pleased he was to have such a clever and ambitious young man working with him. Many of the seasoned detectives on the Task Force were excellent investigators, but Brody felt most of them were stressed by the aftermath of the storm, worrying about displaced families and trying to stay on top of the day-to-day murders in the city. It was easy to crumble under that weight and lose focus. Williams was eager to make a good impression and he had demonstrated sharp instincts so far.

Brody felt good about the day's progress and sat behind his desk to start reviewing the stack of files Sarge had brought to him. He needed to find Number One to help him put this case into perspective, so with a haggard sigh he opened the first of the case files.

†

Talis drove deep into the night and when the sun rose, he caught his first glimpse of the Atchafalaya Bay. The calm water of the bay was surrounded by cypress bogs and was the home of some of the state's best fishing and hunting. It was also home to the one person Talis had ever really considered a friend.

Three years ago, when he was still in medical school and prior to meeting Anastasia, Talis had signed up as a science tutor to earn some extra cash. He was a gifted student and science and mathematics had always been a breeze for him. They weren't as easy for Lute Strider, a football scholarship star. Talis was assigned as his personal tutor to help him get through a freshman biology class and after Lute passed with a B, he and Talis remained friends.

Lute was not your typical testosterone-loaded jock. Although he was a mountain of a man at six foot eight inches, there was a peacefulness about him that Talis had always found intriguing. Talis went to every home game that season and watched as his friend destroyed opponents from his position on the defensive line. He was being considered as a top prospect for the professional league. It was during the last home game of the season where a win would send them to the playoffs when Lute's life changed. The rains had been relentless during the entire game, but the officials would not halt the game and conditions on the field rapidly deteriorated.

As the final minutes of the third quarter approached, the opposing team called a rushing play. As Lute rose from his three-point stance, he was double-teamed, and Talis watched in horror as two large offensive players went directly for Lute's knees to perform a cut block. The maneuver literally cut the legs from beneath the defender, but in this instance, the collisions shattered both of Lute's knees and he suffered career-ending injuries.

Talis watched as a golf cart carried his friend off the field, in obvious pain, and headed to the locker room. Talis rushed for the exit and ran to the fieldhouse where Lute would be x-rayed. He did not make it before they took Lute in for x-rays, so he waited in the pouring rain to hear word of his friend's condition.

Talis raised his dark eyes off the muddy field when he heard the approach of the ambulance. He watched as the paramedics opened up the back of the large bus and pulled out a long stretcher. They returned a few minutes later, with Lute secured on the stretcher, heavily sedated to ease his pain.

Lute was conscious enough to recognize Talis as he stood watching.

"They got me good, my friend," he said as he lifted his huge paw of a hand to Talis.

Talis stepped forward and took Lute's hand in his. "I saw what they did to you."

"Everything will be okay, Talis," Lute said.

"We need to go," one of the ambulance staff said.

"I will see you at the hospital later tonight," he promised as he released Lute's big hand.

Lute smiled at him through a delirium of drugs. “It’s going to be okay, Doc,” he repeated.

“Yes, my friend, you are going to be just fine,” Talis said to reassure his friend.

Shock was beginning to set in as Talis watched the ambulance pull away from the fieldhouse, carrying away the one person who truly ever seemed to care about him.

Later that evening, Talis sat beside Lute’s bed and watched his face contort with pain. He had been rushed through emergency surgery, but the severe damage to his knees could not be reversed. The surgeon told him that Lute would walk forever with a limp, and there would be no more football in his future.

Lute’s sole purpose for being in college was to play football. He was a good student, but Talis knew that after his playing days were done, Lute wanted to return home to fish, shrimp, and hunt until the end of his days. His heart was in the bayou where he was born and raised.

Talis spent the night at the hospital that evening, sitting patiently beside Lute’s bed, watching over him until his need for sleep won out. When he woke the next morning, Lute was propped up in his bed watching him sleep.

“Good morning, Doc,” he said, forcing a smile. “Have you been here all night?”

“Yeah, Lute, I was afraid you might go chasing after one of these cute nurses if someone wasn’t here with you,” Talis said.

“I won’t be chasing much of anything for a while.”

“It will be a long and painful process, but you will be back on your feet in no time.”

“Yes, the doctors have said I will need months of therapy and maybe some additional surgery,” Lute said.

A deep silence fell between them at that point. Talis knew what was coming, but asked his question anyhow. "What's next? Are you planning to finish your degree?"

"The university has promised me an education, but I will only stay long enough to finish this semester and if my therapy is done, I will head home."

"I will hate to see you go."

"It's okay Doc, I just get to start my hunting and fishing earlier than planned. I can work on the shrimp boat with my father and still make a good living."

"I would still love to take a baseball bat to the two that did this to you," Talis said, the anger obvious in his voice.

"Easy, Doc," Lute said. "The maneuver was legal to an extent, but athletes run the risk of injury every time they suit up."

"I know, it just seemed like such a dirty blow."

"What's done is done. It cannot be changed and this happened for a reason."

"I'm happy you can have such a positive outlook on it," Talis said. "I still want to kill the bastards."

"Good, I will need your energy to get me through all this rehab."

Talis became his rehab partner and for months watched his friend suffer through the agony of learning to walk again. Even when he finished rehab, Lute would need the assistance of a cane for several more months until his strength and endurance built back up.

When the semester ended, Lute's father arrived to take him home. Talis felt empty after he hugged his large friend and watched him drive off in his father's old beat-up truck. "Come visit when you can," he still heard ringing in his ears.

Talis had no idea what made him think of Lute. Maybe it was his need to be away from the city for a while until his face in the papers faded from memory. But as he lay on his bed thinking of what to do, Lute popped into his mind. "Come visit when you can," he heard him say.

Talis dug out a telephone number and he hoped that after two years his invitation was still open. He dialed the number and was relieved when her heard Lute's booming voice answer the telephone.

"Lute, this is Doc, how are you doing?"

"I couldn't be finer and you, Doc?"

"I have seen better days," Talis admitted.

"What's wrong, Doc?"

"It's a long story Lute, but I was wondering if my invitation to come for a visit still stood?"

"Oh hell yes, Doc," Lute said. "I have a small cabin on the bay. It's not much, but you are welcome to stay as long as you want. When you coming?"

"Would tomorrow be too soon?"

"Nope, come on down."

"Thanks, this means a lot to me," Talis said.

"I will see you tomorrow then, just call when you get close and I will give you directions."

†

By the end of the night, Brody had narrowed the stack of case files down to five possibilities. His eyes continued to search out the file of Lynn Frost, a businesswoman who had died in a local hotel while attending a conference in the city. Brody was reviewing the file when Crawford came into his office.

"Chief, what do you know about this case?" Brody asked as he handed him the file.

The chief flipped through the report. "I can't remember ever seeing this one, or if I did it doesn't click in my memory." He continued to look through the file. "Why?"

"Well, TBS said that Number One had been swept under the rug by our own," Brody said. "The investigation doesn't seem very thorough," he said. "I don't think it ever reached our desks because it was ruled as an accidental overdose. What are the possibilities that, because of the timing, it was left at that?"

"I would hate to think that could really occur, but her death was just days before Katrina hit and all hell broke loose," Crawford said. "I guess it is a possibility though. There seems to be more to this case than just an overdose."

"I think I will head down to the coroner's office tomorrow and see what I can find out."

"Good idea, but for now, you need to go home and get some rest," the chief said. "We've learned a great deal today and hopefully tomorrow will bring us more good luck."

"All right, you are the boss," Brody said as he tucked the file in his briefcase.

"Damn right I am," Crawford said with a chuckle.

Brody and the chief walked out to the parking lot together. "You've done a good job on this so far, Brody. I'm confident you will bring this bastard into custody," he said as he slapped Brody on the shoulder.

"The quicker, the better," Brody added then slipped in behind the wheel of his sedan. Williams had returned his car to him earlier that evening as he went off duty. He had been exhausted and disappointed that he was not able to pick up any additional information on TBS.

"This will be a long and involved case before we bring him in," Brody had told the young officer. "You've done well so far, and I feel you will be an important player in catching TBS."

Brody stopped off for a po'boy sandwich on his way home. While he ate the sandwich and drank a few beers, he looked at the file on Lynn Frost one last time for the evening. He pulled out the medical examiner's report and slowly read over it word for word. There had not been a full autopsy completed when toxicology revealed such a large amount of cocaine in her system. It was noted that upon visual exam, her body had evidence of recent sexual activity, but because there was no evidence of foul play, the case was closed as a drug overdose.

"Sloppy work," he said aloud. He wondered just how much information he would be able to uncover on the case that had not been included in the report. Brody was still contemplating the report when his eyelids slid down and he fell sideways onto the couch. He woke hours later with a stiff neck and quietly made his way through his house to his bedroom. He stripped out of his clothes and collapsed onto the bed.

†

Sasha and Kara had returned from their trip to Baton Rouge early in the afternoon and pulled the new car into the garage out of view of Milly's eyes. Sasha would leave her truck in the driveway for now so they could conceal her present as long as possible. She and Kara were sitting on the front porch sharing cocktails when James and Milly pulled up in his old truck. They shared a look between them and giggled together as they thought of how shocked Milly was going to be to see the new car.

Milly saw them sitting on the porch giggling when she got out of the truck and walked over to them. "What are you two up to?" she asked. "I could hear your giggles across the yard."

"Who says we are up to anything?" Sasha asked.

"Now if Kara had said that I might have thought you just had a private joke, but you, on the other hand, are up to no good; it's written all over your face," she said to Sasha.

"Why Milly, I am so hurt by your accusation," Sasha protested.

"Uh-huh, sure you are," the young woman replied. "So what are you up to?"

"We were just discussing the need to buy a certain someone a birthday present," Sasha said. "What would you like?"

"A million dollars, a trip to Paris, a whole new wardrobe," Milly teased.

"You already have more clothes than Kara and I combined," Sasha said.

"I most certainly do not," Milly said and then looked at Kara who just smiled at her. "Okay, so no clothes."

"I am fresh out of million dollar bills too."

"I will gladly take it in small bills, unmarked of course," Milly teased.

"Paris isn't such a bad idea, but you are still in school for several more months yet," Sasha said with a sigh.

"What about a trip to Ft. Lauderdale for spring break," Kara said.

"Thanks, but my classmates all act so juvenile," Milly said. "I would rather spend the time here and save up for a trip to Paris," she hinted again.

"What is the sudden urge to see Paris?" Kara asked.

"I really don't know, but somedays it seems it is all I can think about," Milly said.

"Paris does have a romantic allure like that," Sasha said. "It has always been one of my favorites."

"See, you and Kara could come and chaperone me," Milly said.

Sasha chuckled and just shook her head.

"I need to help Mom with dinner, so I'd better be going."

"See you later," Kara and Sasha said together.

"That might not be a bad graduation present," Kara said.

"Would you help me chaperone?"

"We will have to see how my court dates fall out," Kara said. "It is a possibility, though."

Sasha felt a tingling in her head. Milly was trying to dip into her thoughts to find out what she and Kara were going to buy her for a birthday present. Sasha smiled to herself as she watched Milly walk away. Milly's powers were not strong enough yet to weave through Sasha's protections and Sasha was not ready for Milly to be able to project thoughts to her. She did not know how it was possible, but she could feel Milly's powers growing stronger every day.

Kara saw the smile on Sasha's face and asked, "What are you thinking about?"

"I was just thinking about how fast she has grown up. It seems like only yesterday she was still a little girl, bouncing around here in her pigtails."

"The years do seem to be flying by."

Sasha did not think that Kara was aware of Milly's powers and, for some reason, she did not want to bring the subject up, so she kept her observations to herself, at least for now.

"I'm starving," Kara said. "What's for supper?"

"Let's ride into town and grab something," Sasha suggested. "Do you have any idea what you are starving for?"

"Baby back ribs and lots of them," Kara said with a grin. "I'll even let you drive since your truck is in the driveway," she added.

"Let's get a move on then."

Sasha stopped at the end of the driveway and picked up the newspaper delivered earlier. She placed it between them on the seat and drove into town to one of their favorite BBQ places. They ordered ribs and as they waited for the food to arrive. Sasha opened up the paper. Her eyes went directly to the artist's rendering of the TBS killer.

"Well, well," she said. "We now have a face to go with the name."

"What name is that, honey?"

"The TBS killer," Sasha said.

"Oh really, let me see." Kara studied the sketch and looked back up at Sasha. "Handsome, isn't he?"

"If this is accurate, I can see why the ladies were attracted to him."

"How can such a beautiful face disguise such a monster?"

"I don't know," Sasha answered and then returned to read the short article. "They haven't gotten much else on him from the sound of it, but a face, that's a good start."

"I just hope someone will recognize him and the authorities can put an end to this once and for all."

"Me too, my love," Sasha said as the food was delivered and she set the paper aside.

†

"Hello, this is 911, how may I help you?" the operator asked.

"The man in the newspaper, this TBS killer, I know who he is," the caller said.

"May I have your name?" the operator asked.

"No, but his name is Thomas Dubais and he lives on Third Street in Kenner," the caller said and hung up.

The operator quickly noted the number of the caller and tracked it down to a pay phone near Jackson Square. She then contacted the chief of detectives and gave him the message.

Crawford called the precinct house, got them started searching for information on the potential suspect, and then paged Brody.

Brody called back within minutes. "What's up, Chief?"

"We got a tip from the artist's sketch, and I wanted you in so we could plan on picking this guy up," Crawford said. "I have them researching the name now."

"I will be there in twenty minutes," Brody said and hung up.

Brody quickly showered and dressed. He used the car's blue lights to race through the streets. Traffic was light at this time of morning, so there was no need for sirens to move traffic out of his path. He arrived just in time to see Williams walking in.

"You are early," Williams said.

"Come with me, we may have a break," Brody said as they rushed to the building.

"What do we have?" Brody asked Crawford.

"Thomas Dubais, twenty-six years of age, no prior record, and an address in Kenner," the chief said.

He showed them the DMV photograph on his driver's license. "Those things always look like mug shots," Brody growled. "There is a striking resemblance to the sketch though."

"Are we going to get him?" Williams asked.

"I thought you two would never ask," Crawford said with a grin. "I have a marked unit outside his home now, just waiting for us."

When they reached the address on the driver's license, Brody pulled up next to the marked cruiser. "Have you seen any signs of movement in there?" Brody asked.

"No sir, if anyone is home, they are still asleep," the uniformed officer said.

"Well, let's find out for sure," Brody said. "I assume you have a warrant?" he asked Crawford,

"I've got it covered," the chief said.

The uniformed officer knocked on the door and shouted, "NOPD, open up." There were no sounds coming from inside the small house or any signs of movement around the outside.

"Take it down," Crawford ordered and the officer swung backward with a battering ram and smashed the door open with one strike.

The officers rushed into the darkened home and flipped on a light switch only to find the house powerless and empty. "I don't think anyone has lived here in a while," Brody said.

"Let's head back to the precinct and see if we can find out who owns this place. We owe them a new front door if nothing else," he said.

"Williams, I want you to stay with the uniforms and see what you can find out from the neighbors," Brody said. "When you get done, ride back to the house with them."

"Yes, Brody," Williams said uneasily.

"Well, fuck," Crawford said once they were back in Brody's sedan.

"It would have been too good to be true," Brody said. "At least we have a starting point."

"That's true. Two days ago, all we had were dead bodies. Now we have a face and hopefully a name to match."

"Would you mind if we run back to my place? I forgot that case file in my rush to get in," Brody explained.

"Of course not," Crawford said as Brody turned toward his home.

When Brody turned into his small driveway, the chief chuckled. "You better empty your mailbox too, it's overflowing."

"That can't be, I just emptied it yesterday," Brody said with a look of concern.

Crawford stepped out of the car and looked around quickly, but in the darkness, he could see no one or see any signs of movement. Brody rushed to the mailbox and used the barrel of his pistol to lift the lid to a standing position. A white envelope fell from the box and when Brody looked inside he saw a black object. "Bring me the flashlight from the glove box, please, Chief," he said.

Crawford handed it to Brody. "Here you go."

Shining the flashlight into the box Brody reached in and retrieved a pair of silk stockings. He picked up the envelope and pulled out the note. *So close and yet so far away.*

"Chief, that's not the same handwriting," Brody was quick to point out.

"No, it's not," he agreed. "What are we to make of this?"

"Was the tip from an anonymous caller?"

"Yes, of course, there is no reward money posted yet," the chief said. "The caller was male and the phone was traced to a pay phone near Jackson Square." He looked at Brody. "What are you thinking?"

"Either TBS has an accomplice, which I seriously doubt, or we have a copycat," Brody said.

"That is all we need. Another sick fuck running around the city," Crawford growled. "Get your file and let's head back to town."

Chapter Eight

It did not take long to search the tax records to find that a George Calvin owned the house in Kenner. Brody left the phone call for the chief and headed down to the city morgue to have a chat with the medical examiner about Lynn Frost. Something about the case was eating at his gut and Brody had to find out why.

"Calvin here, do you know what fucking time it is?" a harsh voice spoke into the phone.

"I am very sorry to disturb you so early, Mr. Calvin, but do you still own a small house on Third Street in Kenner?" he asked.

"Yes, I do, why?" the man asked. "Who is this anyway?"

"I am the Chief of Detectives, Truman Crawford. Your house in Kenner was listed as the address of a possible suspect in one of our cases," he explained.

"Was it that no-good fruit, Dubais?"

"Yes, that is exactly who we are looking for," Crawford said.

"That makes two of us. The bum skipped out on me last week owing me two months' rent."

"What can you tell me about him?" the chief asked.

"He was one of them pretty boys, waiting to be "discovered" by Hollywood while he was partying his ass off and fucking everything he got his hands on," Calvin said with a sneer in his voice. "Too damned good looking to go out and get a real job, but always came up with money to party."

"Do you have any idea where he might have gone?"

"Not a damned clue," Calvin said. "I know he escorted several older ladies here in town, but that's all I know. Knowing his luck, one of them probably set him up in a suite in the Quarter."

"Thank you for the information, Mr. Calvin, and we will have a carpenter stop by today to repair your door."

"What did you do to my door?"

"We broke it in when there was no answer, so the city will be replacing it today with our deepest apologies."

"Just add it to the prick's bill when you find him," Calvin said.

"Will do, Mr. Calvin, goodbye," Crawford said and hung up.

Williams returned just as the chief was hanging up the phone. "Did you find out anything?"

"Moved out a little over a week ago, with no forwarding address, but one of the neighbors said he was moving on up, had found him a little place in the Garden District."

"From Third Street in Kenner to the Garden District with no full-time job, I don't think so," Crawford said.

"Are you thinking a hustler of some sorts?" Williams asked.

"That's what I am thinking. Take this DMV photograph and hit those all-night diners in the Quarter and let's see if our boy is a regular there."

"On it," Williams said as he stepped out into another muggy New Orleans morning.

†

Brody met with Dr. Sebastian who had signed off on the death certificate for Lynn Frost.

"So, what you are saying is that you ruled the cause of death as a drug overdose?" he asked the attractive brunette.

"Yes," she looked at her file, "that was it exactly."

"You also noted petechial hemorrhaging, which would suggest some form of asphyxiation, if I remember correctly."

"Someone paid attention in class," she teased. "Yes, you are correct."

"So why was that not listed as a secondary cause of death on the death certificate?" he asked.

"Because there was no sign of strangulation marks in the soft tissue of her neck, or any signs of a struggle that would indicate a pillow or other object had been used to smother her," Sebastian said. "The ME said to write it off as a drug overdose and I follow orders, Detective."

"So, in your professional opinion, off the record of course, could there be more to her death than an overdose?" he asked.

"On the record, her death was caused by the drug overdose," the doctor said, holding her ground. "That is not to say that she was alone when she died. There was ample evidence that she had recently engaged in sexual intercourse very close to the time of death." She looked up at him with a cute smile. "There was no evidence, however, that her partner or partners had anything to do with her death."

"I don't see a record of the disposition of the deceased," he said. "Do you have knowledge of what happened to her remains?"

She looked deeper into her file. "Her parents had her flown home the day after the airport reopened."

"Do you have a phone number or address for her parents?"

"Yes, and I supposed you want it?"

"Of course," Brody said with a charming smile.

"I hate to be the one to burst your bubble, but the body was prepared for cremation before it left New Orleans. If you are looking to gain further evidence from her, you will not have that chance."

"Well damn, I can't get a foothold here."

"Why are you so interested in this case?".

"Have you been following the TBS case?"

"The serial killer, yes, I have seen several of his victims," she said.

"I think Lynn Frost was his first victim," Brody said.

"You know what? You need to take me for coffee and beignets."

"Okay, when can we do this?"

"Let's go now before I change my mind," Dr. Sebastian said.

She stepped out of her office, informed her secretary that she would be back in an hour, and walked out to Brody's sedan. They drove down to Jackson Square and he used his police pass to illegally park.

They ordered coffee and beignets and as they waited on their order, he asked, "So what couldn't you tell me at the office?"

"When you mentioned TBS, something snapped in place for me," she said. "I did the autopsy on his latest victim and now that you have brought the Frost woman to mind, there are similarities."

"Such as what?" he asked.

"Both women had evidence of engaging in intense sexual activity, but there was no evidence of force that would indicate rape." She looked around nervously. "They willingly engaged in prolonged rough sexual activity including sodomy and oral sex."

Brody leaned forward on his elbows. "So, how do you think Frost was suffocated?" he asked.

"I think she did the cocaine and was engaging in a vigorous blow job, that blocked her airflow for too long and when she passed out the drugs took her the rest of the way," Sebastian said. "That is just my opinion. I don't have and will never get the evidence to back that up."

"So, do you think Lynn Frost could be his first victim?" Brody asked.

"Yes, I do. Why is it so important to find out who his first was?" she asked.

"It may help us with some clues that we may have overlooked in some of the other cases," Brody said. "Anything to help identify this freak and his motives may help to tie the cases together."

"I wish there was more I could give you. He's got to be stopped soon," she said.

"You have been very helpful and I appreciate your candor," Brody said. "I realize the precarious position you could be in just by sitting here with me now."

"If I can be penalized for stating the truth and my professional opinion, then I don't need to be working in this city," she said.

"I will keep our conversation between us," he said. "I just needed validation that I was on the right trail and you gave me just that."

"I'm glad I could help," she said with a brilliant smile. "Sometimes I feel like our skills are so wasted when we don't truly have the opportunity to investigate cases like we should, but since Katrina, we have spent months just trying to identify victims. I know to the families that is important, but because of the overload, important evidence was not thoroughly investigated."

"I will get this bastard, Dr. Sebastian. I want Lynn Frost and his other victims to get justice for the things he did to them, willingly or not."

"I have every confidence you will solve this case and bring him to trial," she said as they finished the last of the coffee. "Would you drop me back at the office?"

"Of course I will," he said. "Thank you for everything."

"You are very welcome and thank you for a late breakfast," she said.

"My pleasure." He handed her one of his business cards. "Call me if you miss breakfast again," he said with a wink.

"Thanks, I will," she said as she climbed from the car and walked the steps to the morgue.

"Such a beautiful woman in all that ugliness," he said as he shook his head and drove back to the precinct house.

†

"The owner seems to think Dubais is living down in the Quarter," Crawford said.

"Well, that is certainly a step up the social ladder for him," Brody said.

"I have Williams checking the all-night diners to see if our boy is a regular. His ex-landlord said he was quite the lover and had provided escort services to some mature ladies of New Orleans," Crawford said.

"Are you thinking he's some sort of hustler?" Brody asked.

"Well, he has no job that we can discern, but he can afford to live in the Quarter? He must have a Sugar Mama providing for him."

"There are plenty of candidates for that," Brody said. "Rich widows who enjoy the company of a young stud or a younger woman with plenty of daddy's money. Take your pick."

"If he is a hustler, he will have a regular hangout in the Quarter," Crawford said. "The place is full of them after two or three in the morning."

"Chief, I am beginning to worry about why you would know all this," Brody teased.

"I did a few years in Vice as I was coming up and some things never change," Crawford said with an amused smile.

"Do you think Dubais could be our anonymous tipster?" Brody asked.

"Looking for his fifteen minutes of fame, who knows?" Crawford said. "It would certainly add to his celebrity."

"Yes, it would. I would think he was having a good laugh on us, by now," Brody added.

"Would he be clever enough to send you the note and stockings to taunt you?" Crawford asked.

"Without a doubt," Brody said. He was about to explain himself when Williams came rushing in.

"I would say you have good news by that smile of your face," Crawford said.

"I don't have an exact address, but Dubais is now living on St. Charles, according to one of the waiters I interviewed. You were right, he visits the diner almost every night," Williams said.

"Is he a hustler?" Crawford asked.

"Oh yes, he swings both ways, but makes his bigger dollars with some of the older ladies of the city," Williams said. "If the stories are true, he gets paid quite handsomely for his services too."

"Do you want to set up surveillance at the diner or in spots on St. Charles?" Brody asked.

"He is a night creature, so he will probably sleep the day away so setting up spotters on St. Charles would probably be fruitless," Crawford said. "I think our best bet is to plan on surveillance at the diner and follow him home."

"Are you up for it?" Brody asked Williams.

"Count me in. Just tell me when and where," Williams said.

"Meet me back here at ten and you can take me to that diner of yours," Brody said. "Until then, you need to go home and get some rest. This is going to be a long night."

"Yes, sir," Williams said and left the office.

"That goes for you too," Crawford said. "You look dead on your feet."

"I am exhausted," Brody admitted.

"I'll stay a bit longer to review a few more of the leads and then I'll head home too," Crawford said. "Call me tonight if this venture pans out," he said as Brody walked to the door. "If not, I will see you tomorrow."

"Keep your fingers crossed," Brody said then disappeared down the hall.

Brody barely remembered the drive home and was relieved when he opened his mailbox and it was empty. He dropped his keys on the kitchen table and walked directly to his bedroom. Brody barely got his clothes off before he gave way to utter exhaustion and he collapsed face first on the bed.

†

"Lute, this is Doc. I am at the crossroads."

"Hello Doc. Take a left onto Highway 13 and drive two point four miles until you come to a small road, more of a path actually, that leads off to the right. Take that and it will lead you right to me."

It was so good to hear Lute's voice. "I will see you soon, my friend."

"I will be waiting, Doc," Lute said.

Talis turned left and watched his odometer as the distance approached and turned down the path as Lute had instructed. He smiled when he reached a small cabin and saw Lute standing on the porch.

Talis parked his car and walked up to the porch. He hugged his friend and smiled. "You can't possibly have grown more since you left New Orleans, but I swear you look bigger," he said.

"Naw, just the same old me, Doc. You just haven't seen me for a while," Lute said.

"Let's walk around to the back porch. I have some Abita on ice just waiting for us."

"Don't tell me that's your dad's old truck," Talis said as they passed an old clunker in the yard.

"Yes, it is. Dad finally broke down and bought him a new, used truck," Lute said with a chuckle. "It still burns a bit of oil, but it gets me where I need to go."

He noticed the still visible limp Lute walked with, but he appeared to be well adjusted. "You're looking great. How you feeling?" he asked.

Lute handed Talis a beer and they sat in rockers on the back porch facing the bay. "For the most part, I do really well. The cold winter mornings get to be painful sometimes, but I just work my way through them."

"Are you still working the shrimp boat with your dad?"

"Dad has pretty much retired from the boat. He still handles sales, but my brother and I do all the harvesting these days." Lute looked at his friend. "What has been happening with you, Doc?"

Talis took a long drink from his beer. "Not long after you left school, I met a woman. She was the most beautiful woman I have ever seen," Talis said. "I became obsessed with her and for two years nothing else mattered. She was like a poison in my system that I couldn't purge, nor did I want to. I quit school to be with her."

"I hate to hear that, Doc, you were destined to be a great one, but I guess it is not too late to go back and finish is it?"

"No, but my heart really isn't into being a doctor anymore," Talis said. "She was everything to me, including the very breath in my body, so when she decided to leave and go back to Russia, I was devastated."

"I am sorry, Doc."

"She used me to meet her needs, and once she had tired of me, she cast me aside like a child's toy," Talis said. "So for nearly a year now, I have been pretty worthless."

"I wish you would have called before now."

"I have been trying to work things out on my own, but the trauma of the hurricane just made things worse."

"I don't know what your intentions are, but you can stay here as long as you like," Lute said. "If you have a mind to learn how to shrimp, I can always use an extra pair of hands."

"I think I would like that," Talis said. "I have no clue what you do, but I am a quick learner."

"I know you are, Doc. I also know that some time out on the water can be good for a troubled soul too."

Lute excused himself to use the bathroom and Talis walked out onto a pier leading into the bay. Moss-covered cypress trees sheltered the surrounding area. Large cranes that inhabited several of the huge nests atop the trees called forlornly across the smooth water. The silence closed in around him until Talis imagined hearing his own heartbeat. Enthralled by the serenity, he did not hear Lute return to the porch.

†

Lute was gravely worried about his friend. Some dark force seemed to grip his soul and Lute hoped that some time in the bayou would help lift his spirit. He settled back into his rocking chair and allowed his friend the solitude he needed for the moment.

Lute reached inside the cooler and twisted off the cap of another beer. He rarely took a day off from trawling for shrimp and he planned to make the most of it. His father was dropping by later in the afternoon to bring them a fresh boiled batch of crawfish to welcome Talis and they would spend the day relaxing.

Talis breathed in the fresh air as he slowly began to relax. Maybe, just maybe, time with Lute would be exactly what he needed to purge the evil thoughts from his mind. He turned back toward the house and saw his friend sitting in the rocker. Talis walked back to the house with a smile on his face, the first one that felt real in weeks.

†

Williams was waiting for Brody when he got back to the precinct house later that evening. Sleep and some hot food had done wonders for Brody. He was dressed in jeans and a pullover shirt in hopes of looking like a casual customer of the diner. He and Williams would stake out the diner for the first several hours and then move inside separately to enjoy an early breakfast while they waited for Dubais to arrive.

He felt good about their chances of tracking Dubais back to his home, where they would wait until Crawford called him with an arrest warrant. Then they would arrest him and the game would be on. He would accompany Dubais back to the precinct house while Williams and crime scene techs would go through Dubais's home. They knew TBS was collecting trophies, so they had some very specific items to search for.

†

Kara and Sasha were also prowling the streets, looking for the evil presence they had felt on the way to dinner the previous week. There was no sign of the predator they had sensed before and after driving the streets for several hours, they headed for home. They had seen plenty of street hustlers and more than one drug exchange go down, but the pure evil that man exuded was not within their range.

"I have a feeling our guy has flown the coop," Sasha said. "Even if he had gone underground, I think we would still have some sense of him and I get nothing."

"Me either," Kara said, disappointed that their hunt continued to be unsuccessful. "We can try again tomorrow night," she said as she turned into their driveway.

†

Brody gave Williams some final instructions when they arrived at the diner. "If our boy shows up, I want you to follow him on foot. I will follow behind in the car and when he lands, I will radio in for a warrant. As soon as it arrives, we'll take him down." Brody looked at a smiling Williams. "You excited?" he asked.

"Yes, can't you tell?"

"You might want to wipe that shit-eating grin off your face," he teased. "If Dubais doesn't stay put at home, I want you to continue to follow him and stay in radio contact. Understood?"

"Yes, Brody," Williams said. "What time do we move inside if our boy hasn't shown up?" "Two, should be good," Brody said. "Do you smoke?"

"No sir."

"Good, you can be the wino then," he said as he handed Williams a paper sack with a bottle inside. "It's actually apple juice, but I figure your bladder is much younger than mine."

Williams grinned back at Brody as he took the bag.

Brody was really beginning to like this kid. If he continued his excellent work, Brody would see what he could do about bringing him on board as a rookie detective.

"I will take that stoop down on the left. You go up a half a block on the right and call me if you see anything."

"Happy hunting," Williams said as he lifted his bag in salute to Brody.

Brody slipped from behind the wheel of his sedan and took his position on the steps of the stoop. He lit a cigarette and leaned back against the wall to begin his wait. His mind flipped through the files of TBS's victims, looking for a common thread. All but the first were college students. All but the fifth were female. All asphyxiated in some form or fashion and all seemed willing sexual partners, at least in the beginning. Was it his charisma that attracted them to him or was it something more physical? Brody remembered the waiter's description of "a cock to die for," and had to suppress a chuckle.

He watched as a pair of men approached and slipped into the diner, but neither of them fit the description they had of Dubais. He crushed out the butt of the cigarette on the bottom step and continued his wait. Brody hated this job most. He knew it was vital, but he felt so nonproductive during surveillance. On any other case, he would have chosen other detectives to perform this duty, but until they could discover who the leak was in their department, he and the chief would keep vital information close to their vests. The last thing they needed was Dubais's name leaked to the media, further compromising their investigation. Brody made a mental note to make it his priority to discover the mole in the precinct, just as soon as TBS was dealt with. Investigations were hard enough without vital information shared by a dirty cop for profit.

Brody watched couples and singles come and go for the next four hours as they wandered in from the various bars in the Quarter to fill their stomachs before heading home. It was no wonder it took so many of the college kids six to eight years to graduate at the rate he saw them leave the bars well after midnight. He picked up his radio. "Are you getting hungry?" he asked Williams.

"I can taste some pork chops and eggs as we speak," Williams said.

"I will see you inside," Brody said. "If he doesn't show by three we will return to our posts for another two hours before we scrub the mission."

"He will show tonight. I can feel it."

"I hope you are right. These old bones are starting to ache."

Brody stepped from his concealed location and walked toward the diner. Williams waited until Brody got inside and took a seat before he approached. He found a seat near the far door and took up his position.

Brody reviewed the menu and ordered grilled pork chops, fried eggs, hash browns and toast with a pot of coffee. The smell of the place made his mouth water as he waited for his meal, while keeping an eye on the door. He was almost finished with his meal when the door opened and two men stepped inside the diner. The first man he ruled out, not because of his hair color, but because he was barely five foot six inches. The dark-haired man with him was a perfect ringer for the artist's sketch and was easily over six foot tall. He also had a large bulge in his crotch, which failed to go unnoticed as he and his friend walked in. Heads turned to watch him as they found a table very close to where Williams was sitting.

Brody caught Williams's eye and he nodded. Their man had finally shown up and Brody smiled as Dubais checked Williams out very closely and leaned in to whisper something to him as he passed by. Williams blushed and smiled at Dubais as he replied to the handsome man.

Brody was relieved when they ordered sandwiches as he hoped they would not camp out in the diner for the rest of the morning. He asked the waiter for a take-out cup and prepared a cup of coffee to take with him, then paid his bill. With a slight nod to Williams, Brody left the diner, walked down to the sedan, and lit another cigarette before slipping in behind the wheel.

Dubais was in his line of sight. Now he just had to wait until he was on the move. Brody picked up his cell and dialed Crawford. "We have him in sight," Brody said. "You might want to go ahead and start working on that warrant. I will call you back when I have an exact address." Brody closed the phone without waiting for a response.

"Soon, very soon, we shall dance, you and I, Thomas Dubais," Brody said as he watched Dubais and his companion laughing while they shared a meal.

Chapter Nine

Williams watched the two men finish and pay for their meal before departing from the diner. He paid his check and left to follow him with a glance toward Brody, who nodded to him, before he turned to follow Dubais. The men walked for two blocks and then stopped at an intersection. Williams watched as the two men hugged and the blonde walked away in a different direction. Now it was just he and Dubais. Williams waited for Dubais to start walking again and then stepped from his shadowy cover to follow Dubais further down the street. As they approached the Garden District, Brody passed by in the sedan and parked several blocks ahead.

Brody smiled as the two men approached and watched as Dubais turned off the sidewalk and walked past a large home, down an alley, to a small guesthouse on 1122 St. Charles. He picked up the phone and dialed the chief to give him the exact address for the warrant.

"Go ahead and call for backup and I will call you back in just a few minutes," Crawford told him.

"Backup is on the way and the chief is working on the warrant," Brody said as Williams got in the vehicle.

Minutes took an eternity to pass and when Brody's phone vibrated with an incoming call, he noticed that Williams jumped in his seat.

"You okay?" Brody asked after taking the call.

"Yeah, just excited. It's like every nerve in my body is alive waiting for his next move."

"Relax and remember your training. We do not know if Dubais is armed or not, so be careful," Brody warned.

When a cruiser pulled up behind them Brody got out. One of the officers handed him a warrant with a grin. "The Chief told us to deliver this to you personally."

Brody took the warrant looked it over and nodded. "We don't know if he is armed or not so be ready for anything when we go inside."

As they approached the house, they drew their guns and cautiously approached the door. Brody could hear the television through the door when one of the officers banged on the door and shouted "NOPD open up."

Dubais came to the door and had a look of surprise on his face when the four men rushed in and tackled him. One of the patrol officers cuffed him, read him his rights, and sat him down on the couch.

"Are you Thomas Dubais?" Brody asked.

"Yes, I am. What the fuck is going on here?" Dubais demanded. "I was just about to take a shower. Did that fucker Calvin report me for skipping out on his rent?"

"This is much more serious than rent," Brody said. "Take him out to the cruiser while we have a look around."

"Do you have a warrant?" Dubais asked.

Brody pulled the warrant from his pocket and showed it to Dubais. "As a matter of fact, I do," he said with a smile.

"Get him a shirt and take him out of here," Williams said.

The officer who had cuffed Dubais picked up a T-shirt and led Dubais out to the cruiser.

"Let's take a quick look around," Brody said as he walked toward the bedroom. If Dubais was the killer, his shrine would be very close to him and he prayed they would find it.

The bedroom was immaculate compared to the living room they had just left. The king-sized bed was made and everything in the room was well organized. Designer name brand clothing filled the closet and dresser. Nothing sent up any red flags.

"Look at this," Williams said after he opened up a bedside drawer.

Brody rushed over and looked into the drawer. Inside was a packet of white powder and a small straw. "I bet it will test to be cocaine. What do we have here?" He used his pen to push the packet out of the way. Underneath was the daily paper and it was folded open to the artist's sketch of TBS. "Obviously he noticed the resemblance," Brody said. "I wonder why he didn't say anything when we arrested him?"

"Don't know." Williams pulled back the clothing in the closet to find only a bare wall. "No sign of a shrine in here."

"I am going back to the precinct to begin interrogating Dubais. Keep looking and call me directly if you find anything related to a shrine."

"Will do, Brody."

†

At the precinct, Brody found Dubais in interrogation room one. He stood behind the two-way glass and observed him as he sat numbly in the chair. Something didn't feel right about him and Brody knew before he walked in that this wasn't his man.

He stepped inside the interrogation room, took Dubais's face in his hand, and turned his head to the left. As suspected, there was no scar on his right temple as the waiter had described.

"What is this all about?"

"You have been reading the papers, Dubais, you should know why you are here," Brody said.

"What are you talking about?"

"I am talking about the newspaper under your stash of coke in your nightstand. Even someone as dumb as you can see the resemblance between you and the TBS killer."

"You think I'm the serial killer?" Dubais asked as he sat up in his seat.

"We received an anonymous tip saying you were TBS," Brody said. "Too bad it didn't pan out."

A uniformed officer walked into the room and handed Brody a report. The fingerprints of Thomas Dubais did not match the ones of TBS. Nothing he didn't already know.

"Tell me something. How does an obvious loser like you score a crib in the Garden District?"

Dubais flashed Brody a charming smile. "I have several rich benefactors who see to my needs after I see to theirs," he said smugly.

"So you are just a piece of meat?"

"That would be prime meat. I probably get more action in one week than you see in a year," he said with a leer.

"And you get paid for your services too."

"By some of New Orleans's finest," Dubais crowed.

"It's such a shame that the word is going to get out on the street that you have something antibiotics can't cure," Brody said with a brilliant smile. "That should take you from a thriving organization to a non-profit real fast." He watched the smug grin disappear from Dubais's face.

"That's slander," Dubais shouted.

"What you are doing is called prostitution," Brody said. "Get a real job and stop taking advantage of the women of New Orleans."

"Deprive them of their pleasure? No way I can do that."

"Then you force me to call my friends in Vice."

"That's harassment," Dubais complained.

"It's called cleaning up the streets," Brody said. "You're in the system now, my boy, so clean up your act or take it to another town."

Brody left the room. "Cut him loose. He doesn't have the brains to be TBS," he said to the officer outside of the interrogation room. "Then make sure our boys in Vice start paying visits to his customers, starting with his new landlady, to explain about a nasty little infection our boy has."

"Oh, I am all over that," the officer said.

Brody walked back to his office and slumped behind his desk. Strike one, he thought. Dubais had been a good lead, but he wasn't TBS. He would take one piece of scum off the streets, but not the one he sought.

The chief walked into his office sometime later. "Dubais didn't pan out, but we will get him, Brody."

†

Sasha and Kara made routine drives through the Quarter for the next two weeks, failing to pick up any sign of the TBS.

"He must be gone," Kara said as they drove for home.

"Gone, but not forgotten," Sasha said. "He will be back."

†

Lute shook Talis awake the next morning.

"Sorry to disturb your sleep, my friend, but it's time to get moving. Dress warmly. It's cool out this morning." Lute left Talis to get dressed.

Talis looked at the clock to see that it was four in the morning. He must be crazy to have agreed to go out with Lute, but he had promised. He crept from the bed and pulled jeans and a heavy sweatshirt from his suitcase. His eyes fell on a small box and he smiled to himself. He opened the lid and sorted through the objects as he drew power from them. He tucked his prize back into his suitcase and joined Lute in the kitchen.

Lute handed him a cup of coffee. "Good morning, Doc."

"Good morning, Lute," Talis said. "Are you ready for work?"

"As ready as I'm ever going to be," he said. "Here, you better take this." He handed Talis a heavy coat. "It'll be cold out on the water."

Talis took the coat and slipped it over his shoulders before following Lute out to the old truck. Lute had come outside earlier to crank it and when he sat on the worn-out seat, he could feel the heat surrounding his feet.

"I'm glad to see the heater still works," he said to Lute with a grin.

"Like a charm," Lute said as he put the truck in reverse and drove toward town.

He pulled up at the small harbor and they walked to a small boat. The *Lucy Ann*, named after his mother who had passed away years ago. They stepped on board and were welcomed by Lute's brother, Harris.

"Good morning," he said a bit too cheerfully.

"Harris, this is Doc," Lute said.

Harris offered his hand to Talis. "I am pleased to meet you. Lute has told me so much about you."

"Nice to meet you too," Talis said, a bit surprised by Harris's size. Standing next to Lute, he was much smaller and had he seen them together he would never guessed them to be brothers.

Harris saw Talis looking at him. "I know, we look nothing alike and he is so much bigger," he said. "We really are brothers though, I just got mother's smaller genes."

"I got the size, but he got the brains," Lute said as he punched his brother's shoulder. "Are you ready to learn how to shrimp?"

"As ready as I can be."

"Great. You can start by tossing me those mooring lines."

Talis unraveled the lines and tossed each one to Lute who carefully coiled them on deck.

Harris started the engine and, after securing the mooring lines, he pulled the boat from the slip and headed out of the bay.

Lute gave Talis a short tour of the equipment they would be using and told him how they would start sending out their nets when they got to a good spot and continue until they had made a large circle. Then they would use the winch to slowly draw the net back in. Once they hoisted the net above the deck, it would be lowered, emptied and they would quickly sort through the catch.

"You will see everything from hubcaps to baby dolls in the net," Lute said. "The trash we put in that large canister and then we begin to cull the harvest. The shrimp we deposit into the pit," Lute said as he lifted the lid covering a large storage compartment beneath the deck.

There were several other large tubs secured to the side of the boat. "What are those for?"

"We will also catch crabs and some larger fish in the nets, and we keep the ones we can sell at market and toss the rest back."

"I can't tell a tuna from a grouper."

"We will help you learn," Lute said. "If we are lucky we may have enough crab for our dinner tonight. If not I will show you how to crab once we return home."

"That sounds interesting," Talis said with genuine sincerity.

"Are you warm enough?"

"Quite toasty, thank you," Talis said with a grin.

"We have time for another cup of coffee before we get to our favorite spot."

"That sounds good to me."

Talis followed Lute into the cabin where he poured coffee for himself, Talis, and Harris. They took the coffee and joined Harris in the wheelhouse.

"Thanks," Harris said. "So are you educated on trawling for shrimp?"

"Lute gave me a rundown, so I have a general idea."

"Just do as Lute tells you and you will be an old hand at this by the time we head for home," Harris said with a grin. "I swear he could do this in his sleep."

Lute gave out a hearty laugh. "I feel like I have done it in my sleep several times."

There were other shrimp boats out on the water and Talis hoped there would be enough to go around.

"Here we are," Harris said. "Do your magic, Lute."

"Let's do it." Lute dropped the first portion of the net into the water. "Help me make sure the net stays straight as I guide it into the water."

Talis moved quickly to untangle the net as he fed it to Lute. With the two of them dropping the net, Harris was free to move the boat forward allowing gravity to assist them with the job. For thirty minutes they fed the net into the dark blue water and when they reached the end, Harris turned the boat to begin the circle to close the net.

"Pull that lever down."

Talis did as instructed and heard the powerful winch go into motion, slowly gathering the ends of the net together. He listened to the whine of the motor and when he heard it begin to make a surging sound, he looked at Lute.

"The nets are filling up, causing the winch to work harder," he explained. "That sound is music to my ears."

Talis smiled at his friend. He watched the lines draw closer to the boat, and when the net was close enough to raise on deck, Lute pressed another lever as Harris killed the engine, setting them adrift. Talis could see a variety of creatures roiling together in the net. Lute pressed a button and the net purged its contents.

Talis began sweeping the larger shrimp toward the bin and when he came across a fish, Lute would identify it for him and tell him "keeper" or "trash." Talis would toss the keepers in a bin and the trash went overboard. They had netted a dozen or more large blue crab that Harris carefully placed in a separate bin. With the first haul taken, they had filled the shrimp pit one third full, had reaped a dozen marketable fish and the crabs they would have for dinner.

Harris and Lute quickly checked the net for any damages and finding none, Harris asked, “Ready for another pass?”

“Go for it. See, that’s all there is to it,” Lute said. He and Talis began feeding the net as Harris pulled forward slowly and in another thirty minutes, they were ready to reap the next haul.

The next two passes the nets filled mostly with shrimp, which was good for business and Lute said, “Just one more pass should meet our quota for the day.”

They ended the morning with a full take of shrimp, three dozen fish, and thirty crabs. Lute was all smiles as they headed back into market.

“You brought us good luck today,” Lute said. “Generally it takes us until well after noon to catch our quota.”

Talis smiled at the thought of bringing anyone good luck. Over the past few months he had been the harbinger of bad luck for the people he had chosen as his victims, so this was a much-needed change of pace for him.

Lute called ahead to alert his dad of their return and when they pulled back into the harbor he met them with a huge motorized dolly that they hooked up to the shrimp pit. Talis watched with awe as the dolly lifted the pit canister that held almost five hundred pounds of shrimp.

“Grab that side, will you?” Lute said as he pointed to a handle on the bin holding the market fish. They carried the bin into the fish market and then waited as one of the clerks weighed and graded each of the fish.

“One eighty-five,” the man said.

“Fair enough,” Lute said. “Add it to today’s shrimp.”

“You had a good catch today.”

"We had a first-timer on board who brought us good luck," Lute teased.

"You need to keep him around for a while then, son," Lute's father said with a grin.

"I think we will, Dad," Lute said, turning to Talis. "You did good, Doc, and I didn't have to go swimming to rescue you," Lute added with a chuckle.

"Does that happen often?" Talis asked.

"We had a brother-in-law from Shreveport go out with us once and Lute had to go in the drink when the dullard fell overboard," Harris said with a roar of laughter.

"Needless to say that was his first and last trip out with us," Lute said.

"Poor Harold," Lute's father said.

Harris chuckled. "I don't think the poor man has eaten shrimp since that trip."

Lute and Talis returned to the boat and dumped the crabs into a five-gallon bucket. They walked to the truck and made the short drive back to Lute's home.

Talis took off the coat and hung it on a peg just inside the door. "Are you tired?" Lute asked.

"Not as bad as I would have thought," Talis said.

"Good, let's do some crabbing."

Lute opened a small chest freezer and pulled out a package. "Chicken necks," he said to a curious Talis.

Talis followed Lute out onto the back porch. "Grab that fishnet, please."

Lute picked up the bucket of crabs and carried it out to the end of the pier. Talis followed closely, very curious of what was about to happen. Lute pulled up a thin line tethered to a post on the pier and tied the chicken neck to it.

"Watch," he said to Talis.

Lute swung the chicken neck backward and tossed it out in front of them about fifteen feet. For a few minutes, nothing seemed to be happening, but Talis continued to watch.

"It takes a few minutes for the chicken neck to thaw and send out a scent. Anytime now we will have a taker."

Talis caught a glimpse of movement out of the corner of his eye and he watched as a large blue crab moved sideways as it approached the chicken neck. Lute let the crab pick up the scent of the meat and he slowly started reeling the line toward the pier.

"Lower the net into the water as quietly as you can and extend it toward the line."

Talis barely made a sound as the net broke the surface.

"I will lead him right to you and when he is in reach, scoop him up with the net," Lute instructed. "That's it, come just a little closer, okay now, Doc."

Talis lifted the net with the crab firmly in the net.

"Good catch, Doc," Lute said. "Now drop him in the bucket with the others. Here, you try the next one solo while I go get us a beer." He smiled when Talis swung the chicken neck and released it just as he had showed him. "I will be right back. Happy hunting, Doc."

Talis froze when Lute said that statement. For almost a whole day, he had forgotten his life in New Orleans and the evil that had gripped him. "Happy hunting," he repeated. Soon he would be hunting again and that would definitely make him happy.

Talis watched the crab approach, he started to retract the line toward the waiting net, and when the crab reached the right spot, Talis lifted the net trapping him inside.

"If I didn't know better, I would say you grew up in the bayou," Lute said as he handed Talis a beer. "Three or four more and we should have a fine dinner."

Talis took a sip of the beer and then set it down on the pier. He tossed out the bait and caught three more crabs, grinning with delight at his new learned skill.

"That should do. Finish your beer and later we will cook us up a batch of crabs."

"That sounds good," Talis said, realizing they hadn't eaten all day. "I'm starving."

"Do you need a sandwich to hold you over?"

"No, but I do need a shower."

"Fine, you go ahead and I'll get the cooker set up on the porch," Lute said. "It looks like we might get some rain this afternoon, so I'll move it under shelter."

Talis looked at the clear blue sky. There were no clouds in sight, but somehow he knew Lute would be correct about a rain shower. He went into the guest room, slipped out of his clothes, and stepped into the warm water.

Dressed in baggy shorts and a T-shirt he returned to the porch to find Lute reading the paper.

Putting the paper aside Lute stood and said, "I will be back soon."

Talis sat down with a fresh beer as a light rain began to fall and picked up the paper Lute had been reading. He flipped to the section on state news and the front-page headline, *Possible Suspect in TBS Case Released from Custody,* caught his attention.

Talis cringed at the possibility that someone else could have taken credit for his handiwork and read the short article. A suspect had been taken in, and released when the fingerprints and physical description had not matched. An anonymous caller identified the suspect, described as a street hustler.

"Don't get too distracted, Brody," Talis warned. He took the section of paper to his room; he would add the article to his collection later.

"Street hustler," he spit out with venom in his voice. "I hope it didn't take you too long to figure him out for a fake, Brody," Talis whispered to himself.

Talis heard a scraping sound and looked over at the bucket. The crabs were scrambling around as they tried to climb the smooth walls of the bucket. As they failed and fell back amongst the group, the next crab would take up the challenge. Talis smiled at their failure and a word popped into his mind: *oubliette*, a French word for a deep pit, generally used to punish prisoners. Talis was concentrating on this word when Lute came back out onto the porch.

"I knew it was going to rain," he said as he took a seat next to Talis. "You okay, Doc?"

"Yes, I am fine, Lute," Talis said with an eerie smile.

Lute smiled back at his friend, but felt very uncomfortable with the look on Talis's face.

†

Sasha was napping in the sunshine on the front porch when she felt a presence moving toward her. She opened her mind to find that Milly was trying to sneak up on her.

She could feel Milly probing her mind and sensed her frustration when her efforts failed.

"Don't you know you have to be invited in?" Sasha projected.

Milly stopped dead in her tracks, ten feet from the porch.

Sasha opened her eyes and smiled at Milly. "You are home early today."

"I finished midterms early, so I got to come home."

"Your parents are in town shopping for tomorrow's big party."

"All five of us," Milly chuckled.

"So why didn't you invite some of your classmates?"

"If I considered any of them friends I probably would have," Milly said. "I just don't have much in common with them, so I go to my classes and pray for graduation to come soon, so I can start some real studying."

"Little miss lack of patience," Sasha teased

"Is Kara at home?"

"No, she won't be home until about seven,"

"So, I have you all alone?"

"Well, yes, is that so unusual?"

"As a matter of fact, yes, it is, I hardly have time with you without someone around."

"Does that bother you?" Sasha asked curiously.

"Usually no, but I have wanted to talk to you for a while and there always seems to be someone else around."

"What do we need to talk about that you need privacy for?"

"My future," Milly said.

"Okay, I am all yours."

"Come with me."

Sasha stood and followed Milly into the parlor, and they stood directly in front of the portrait of Milly.

Sasha watched as the younger Milly's finger reached out and traced the words, "I love you," that Milly had painted in disguise into the foliage of the trees. No one not even Kara had ever seen that message Milly had left for Sasha. Sasha herself did not find it until after Milly's death.

"How did you know that was there?"

"Because I put it there," Milly said.

Sasha felt faint as she sat back on the love seat, joined by Milly.

"I guess I should explain that,"

"I wish you would," Sasha said.

"I can't guarantee all the facts, but when I was born, I think somehow Milly attached all her memories to me, and as I have grown more mature I have been remembering more and more of her life with you."

Sasha had turned a ghostly white. "How can that be?"

"I have no idea, but, I know what you are, what Milly was, and how you came to be a couple."

"I can't be hearing this," Sasha said as she rushed from the room and left the house.

Milly watched Sasha walk across the yard and disappear into the woods. She knew where Sasha was going and gave her a few minutes head start before following her.

†

Milly's revelations left Sasha extremely disturbed. How could it be possible that Milly's memories were transferred to her when Milly had been dead long before the young Milly was born. Sasha's head ached from thinking so hard. Her feet took her down a path and before she knew it, Sasha was at the special place she and Milly had held so dear. She walked over to the spring and splashed some of the cold water on her face. Sasha then made her way to the old oak and sat down, leaning back into the solid tree.

What was even more eerie to Sasha was that as Milly grew older she looked more like her beloved Milly. It was as if she was looking at her Milly at age eighteen. This was too much information for Sasha's emotional state and she hid her tears in her hands as the raw pain of losing Milly resurfaced.

†

Milly walked around the tree and found Sasha crying. Milly knelt down next to her and wrapped her arms around Sasha. "I am so sorry for just dumping this on you like that," she said.

"I just don't know how it can be possible."

"I don't have an explanation either, but it is true. I know this was one of our favorite spots, and we made love often on this very ground."

Sasha's head whipped up as she looked at Milly in shock. "How can you know that?" she demanded to know.

"Because I am Milly," she said. "Not just her namesake, as my parents had intended, but I am Milly, reincarnated somehow."

Sasha stared into the eyes she once fell in love with.

"I know how much you loved me and how much you now love Kara," Milly said.

"You were my first and greatest love," Sasha said, admitting that what she thought impossible was true.

"As you were mine, Sasha," Milly said as she lifted Sasha's chin in her hand. "I will not ask for that love again, as your time is now with Kara, but I will ask for one thing."

"Which would be what?"

Milly sat down in front of Sasha and gazed into her loving lavender eyes. "I have Milly's memories, some of her abilities, but I do not have her greatest gift. I want you to transform me, Sasha."

Sasha stared into the intense blue eyes as she had done for many years. She could sense Milly in them and she had to force herself to remember she was talking with a child, not the woman she adored for years.

"I want you to make me immortal, Sasha," Milly stated.

"Leave me now," Sasha said as she turned away from Milly's pleading eyes. "I need to think and I can't do it with you here with me."

Sasha saw tears welling in Milly's eyes as she stood and left the clearing.

†

Milly had been her mate, promised for eternity. If she really had been reborn with little Milly, how could she deny her request. She was her maker, connected to her forever. Even if she refused to transform Milly, her thoughts would continue to haunt little Milly and she would not be able to fully realize the gift of powers Milly had given her. But, she was too young to be making such a serious decision. Barely eighteen and had not experienced life fully as a human yet.

Sasha could not deny Milly's request, but she would have one condition. She opened her mind and projected to Milly. *Come back to the clearing,* she projected.

Yes Sasha, I will be right there, Milly answered.

"Sit down with me, Milly," Sasha said when Milly returned.

Milly sat down facing Sasha and waited for her to speak.

"Milly, as you know, was my creator as well as my greatest love and I cannot deny her wishes," Sasha said. "I do have one condition, though."

"What is that?"

"I will agree to transform you, but not until you turn twenty-one."

"But that is three years away, Sasha."

"You need to experience life as a human adult before you make this decision," Sasha said. "Once it is done, there is no turning back."

"But, you weren't much older when I transformed you."

"And that was a much different era. When I was your age the world was a very different place than it is now."

Milly pouted, but it had no effect on Sasha. "I have made up my mind."

"I guess that is better than an outright no," Milly said, disappointed.

"Have you been trying to pick Kara's brain, like you have with me?" Sasha asked.

"No, I don't have a connection with her," Milly said. "Will you tell her about my request?"

"Eventually, but I have to come to terms with our agreement before I can explain it to her."

"So, since I can't pick your mind, what did you get me for my birthday?"

"If everyone is home, you will find out," Sasha said.

"Really? Tonight?"

"Yes, I don't see why not."

Milly jumped to her feet and offered Sasha a hand. "Let's go then. Thank you, Sasha."

"There is no need to thank me yet," Sasha said. "Three years and I am sticking to it."

Milly smiled as she pulled Sasha to her feet. "That gives me three more years to pester you," she said with a grin.

"Come on," Sasha draped an arm around Milly's shoulder as they walked back to the house.

Kara had just parked her car and slammed the garage door shut when she saw Milly and Sasha approach.

"It's okay, I told her she could have her present tonight," Sasha said.

"You hid it in the garage?"

"Yes, we did. Go see if your parents are home yet,"

"Hello, my love," Sasha said as she took Kara in her arms and kissed her. "I am glad you are home."

"Is everything okay?"

"Yes, things are just fine. Why do you ask?"

"I got a feeling of distress from you when I was driving home," Kara said.

"I had egg salad for lunch and you know what that does to me."

Sasha heard the screen door slam and looked up as Milly came rushing back outside, literally dragging her parents behind her, as she crossed the yard toward Kara and Sasha.

"Did you really tell her she could have her present tonight?" James asked.

"She was driving me nuts," Sasha said with a grin.

"Go ahead and open the garage door," Kara said as Milly approached.

Milly reached for the door and swung it open. "Oh, my word," she screamed. "You bought me a car?"

"If you don't like it we can take it back," Kara teased.

"Don't even think for a second I don't love it," Milly squealed.

"The keys are in it," Sasha said.

Milly climbed inside the car and cranked it. She sat behind the wheel staring at the inside of her first car.

"You have to move the gearshift to R, honey," James shouted.

"I know, Father, I just can't believe I have a car," Milly shouted back. She put the car in reverse and backed out of the garage.

"Can we go for a ride?" Milly asked.

Sasha looked at Kara and James. "Do you think it's safe?"

"I think I'm going to stay and put some supper on for all of us, so why don't you three take a ride with our birthday girl," Marie said.

"We will be back soon," James said as he kissed his wife and climbed into the passenger seat next to his daughter.

Kara and Sasha climbed into the backseat. "Buckle up," Kara said.

When they all were safely seated, Milly put the car in drive and headed down the driveway. When she reached the hard road, she turned right to drive deeper into the bayou instead of into town, much to Sasha's surprise.

They took a drive of twenty minutes and when they returned home, Milly hugged both Kara and Sasha. "Thank you for such a perfect gift."

Chapter Ten

Talis worked with Lute for three weeks before the burning in his body started to grow unbearably. He had quickly learned the task of harvesting shrimp and as Lute had predicted, he was good at the skill. Each day when they went out on the water, Talis felt relaxed and even enjoyed the physical activity and the time spent with Lute. But the nights seemed to grow longer, his dreams filled with vile acts that left him aroused and frustrated. On the third night of these dreams, Talis decided he would return to New Orleans.

The next morning, he spoke with Lute. "I think it is time for me to return to New Orleans," he told his friend.

"I understand, but I wish you would change your mind," Lute said. "You have brought us such good luck, I hate to see you go."

"I appreciate your hospitality and hope I will be welcome in the future," Talis said.

"You are welcome back at any time," Lute said, then he pulled out three one hundred dollar-bills and handed them to Talis.

"What is this?"

"A down payment on your share of the shrimp we have brought in since you have arrived," Lute said. "You have earned much more, but that is all the cash I have on me."

"I don't deserve your money, Lute."

"You worked just as hard as Harris and I, so you share the profits," Lute said. "If you will give me your address, I will send you the rest."

"Hold onto it for me," Talis said as he took the cash.

Lute hugged his friend. "Take good care, Doc."

"I will. Say goodbye to Harris and your dad for me, please."

"Will do," Lute said and walked from the small cabin to climb into his truck.

Talis packed his suitcase and loaded it into the trunk of his car. With a final look at the cabin, he pulled from the drive and headed for home. He drove straight through, stopping only for gas. He ached to be home in New Orleans. He had work yet to do, and had been idle for too long.

He parked the car in the garage and took out the suitcase, locking the door securely behind him before he walked to his flat. He opened the windows to air out the flat as he took the box from his suitcase and returned his trophies to their rightful shrine above his bed. He took scissors and carefully trimmed the article he had torn from Lute's newspaper. Talis turned on his laptop and pulled up the newspaper archives to see what he had missed while he was gone. There were several small articles that he printed out and then posted to his wall. Talis was particularly interested in the article on Thomas Dubais, the imposter the police had arrested. Talis would make sure that mistake would never happen again.

Talis pulled on a worn pair of jeans and a clean shirt. The time on the shrimp boat had done wonders for his body, strengthening muscles that had grown weak from disuse. Talis sprayed a small amount of the cologne on his neck and smiled back at his image in the mirror. He left the flat well after dark. "Time to hunt," he said as he closed the door behind him.

†

Brody had made good on his promise to Dubais. Word got out on the street that he had a sexually transmitted disease and his female benefactors quickly turned away from him. He found himself reduced to trolling the gay bars searching for tricks. It was never difficult for him to find a date, but the pay he received was barely enough to keep him fed. He remembered Brody's suggestion to leave town and was giving it serious consideration. *Baton Rouge maybe.* He headed from the small room a friend had allowed him to move into after his high-and-mighty landlady tossed him to the street. "Damned Brody," he said as he hit the sidewalk.

†

Not only had he grown stronger during his stay with Lute, but Talis's appearance had changed some as well. His hair had grown, no longer short cropped, and had a slight bit of curl to it. It also had blond streaks running through it from the hours he had spent in the sun, which also tanned his face and upper body.

Talis was hungry. He had not eaten since the night before and he needed nourishment, especially if he was going to have an active night, which was also certain in his mind. He stopped by an all-night diner and sated his hunger with a cheese steak sandwich and fries, topped off with a slice of apple pie.

"That's a healthy appetite you have there," the waiter commented.

"Time to refuel so I can do some dancing." Talis gave him a charming smile.

"I would love to see your body in motion." The man was obviously, flirting with him.

"Maybe later, I plan to be out for a while."

"What a shame, I am on duty until four," the man replied with disappointment.

"How about a rain check then? I will be in town a few more days."

"Sounds good to me. Just drop by tomorrow night, I'm off at one," the waiter said, returning Talis's smile.

"I will see you tomorrow then." Talis paid the tab and slipped a nice tip in the man's front pants pocket.

"I look forward to it." He watched Talis walk from the diner.

Talis walked farther into the Quarter and stepped inside a packed bar. He was lucky to find an empty barstool and ordered a cold beer while he watched a beautiful blond male dancer gyrating on top of the bar. A rivulet of sweat rolled down the man's hairless chest as he smiled down at Talis. Talis returned his smile and the man dropped to his knees, thrusting his hips toward Talis, who reached into his pocket and pulled out a five-dollar bill. He took great pleasure in sliding the bill into the man's G-string, the back of his hand grazing the erection the young man was enjoying. The music tempo changed and the young man jumped to his feet and, with a wink to Talis, danced his way back down the bar.

Talis surveyed the room but did not find his prey on the first pass. Several men offered to buy him drinks or requested he dance with them, but he politely turned them all down. He had one particular man in mind for tonight and would settle for nothing less. After finishing another beer, Talis heard the name "Thomas" called out from the dance floor, and he looked up as a darkly handsome man stepped inside the bar.

A young man placed his hand on Talis's shoulder. "Dance with me please?" he begged.

Talis gave a slight chuckle then pulled the shirt over his head as he approached the dance floor. The music was pounding out a furious beat and he let the frantic rhythm take over his body. He caught a glimpse of Dubais as he approached the dance floor and stood watching him move. When Talis turned to face him, their eyes locked and he shared a soft smile with him. He danced with his young partner until his chest was soaked and he was gasping for air.

"Thanks," he said to the young man and then slipped the shirt over his head.

"That is a crying shame," a voice spoke from behind him.

Talis turned around to find Thomas standing close to him. "What is a shame?"

"That you would deprive the rest of us a view of that gorgeous body of yours," Thomas said. "May I buy you a drink?"

"Sure, I'll take a beer," Talis said as they moved toward the bar.

Thomas returned carrying two beers. "You want to find someplace a little more quiet?"

"Lead the way," Talis said as he took the beer and followed Thomas up a small staircase to a second level of the bar. It wasn't any less crowded, but at least it was quieter. Talis turned and leaned on the railing and looked down at the dance floor. "All those gyrating bodies with erections from hell."

"Pardon me, what did you say?" Thomas asked.

"I was making a comment about all those hard bodies," Talis said.

"There are some nice ones, but none like yours."

"I'm glad you approve," Talis said as he turned toward Thomas.

Thomas was a good three inches shorter than Talis and had to look up slightly to meet his eyes. "I noticed your chest isn't the only thing hard about you," he said as his hand rubbed across Talis's crotch.

Talis smiled.

"I haven't seen you in here before, are you new in town?" Thomas asked.

"I'm visiting an uncle in town for a few days," Talis said. "If I find something I like, I might just make a move down here." He ran his hand through Thomas's hair, pulling his head back. He stepped into Thomas as he reached out with his left hand to stroke him. "It appears I am not alone in being hard," he whispered into Thomas's ear as he fondled his shaft through his jeans.

Talis turned Thomas toward the dance floor and pressed his body into his ass as he moved in rhythm to the music thumping through the bar. He could feel himself grow harder as he ground his crotch into Thomas.

"Come with me," Thomas said.

"I would love to. Does this bar have a lube dispenser in the bathroom?"

"Yes, it does."

Talis handed him several dollars. "Go buy a packet and meet me out front," he said. "Then we'll take a little walk."

They walked past the mass of bodies making out on the balcony, then down the stairs. Talis stepped outside into the cooler air and waited for Thomas. When Thomas joined him, they walked to the same park where weeks earlier he had fucked Susan. Just remembering how wet she was, made him grow harder.

Talis led Thomas over to the picnic table and spun him on his heels to face the table. There was need burning between them and Talis wasted no time on foreplay. He thrust in and out of him and felt Thomas come as his body coiled and released before he fell exhausted onto the picnic table. Buried completely inside him, his hands closed around Thomas's neck. When Thomas could not breathe, he began to struggle, trapped beneath Talis's body. Thomas passed out and Talis thrust wildly until he was sure Thomas was dead and then came violently inside him. He withdrew and pulled Thomas's jeans up and took out his wallet, removing the driver's license, before rolling him over and leaving his lifeless eyes staring up at the sky. He also dug a cell phone from his front pocket.

Talis tucked himself away and picked up the empty lube packet. He dropped it in the trash on his way out of the park and slipped the driver's license inside his back pocket. Talis walked a few blocks south, toward Jackson Square, flipped open the cell phone and dialed 911.

"Hello, this is 911, what is your emergency?" the operator asked.

"I need to speak to Detective Brody to report a murder," he said calmly.

Talis kept walking as he waited for the call to transfer to Brody.

"Detective Brody speaking."

"I just wanted to let you know that I am back in town, but I couldn't wait on you for number nine," Talis said.

"What have you done?"

"I took your imposter to the doggy park for a little doggy style," Talis said. "You won't have to worry about him interfering again."

"Thomas Dubais?"

"Yes, that is the one. I will be in touch soon," Talis said and hung up.

†

"Fuck!" Brody slammed down the phone. "Did we get a trace?" he shouted.

"No, ironically he was using Dubais's cell phone as he walked around," Williams said. "What did he say?"

"He took care of Dubais and said we would find him in the doggy park."

"There is one not too far off the Quarter."

"Let's go and you drive," Brody said as he tossed the keys to Williams.

Brody called Crawford from the car and filled him in on the call.

"I guess TBS didn't like the thought of someone else getting credit for his handiwork. At least he didn't take an innocent victim," Crawford said.

"That's true I guess."

"Call me after you get done at the scene."

"Will do, boss."

They arrived at the park and found Dubais, and Brody called in the crime scene techs. "Hit some of the gay clubs and see what you can find out about Dubais's partner tonight," Brody said. "Take the sedan and I will walk back, I need to think."

"I can see the physical toll this case it taking on you." Williams turned away then back again.. "I see you sitting in front of the board for hours staring at the evidence, trying to piece the clues together. I sure hope we unravel this case soon.

"Yeah me too." Brody waited at the scene for the crime scene techs and the ME to arrive to pronounce the death. When they took over, Brody started to walk back through the Quarter to the precinct house. Somehow, he had to get inside this guy's head and begin to think like him.

Talis watched as Brody left the crime scene on foot walking in his direction where he sat concealed in the shadows to watch over his victim. When Brody got within a block of where he was hiding, Talis left the cell phone on the steps and slipped into the darkness to walk back to his flat.

Brody stopped, mere feet from where Talis had stood seconds earlier. Something was in the air. Brody stepped toward the smell and stood almost identically where Talis had been. When he recognized the smell, Brody smiled. The smell was the cologne TBS had worn and now Brody knew that he stuck around the crime scene to witness the discovery of Dubais. He turned into the direction the smell was coming from and Brody saw the light of a cell phone shining brightly up at him. He picked up the phone and closed the lid, extinguishing the light. Brody hoped he could use that knowledge to his favor in the future. He turned down the same street TBS must have taken to elude capture and followed it for two blocks. Brody did not smell the scent or see any evidence of the killer, so he returned to the corner and walked the rest of the way to the house.

Williams was adding the DMV photo of Dubais to the board when Brody walked in. He dropped the cell phone on the desk. "Our boy left us a present."

"Where did you find that?"

"He left it on the steps about a block away from the crime scene."

"So he is sticking around the crime scenes now?"

"It would appear so, yes. At least until the victim is discovered."

"It must really add to his high to see the crime scene swarming with activity, knowing he was the cause of all the turmoil," Williams said.

"Yes, I think our boy gets quite the kick out of seeing us at work."

Crawford walked into the office. "Anything of value?"

"TBS is hanging around the crime scene."

"How did you determine that?"

"I started walking back to the precinct house to clear my head, and when I reached a corner a block from the crime scene, I smelled his cologne and found that," Brody said, pointing to the cell phone.

"Do you think you have the scent well enough to try to track it down?" Crawford said. "I bet our boy doesn't use the bottle with a ship on it."

Brody smiled. "It was definitely not Old Spice."

"Tomorrow, I want you to go down to the Quarter and hit some of the perfumery shops to see if you can determine what the scent is and maybe who bought it," Crawford said with a grin.

"It is worth a shot. I agree with you that he would not wear cologne that is common." He smiled at Williams. "How did that crime scene tech describe it?"

Williams thought for a few seconds. "Something rich and sensual is what she said."

"Maybe we will luck up and it will be a special blend, something very limited, or better yet, something made specifically for him," Brody hoped.

"I didn't get much from the canvass of the gay bars. I found out where they met, but no one had seen the man Dubais left with in the bar before," Williams said to a disappointed Brody.

"Let's call it a night and you can meet me back here at eight in the morning," Brody told Williams. "There isn't much more we can do tonight."

"Very well, goodnight you two," Williams said and left the office.

"That young man has a world of potential," Brody said to Crawford. "I would like to bring him on the squad once this case is over."

"I can arrange for that. He does seem to have a quick and clever mind," Crawford added.

"He has very good senses about him and will make a great addition to the squad."

"Yes, he will, and under your tutelage he will become a great detective. Now go get some rest and I will see you tomorrow."

"Goodnight, Chief," Brody said as his friend left the office. He turned back to the board, studying the growing number of pictures. "You like to watch, don't you?" Brody wondered if TBS would be bold enough to attend a funeral and made a note to contact the family member or friend who claimed Dubais's remains to see if there would be a service. It was a long shot, but worth sending a couple of detectives to survey the crowd if there was going to be a funeral.

Brody's eyes felt dry and were starting to burn. He needed sleep badly. He turned off his desk lamp and left the office, intending to go straight home. Brody was passing by the front desk when the sergeant on duty said, "You have a call, Detective Brody."

"Thanks, what line?"

"Line three."

Brody walked to a nearby phone and picked up the receiver. He punched a rapidly blinking line three. "Detective Brody speaking."

"Good evening, Detective, I hope I am not interrupting your evening," Talis gloated.

"I was just on my way out would you like to join me for a cold beer?"

"That does sound rather tempting, but I think I will pass for now. I just wanted to apologize for being so hasty with Number Nine, but I was quite disturbed by the thought that you imagined I could actually be a common street hustler."

"I knew almost immediately he was not you."

"That is a great relief, I have more respect for you now," Talis taunted.

"Why are you doing this?"

"I was getting bored and decided I would spice my life up a bit."

"I wish you would have chosen a different hobby."

"Oh, but this one is so much fun. How else would I be able to meet such a clever detective?" Talis jeered.

"Well, you obviously have my number, so you could have just called if you felt you needed attention," Brody taunted back.

"I need more than attention, Brody. I need to be stopped."

"I would be more than willing to come pick you up right now," Brody replied.

"I bet you would, but that is not how the game is played and you know it. I will be in contact soon." Talis hung up.

Brody replaced the phone on the cradle and left the precinct house. He replayed the conversation over in his head as he drove home. TBS was definitely fixating on him, which was a good thing, but he would also have to remain sharp, in case TBS attempted to make him a target.

Exhausted, he stripped out of his clothes and stretched out across his bed. His dreams were filled with the images of the victims TBS had taken and he slept fitfully all night.

†

Sasha and Kara were making a final pass around the Jackson Square area. "Are you picking up anything?" Kara asked Sasha.

"I'm getting a faint tingle, but he is too far off to determine where he is. I think it is safe to say TBS is back though."

"I was hoping for a much longer break."

"That would have been nice, but the police will need much more information to break this case," Sasha said. "Let's go home for now and we will spend more time in town this weekend when he is sure to be out on the prowl."

Kara drove them home and when they walked into the bedroom, she turned to Sasha. "I need some loving, baby."

"I was hoping you would," Sasha said, taking Kara in her arms for a tender kiss.

Sasha undressed Kara and placed her lover on the bed while she quickly undressed and joined her. Sasha knew that she had become preoccupied with tracking the serial killer and had lost focus on Kara's needs, but intended to remedy that tonight. She found she was also concerned with the conversation she had with Milly and her request to be changed.

Her hands made loving strokes down Kara as she explored her lover. Her fingertips caressed every soft curve in Kara's body and her touches made Kara twitch with desire. Kara's eyes glowed with excitement when Sasha draped her right thigh over hers, and she could feel the wetness of Sasha on her skin.

Sasha gently pushed the hair back from Kara's face. "You are so beautiful, my love," she whispered.

"You make me feel so loved, Sasha," Kara said.

"Because I love you so dearly," Sasha said as her moist lips met Kara's for a slow kiss that escalated into a burst of passion as their tongues swirled together and Sasha's hands flowed down Kara's body.

"I adore the feel of your body next to mine," Kara breathed into Sasha's ear while she kissed the side of her neck.

Sasha moved atop Kara, pressing skin to skin. The heat of their passion increased and their bodies melted and moved together in unison. "I can feel the excitement quivering in your body," Sasha said when her swollen clit rubbed across Kara.

"You make me feel like none other," Kara said, lifting her hips to Sasha.

Sasha's hands covered Kara's breasts, softly squeezing the excited flesh, her thumbs stroking across her throbbing nipples. Their bodies moved together in a rippling blur of passion and the sounds of their lovemaking filled the room.

"I need you inside me," Kara said when their eyes locked together.

Sasha knew what Kara was asking and got up and walked into the bathroom. When she returned to the bed wearing a harness and strap-on, Kara's smile welcomed her.

"Oh yes, baby," she cooed when Sasha crawled from the end of the bed to return between her trembling thighs.

Sasha placed the dildo across Kara's wetness, stroking slowly, coating it with her moisture. Kara spread her thighs wide, Sasha's motion driving her mad with excitement. "Fuck me slowly," she said as she reached down and placed the tip of the dildo at her entrance.

Sasha entered Kara, slowly parting her lips.

"Oh god, yes," Kara said. "You feel so good, Sasha," she purred when Sasha entered her.

Sasha's hands teased Kara's swollen nipples as her hips slowly worked the dildo into Kara. The movement of her hips brought the base of the dildo across her lips and clit causing Sasha to struggle to concentrate on Kara's pleasure, while holding back her own.

She moved fluidly inside Kara and leaned forward to cover Kara's mouth as Kara's legs wrapped around her waist. Sasha could feel Kara's moans deep in her mouth while her hips ground deeply into her body and her hands squeezed her breasts. Kara's nails dug into the skin of Sasha's ass, her hips driving the dildo deeper inside her with each thrust.

Sasha heard the blood rushing through Kara as her climax approached. The pounding of their hearts increased and she picked up speed, thrusting faster into Kara.

Kara broke the kiss to gasp for air. "That feels so good, Sasha," Kara purred. "Come with me, baby," she cried as she erupted with pleasure. Sasha felt the burst of wetness inside Kara and thrust faster until her movements overwhelmed her restraint.

"Oh yes, Kara," Sasha cried out, overtaken by spasms of pleasure.

Kara pulled Sasha onto her chest, their bodies molded together sharing an intense orgasm. She could feel her muscles clutching at the dildo. When her climax began to wane, Kara rolled Sasha onto her back as she held the dildo deep inside her with her knees straddling Sasha's hips. The change of position pressed the dildo deeper into her. Kara tossed her head back and began bouncing on Sasha, filling her completely with the dildo on each down stroke.

"This feels so good, Sasha," Kara wailed as she rode Sasha with abandon.

Sasha watched Kara's breasts bounce with her body as she took her pleasure and ground the mount of the harness roughly onto her clit with each movement. She entered Kara's mind to feel the intense pleasure Kara was feeling while she rode her body and felt the pleasure grow. She reached up to stroke her thumb across Kara's clit.

"Yes, yes, yes," Kara growled as her mind exploded with pleasure. "That's it, baby," she said when Sasha's thumb stroked across her clit.

Sasha felt the rush of wetness flowing from Kara, and then watched her collapse forward into her arms, breathing in rapid gasps. She slowly lifted off the dildo and cuddled in beside Sasha, placing her head on Sasha's shoulder. "That was fantastic."

"I rather enjoyed it as well," Sasha said with a grin.

Kara's hand released the harness from Sasha's hips and when she tugged on it, Sasha lifted her hips to allow her to remove it. Kara's fingers located Sasha's center. "I guess you did enjoy it," she said, dipping her fingers into the wetness. "Why don't we see if I can improve upon that," Kara teased as she stroked through Sasha's wetness.

"That, my dear, is an excellent idea."

"You are so velvety soft," Kara whispered, her fingers slipping between Sasha's lips and entered her, reaching deep inside.

"That feels good," Sasha said, spreading her thighs wider.

"I bet it tastes good too," Kara whispered against her skin.

"Why don't you find out?" Sasha encouraged.

"I think I will," Kara said as her soft lips brushed Sasha's skin, kissing down the front of her, her fingers plunging in and out of Sasha's wetness.

Kara licked the sweet juices from Sasha's clit then wrapped her lips around it while she suckled it deep into her mouth. She slipped a third finger inside Sasha and began curling her fingers, stroking across her G spot.

Sasha's fingers were teasing her nipples while Kara's tongue stroked across the top of her clit, bringing her near climax. Sasha buried her hand in Kara's hair, pressing her mouth more firmly onto her as her inner muscles clutched at Kara's fingers. Kara's moans vibrated on her clit causing Sasha to shake with pleasure. She ground into Kara's face.

"Holy shit, that felt good," Sasha said when she released Kara's head from her grip.

"It tasted good too," Kara said with a devilish grin. "Just like I knew it would."

Kara settled back in on Sasha's shoulder with her hand resting on Sasha's stomach. Sasha listened to Kara's slow even breathing until she fell asleep and it drew her toward sleep. Just when she was about to drift off, Sasha's brain was flooded with memories of making love with Milly. She was startled by the vivid images.

The movement of Sasha's body jarred Kara awake. "Are you all right, my love?"

"Yes, baby, I just had a spasm," Sasha said. She closed her eyes and concentrated on sleep.

Kara snuggled back onto Sasha's shoulder and allowed sleep to reclaim her.

†

Milly awoke to a sense of extreme pleasure as she lay in bed. Her hands softly caressed herself while she thought of Sasha. Her fingers filled her body when she felt Sasha's climax, causing a shudder of release to run through her, soaking her sheets with her juices. Milly floated back to sleep and dreamed of Sasha.

Chapter Eleven

When Milly came home from school the next day, she found Sasha reading the paper on the front porch.

"Hello, Sasha," she said sweetly.

"Welcome home, how was school today?"

"It was okay. I was wondering if I could ask a favor of you."

"Sure, what can I help you with?"

"I need go to the university and register for classes tonight, and I was wondering if you'd go with me."

"What time?" Sasha asked.

"I can go anytime between five and eight."

"Why don't we go at four and we can meet Kara for dinner in town, before you register."

"That would be great," Milly said.

"I'll call Kara and change into some different clothes. Do you want to drive?"

"I think it would be good practice for me."

"Good idea. So, you go get ready and meet me in a half hour," Sasha instructed.

Sasha watched Milly cross the yard and step into her home. She smiled when she realized how attractive Milly had become over the last year as she blossomed into a young woman. She shook the thought from her head and walked inside to call Kara.

"Hello, my love," Sasha said when Kara answered the phone.

"Hi Sasha, this is a welcome surprise."

"Milly has asked me to accompany her to the university to register for classes tonight, and I was calling to see if you could meet us for an early dinner?" Sasha asked.

"I have a late appointment at five," Kara said. "Why don't you two enjoy a nice dinner and I'll see you later when you get home?"

"Okay, sweetie," Sasha said. "I don't think we'll be late."

"Have fun and tell Milly to keep you out of trouble," Kara teased.

"Yes, dear. I'll see you tonight. I love you."

"I love you too, Sasha."

Sasha took a quick shower and dressed in a new pair of jeans and a button-up oxford shirt. She slipped her feet into comfortable leather loafers and walked back downstairs to find Milly waiting for her in the parlor. She was looking up at the portrait and when she heard Sasha, she turned around.

Stricken by the resemblance between the young woman and her Milly, she felt her face grow red with a blush.

"We're on our own tonight, Kara has a late appointment."

"That's not a problem," Milly said as she smiled sweetly at Sasha. "Are you ready to go?"

"Waiting on you," Sasha teased.

They drove into New Orleans in comfortable silence. When they reached the river, Milly asked, "Where are we going for dinner?"

"How does seafood sound to you?"

"It sounds great. Where are we going?"

Sasha gave her directions to an out-of-the-way spot. Milly pulled into a parking place and followed Sasha into the building. They were ushered to a small table and given handwritten menus to select their dinner.

"I think I am having the fried shrimp," Sasha said. "They have fresh oysters too, I see."

"I saw that too. Should we share a dozen?"

"At least one," Sasha said.

Sasha ordered two glasses of sweet tea and a dozen raw oysters. "Have you selected an entrée?" she asked.

"I'll have the fried shrimp too," Milly said.

The waitress took their orders and returned a few moments later with a tray of oysters on the half shell, a bottle of Tabasco, and saltine crackers.

"Dig in," Sasha said.

Both she and Milly placed an oyster on crackers then doused them with Tabasco sauce. "Down the hatch," Sasha said with a grin.

"These are great."

"Can you split another dozen?" Sasha asked.

"Yes, but only one more so we don't spoil our dinner," Milly answered.

Sasha ordered another tray of oysters. "So what classes are you going to take?"

"I thought I would go ahead and get an English and history course out of the way. That'll give me two classes, three nights a week."

"You should be able to handle that pretty well."

"I think so too," Milly said. "My last two classes of the day are study hall, so I should be able to do a lot of the classwork then."

They ate the last of the oysters over light conversation and when the platters of shrimp arrived, Milly's eyes grew wide.

"Those are huge portions," she said.

"In hindsight, maybe we should have split an order," Sasha said with a grin.

"No worries, I'll take a doggy bag to father."

They both made it through barely half their meals and asked for a carryout box. Sufficiently stuffed, Sasha led Milly back out to the car. They drove onto campus and went in search of a parking place.

They walked around campus until they located the hall where Milly needed to register. "Do you want me to go in with you?" Sasha asked.

"No, I think I can manage from here."

"I'll sit out here and wait for you then."

Sasha watched Milly disappear inside the building, and then walked over to a wall of stone to take a seat. The campus was very busy as students rushed to and from classes while younger students came in alone or were accompanied by parents to register.

Sasha felt a pain in her left shoulder as she looked across the courtyard. When Sasha had gone to South America to take care of the last of the Bellfontaine brothers, one of the narcoterrorists had shot her in the shoulder. Her immortal powers had healed the wound almost instantly, but it left a small scar that burned whenever she was in the presence of evil. Between her shoulder and the tingling in her mind, Sasha had ample tools for detecting evil in her presence.

The pain had come first and now she felt a sensation in her mind as she looked around to determine the source. She scanned the crowd of faces, but could not narrow the field enough to discover whom the source of evil was resonating from. There were simply too many people moving around the courtyard. Sasha stood and walked through the crowd, hoping she could move close enough to whoever it was to pick up a stronger signal, but the more she moved, the more confusing the signals were. She ran into a female student who was rushing through the crowd, without watching where she was going and books flew everywhere. Sasha bent down to pick her up and helped her collect her books. When she straightened up to resume her search, the signal had disappeared completely.

"Damn," she said and received a few questioning glances from passing students. Sasha walked back to the wall and sat down to resume her wait for Milly. She was still staring out across the crowd when she heard a voice from behind her.

"Hello handsome," Milly said.

Sasha turned around to find blue eyes smiling at her.

"Are you okay?"

"Yes, I'm fine, why do you ask?"

"You look concerned about something."

"It's nothing, I just thought I saw someone, but I was wrong," Sasha said.

"Would you mind if we make one more stop to buy my books?"

"Chomping at the bit, are you?" Sasha teased. "No, I don't mind."

"The bookstore is only a block over if you don't mind a short walk," Milly said.

"I don't mind at all. Lead the way."

Milly made her purchases at the bookstore and the two started for the car. Sasha felt the burn in her shoulder again and looked around carefully as they walked. She caught a glimpse of a man who seemed to be looking in their direction, but he was not close enough for her to see his face in the growing darkness.

Milly wound through traffic and was driving down on Canal Street when Sasha felt the tingle, stronger this time. "Pull over for a second, Milly."

Milly pulled over to the curb and Sasha stepped out of the car. She walked back to the corner they had just passed and looked down the street in both directions. There was no one in sight, so Sasha turned back toward the car.

Milly had turned the engine off as she sat waiting for Sasha. She looked at Sasha when she climbed back into the car.

"You have to tell me what is going on," Milly said.

Sasha looked at Milly. "I know you have heard about TBS, right?"

"The serial killer, yes, I have."

"I think he has returned," Sasha said. "I've been getting evil vibes from someone, but I can't get close enough to track him down."

"Does Kara know you are doing this?"

"Yes, she does. We have been making routine trips to town at night to drive through the Quarter in search of him."

"Do you want to take a drive through now?" Milly asked. "I assume you felt something when you asked me to stop."

"Yes, if you don't mind a little side trip."

"Not at all," Milly said as she reached down and turned the key.

"Thanks."

"Just let me know if you need me to go in a certain direction."

"I will. I want you to be very cautious when you come to town to school too," Sasha said.

"You think he could be on campus?" Milly asked.

"I felt the first vibes when you were registering," Sasha said. "It may not be the same person, but you must be careful. He's claiming college students as his victims."

"I'll be on the alert," Milly promised.

They drove through the Quarter twice, with no sign of the vibes Sasha had felt earlier. "Have you sensed anything?"

"No, not a thing," Sasha said. "You can head for home now."

Milly slowed and turned into the drive. "Thanks for going with me tonight and thank you for such a great dinner."

"It was my pleasure and maybe we'll go again soon."

†

Milly's heart raced at the thought of spending more time with Sasha. The desire to kiss Sasha had returned burning deep inside her. When she pulled up beside Sasha's truck, she put the car in park and turned the engine off. "Sasha," she whispered.

Sasha looked at Milly when she called her name and saw a familiar sparkle in her eyes. She sat frozen as Milly leaned into her and covered her lips with a soft kiss. Sasha's mind reeled with the softness of Milly's lips as they brushed hers and she parted her lips to allow Milly's tongue inside her mouth without thinking. For just a moment, Sasha responded to Milly's kiss, enjoying the familiar toying of her tongue as it swirled around her own. Then Sasha remembered it wasn't her Milly she was kissing, nor was it Kara, and she broke the kiss.

"Milly," she said. "That should never have happened."

"I know, Sasha, I am sorry, I don't know what possessed me," Milly said, her face drooping.

"Don't apologize. We'll make sure it doesn't happen again, all right?"

"Yes, Sasha," Milly said as she picked up the seafood container and opened her door. She stepped out of the car. "Thanks again for going with me," she said and walked quickly to her house.

Sasha leaned against the car, glad it was dark to hide the flush of her cheeks. She had responded to Milly's kiss and had enjoyed it. That must never happen again she told herself. She stepped away from the car into the cool night air and into the light of her front porch.

†

Kara had heard the approach of Milly's car as she changed clothes in the bedroom. She walked to the window and saw Milly park the car beside Sasha's truck. Kara was startled when she saw Milly kiss Sasha and a surge of jealousy rushed through her. She was even more startled at the length of time it took for Sasha to break the kiss. Anger burning deep inside, she turned away from the window and walked downstairs to meet Sasha.

"Welcome home, love," she said as Sasha walked through the front door. "How was the trip?"

"It was fine," Sasha said. "She's all set to start classes next week."

"Very good. Are you all right, you look a bit flushed?" Kara opened the door for Sasha to explain what she had just witnessed.

"Yes, I'm fine. I got a tingle when we were on campus and another stronger one as we were driving home, but I couldn't track it down. I asked Milly to drive through the Quarter, but I never could pick up the vibes."

"Does she understand what is going on?"

"Yes, I had to explain it tonight, and she promised she'd be careful when she starts classes," Sasha said.

"Good, I'm glad she is aware of the danger. Did anything else happen tonight?" Kara hoped Sasha would take the bait and explain the kiss to her.

"No, all is well." Sasha looked at the floor.

Kara could sense the distress and excitement Sasha felt when Milly kissed her and it was obvious that she had no idea that Kara had witnessed the exchange from the bedroom window.

"Did you have something to eat?" Sasha asked.

"Yes, I fixed a light salad," Kara said. She hid her disappointment in Sasha. Maybe there was a good reason she was unwilling to talk about her feelings for Milly. Kara had thought they could talk about anything, until now.

"Good." Sasha took Kara in her arms and kissed her passionately as her hands stroked down Kara's back to squeeze her buttocks.

"My, my, what did you eat that has gotten you into such an amorous mood?" Kara teased, determined to push aside her questions about the kiss.

"Milly and I each had a dozen oysters before we had shrimp."

"Oysters, hmm. I love what they do to you," she said with a grin.

"Me too, they make me hungry," Sasha returned Kara's grin.

"Should we go take care of that hunger?"

"I think we should," Sasha said as she scooped Kara into her arms and carried her up the stairs to their bedroom as they kissed deeply.

Sasha set Kara onto her feet beside the bed and lifted the shirt above her head. Kara was not wearing a bra, which allowed Sasha's mouth freedom as she moved to cover her left breast. She hungrily suckled Kara's breast as her hands slid beneath the fabric of her sweatpants to cup Kara's ass with her strong hands. Kara pulled Sasha further into her breast as her groans of pleasure echoed in Sasha's ears.

"Yes, Sasha," she groaned as Sasha's teeth raked across her nipple and her mouth moved to cover her right breast.

Kara reached down and pulled Sasha's shirt free from her jeans, her nails leaving trails of gooseflesh on Sasha's back as she pulled the still buttoned shirt up to her shoulders. Sasha lifted her head and arms to allow Kara to pull the shirt from her body then resumed suckling her breast as she slowly moved Kara toward the bed. Sasha lowered Kara's pants and pushed her back onto the bed as she knelt down between her legs.

Kara spread her thighs and draped them over Sasha's shoulders as Sasha's hands kneaded her breasts. "I love the feel of your body," Sasha whispered as her lips kissed down the inside of Kara's thigh.

Kara felt the rush of wetness between her legs as Sasha kissed her skin and she reached down to part her lips for Sasha's approaching mouth. "Kiss me, baby," Kara said as she felt Sasha's hot breath on her clit.

Sasha flattened her tongue and slowly stroked the length of Kara's lips, causing her to shudder with need. "You like that, don't you?" Sasha breathed against her hips.

"Oh hell yes, Sasha, don't stop now," Kara begged.

"I have no intention of stopping," Sasha said as her tongue slipped along her length again.

Kara lifted her hips, trying to reach Sasha's tongue, but Sasha lifted her face just out of reach. "I can see I'm not the only one who hungers tonight," Sasha purred.

"Lick me until you make me come, Sasha," Kara groaned as she lowered her trembling hips back onto the bed.

Sasha intended to do just that as she lowered her face between Kara's legs. Her mind flashed back to the memory of Milly's kiss just as her mouth made contact with Kara's wetness and her tongue swirled wildly around Kara's clit. "Oh god, yes, Sasha," Kara cried out as her shaking fingers held her lips open to Sasha's mouth.

Sasha lapped at the soft folds of skin so lightly she thought Kara would go insane with lust as she cried out for Sasha to go deeper. The tip of Sasha's tongue probed deeper into the silky wetness of Kara's body, lapping the juices into her mouth as she took Kara closer to orgasm.

†

Milly had finished her shower and slipped between her covers when a familiar taste filled her mouth. She opened her mind to Sasha and could peek inside her defenses long enough to know that Sasha was making love to Kara. The thought of them together stirred Milly and she soaked her panties with a rush of juices. Milly could feel the softness of Kara's breasts under Sasha's hands as her left hand rubbed across her own aching breasts. Milly spread her legs as her right hand slipped beneath the fabric of her panties and her fingers reached her wetness, causing her to moan with delight. Her clit was erect and throbbing as her fingers moved past it to enter her wetness. Sasha's tongue was buried inside Kara's body, so Milly penetrated her wetness with two fingers and began curling them deep inside. Her fingers emulated the lapping of Sasha's tongue inside Kara, but Milly knew they didn't feel near as nice as Sasha's hot tongue inside of Kara. Still, she felt herself shivering as her fingers plunged in and out. When she felt she was close to climax, Milly rubbed across her clit with the palm of her hand until she exploded with pleasure. "Oh yes, Sasha," she whispered as the grip of climax took her mind.

†

Sasha felt Kara's inner muscles begin to convulse and she lifted her mouth to cover her clit, sucking it deeply into her mouth. She heard Milly's whisper calling her name and Sasha entered Milly's mind just as she was experiencing her orgasm. The intensity of what she felt in Milly's mind made her groan, sending vibrations onto Kara's clit.

Sasha drove two fingers deep inside Kara's body as she sucked her clit hungrily. Kara cried out, "Yes, yes, yes, Sasha," and then flooded her face with her release.

Sasha slowed the movement of her fingers and softly kissed Kara's clit as Kara gasped for air.

"Damn, that felt good Sasha," she said.

"Good, but I'm not done with you yet." Sasha removed her fingers and rubbed across Kara's clit with the palm of her hand.

"You are going to drive me crazy," Kara groaned as Sasha pulled and stretched her swollen clit.

Sasha used her free hand to open her jeans and slid them down over her hips as she wiggled them off her body. She then climbed onto the bed and straddled Kara's face with her hips.

"Yes, Sasha, I want to taste you," Kara begged as her hands reached up to pull Sasha's hips toward her face.

Sasha could still feel Milly inside her mind as she lowered herself onto Kara's waiting tongue. *If you are going to eavesdrop, you might as well feel it all,* Sasha projected as she felt Kara's tongue drive deep inside her. Sasha ground her hips onto Kara's face soaking her with wetness as her fingers slipped inside Kara and her mouth targeted her clit once more.

†

Milly felt the pleasure Sasha was experiencing and it drove her wild with lust. She filled her wetness with three fingers, thrusting them in and out until she felt Sasha come and Milly came again, leaving her soaked with sweat and shaking violently on the bed.

†

Sasha and Kara came together in a wave of bliss as their bodies convulsed uncontrollably on the bed. When Kara climbed up to rest her head on Sasha's shoulder she whispered into her skin. "I am sending you into town with Milly once a week to have oysters."

"You enjoyed that just a bit, didn't you?"

"Oh my god, Sasha, that was beyond incredible, you were like a woman possessed," she teased.

"Oysters it is then," Sasha said with a grin.

"Would you like to sleep for a while now and then shower before we make a sweep of the Quarter?"

"That's an excellent idea," Sasha said as Kara cuddled into her side.

Chapter Twelve

Brody met Williams at the precinct house at eight the next morning. "Do you want to tag along with me today?"

"Unless you have something else you would like me to do," Williams said.

"Come along then," he said. "I wish I had other leads for you to follow up, but right now we are stuck."

"You want me to drive?"

"Sure," Brody said as he tossed him the keys. "There are four shops that specialize in perfumes and colognes that I think we should visit this morning,"

"I know of three of these."

"Let's hit the one you don't know first then."

"I'm on it," Williams said as he pulled out onto the street.

When they pulled up to the address of the store Brody groaned. "No wonder you didn't recognize this one," he said. The store had received major damage from the flood and had not reopened.

By the time they had visited the next two shops, they were beginning to get disappointed. "Let's hit the last one and then I'll spring for some lunch before we head back to the house."

At the final stop, the shop's owner led them to the back of a small shop.

"What is it that you two gentlemen are looking for?" she asked.

"We are searching for a scent that a suspect we are looking for may be wearing," Brody explained.

"That sounds like searching for a needle in a haystack," the owner said. "Can you describe the scent?"

"It definitely was not your run-of-the-mill cologne," Brody said. "It has a very rich and sensual smell to it, according to one of our female crime scene techs."

"Maybe you should have brought her along," the woman teased.

"We have both smelled the scent," Williams said.

"That was not meant as a slight to you fine gentlemen, but a woman's nose never forgets a scent like that," the shop owner said.

"Williams, get on the radio and see if our lady is on duty today," Brody said. "If so, ask her to get here on the pronto."

"Yes sir," Williams said and rushed back to the car.

"What kind of person would be wearing the scent?" the woman asked.

"Someone who is very physically attractive to both sexes," Brody answered. "Have you been following the serial killer reports in the newspaper?"

"The TBS case, yes, I have," she said. "You think he may be the person wearing this cologne?"

"It is a very unusual scent, but yes we have smelled it at two of his latest crime scenes," Brody said.

"That is very interesting. I will pull out some samples for your lady to try," she said as she left the room.

Williams walked back into the room. "She will be here in fifteen."

"Thanks, what is her name by the way?"

"Samantha Dickens."

"Let me guess, she goes by Sam."

"No, actually, she goes by Samantha," Williams said with a chuckle.

"All right, wise guy. The owner is setting out some samples for us to check out."

It only took Samantha Dickens ten minutes to arrive. Williams waited for her in the front of the shop, and led her to the back room to join Brody and the shopkeeper.

"Thank you for coming so quickly, Dickens," Brody said. "We hope you can help us identify the scent TBS has been leaving behind."

"I'll do my best, Detective," Samantha said.

The shopkeeper had set out a dozen samples. They each tested and discarded those they could immediately rule out. Samantha kept returning to one bottle. "This is the closest, but it isn't quite right," she said.

"What's missing?" the shopkeeper asked.

"It doesn't have the I-could-eat-you-for-dinner smell," Samantha said with a blush.

"The what?" Williams asked.

"The quality of the scent that makes people smell good enough to eat," the shopkeeper said. "I know exactly what you are talking about."

The shopkeeper seemed to be thinking of something as Williams chuckled at Samantha's description of the scent.

"Would this person have money?" the shopkeeper asked.

"That's a good possibility," Brody said. "Why do you ask?"

"Something that good is probably a special blend or made specifically for a certain body heat and would cost ten times more than regular top-shelf cologne."

"Do you make those?"

"I have in the past. Since the storm, business hasn't been what it once was."

"Would you possibly still have some samples of the ones you have made?"

"Somewhere, but it may take a few minutes to locate. Help yourselves to coffee and I'll be back as quickly as I can." She walked back to the front of the store and started rummaging through drawers.

"Would you two care for coffee?" Williams asked.

"No thanks," Samantha said.

"I'll take a cup, black please," Brody said.

Williams poured two cups of coffee and then joined them at the small table.

"Thanks."

They were almost finished when the woman returned carrying a case holding a dozen small bottles. She placed it on the table and opened it up. "Good luck," she told Samantha.

Samantha tested one bottle at a time and when she reached the fifth bottle, she smiled. "This is it." She handed the bottle to Brody.

Brody took the bottle and waved it under his nose and then handed it to Williams. "I think you are right," he agreed.

"I know I am," Samantha said. "On the right person, that smell would be irresistible."

"She is absolutely correct about that, gentlemen," the shopkeeper added.

Williams turned to look at the bottle. "Lust, that's a simple name."

"How much would a bottle this size cost?" Brody asked.

"I only made three bottles of this. The same woman bought the other two at three hundred dollars each."

"Three hundred dollars," Williams groaned. "That's a lot of money for that small of a bottle."

"A woman, you say, bought them," Brody repeated.

"Yes, a tall, dark woman with a Russian accent," the shopkeeper said.

"Would you still have records of the sale?"

"Don't need them. The woman who bought them was named Anastasia, but I never knew of a last name."

"I don't suppose she used a credit card?"

"No, I deal in cash only."

"Do you have any idea when she made the purchase?"

"Late last spring, maybe April."

"Do you have any other information that may be of help to us?" Brody asked.

"No address, but I know she was living in the city."

"You've been a great help."

"Thanks, I hope you get that bastard soon," the shopkeeper shared as she walked them out of the shop.

"We do too," Brody replied as they headed toward the car. He turned and faced Samantha. "Great job, Dickens, can I buy you some lunch?"

"I'd like that," Samantha answered.

"You pick the spot," Brody told her.

"Very well, follow me," she said as she walked back to the crime scene van.

Samantha took them to the same hole-in-the-wall seafood place Milly and Sasha had dined at the night before. "They have the freshest oysters and seafood here."

"Excellent choice," Williams agreed.

They all dined on seafood platters, completely sating Brody's need for food for at least a day. When they finished, Brody thanked Samantha again for her assistance and walked with her to the crime scene van.

"Be careful out there," he warned softly.

"Always, Detective." She smiled at him and drove away.

"What next?" Williams asked as Brody climbed into the passenger seat.

"Back to the house for me, but I have other plans for you. I want you to go down to the hall of records and do a search of any property owner with the first name of Anastasia."

"Now we're talking a needle in a haystack," Williams complained.

"True, but we have to make sure the haystack is empty as we follow up every lead. Drop me at the house and you can use my car."

Williams pulled up to the curb and Brody climbed out of the car. "Call me if you run across anything."

"I will, Brody," Williams promised.

†

Talis stopped and purchased a Cajun sausage sandwich from a street vendor and then walked back to his flat. He finished the sandwich, tossed the cardboard holder in the garbage, and picked up the day's paper.

Nothing caught his interest until he reached the obituaries, where he read…

Thomas Dubais
26 of Kenner

Internment will occur tomorrow at 1pm at Lafayette Cemetery #1 Graveside service only.

In addition to the brief announcement, a picture of Dubais was included. Talis carefully cut the obituary and picture from the paper and added it to his growing shrine. “I guess one of your many patrons took pity upon you and decided to have you sent to a city of the dead,” Talis sneered as he tacked the picture to the wall.

As he sat on his bed, staring up at the many items that made up his shrine, the idea of going to the funeral popped into his mind. After all, the police still did not know what he really looked like, the sun from his stay with Lute had bleached his hair, and his complexion was much darker.

“What the hell. I have nothing better to do on a Saturday afternoon,” Talis spoke out loud. He climbed from the bed and walked into the bathroom to take a long, hot shower. As he was enjoying the feel of the hot water on his skin, the image of the young blonde and the tall, dark-haired woman kept returning to his mind. Either of them would do, but the blonde was so young and fresh-looking. Talis doubted that she had ever been touched and the idea of a virgin made him twitch with excitement. This would definitely take more time and planning. He wasn’t sure if the blonde was a commuter student or if she lived on or near the campus. Indeed, it would take much more of his talents to lure the woman if she did not live close by, but the always-creative Talis was already forming a plan. He stretched out on his bed and allowed his mind to weave through dreams of decadence and debauchery.

†

"Damn, this is frustrating," she growled. "I know that bastard is here somewhere, but I can't find him."

"You're doing everything you can, Sasha," Kara calmly reminded her.

"I know, honey, but he's been quiet for too long and I can sense he is ready to act," Sasha said, unaware of Thomas Dubais as his most recent victim.

"I was sure he would be out hunting on a Friday night," Kara said. "I wonder what he is planning for us now?" she added.

"I wish for just a moment, I could slip into that depraved mind of his to find out what his next move is," Sasha said. "We might as well head for home and try again tomorrow night."

†

Later, as Kara rested in her arms, Sasha's thoughts focused on TBS. *What are you up to, you bastard?* Sasha felt a tingle, but this one was much different than the one she searched for. This tingle had the sensual feeling of Milly. Sasha entered her mind to find Milly awake and lying in her bed. Sasha watched and felt Milly's hands as they moved across her naked flesh. She could feel the rippling of Milly's skin as gooseflesh appeared behind the trail of her fingertips as she reached down between her legs. She could smell the wetness of Milly's excitement and Sasha felt her body react in like, her wetness oozing past her lips.

Sasha did her best to pull her mind back from this private moment, but her thoughts refused to leave and she watched as Milly brought pleasure to her body, softly calling out Sasha's name as her passion grew beyond restraint.

Milly's sensuality had roared back to life in the younger Milly and Sasha knew she would have to devise a way to prevent Milly's allure from entrapping her. Sasha loved Kara deeply, but she could not prevent her body from betraying her desire for Milly. She felt the quivering of Milly's body in her post climactic state and was relieved when Milly's need was quickly sated and she felt her drift off to sleep.

†

Talis awoke bright and early the next morning and decided he would walk down to the Square for coffee and beignets. He purchased a newspaper, which he read as he downed two orders of beignets and several cups of rich, steaming coffee. He made no effort to conceal himself as several police units passed on the street less than ten feet from where he was perched. He was TBS and he might as well be invisible to the clods that called themselves police officers. He smiled his arrogant smile and watched as the morning tourists and late-night partygoers came in droves for coffee and the sweet pastry.

†

Brody had spent the night in the precinct's crib. When he awoke the next morning, he showered and dressed before going into the precinct's break room for some hot coffee. Williams, who apparently arrived early and waited for him to awaken followed him into the break room.

"Good morning, Brody."

"Good morning," Brody returned. "Have you got a suit?"

"Sure I do. What is happening?"

"Thomas Dubais's funeral is this afternoon at one and I thought we might go to pay our last respects. You know, on second thought, I have a better idea for you."

Williams followed Brody back into his office and sat down across the desk from him. "I'm listening," he said.

"I think I will go to the service and have you parked outside the front gate taking pictures of anyone who attends the service. I just have a hunch our boy might make an appearance." Brody looked at Williams. "Yes, I think that will do. Now why don't you go down to supply and sign out a digital camera. Then we will go to the Square. I am having a sudden urge for beignets."

"I hope that craving doesn't mean you're pregnant," Williams teased.

"Okay, wise guy, for that you can drive *and* buy," Brody quipped back.

"Ouch, will they give me a pile of cash from the supply room too?"

"Okay, you drive and I'll buy."

"I'll be right back then."

As Brody often did, he found himself turned away from his desk staring at the crime board, in hopes that some message would jump out at him. He was deep in his study when Williams returned and placed the digital camera on the desk.

"So what time is the service again?"

"It's at one," Brody said as he stood and pulled his jacket around his shoulders. "Leave the camera. We have plenty of time before we leave for Lafayette Number One."

Williams followed Brody out to the car, drove them to the Square, and parked illegally on the curb. *The kid was learning fast.* Brody watched him take the detective placard and hang it from the rear mirror. "You are getting this down pat," he teased as they left the car and crossed the street.

†

They stood in the express line, which was anything but express at nine on a Saturday morning, and then took their trays to an empty spot. Brody set his food on the table and began to remove his jacket. He stopped in mid-movement and looked up at Williams, who was staring back at him.

"Yeah, I smell it too," Williams said. "Very faint, but no doubt it is the same."

Brody knew it was useless, but he looked around at the milling crowd. TBS was nowhere close, but he had definitely been right where he was standing. "We have got to get that bastard soon," Brody said to Williams. "I'm tired of him being one step ahead of us."

"I hear ya, boss. We'll get him soon."

Brody took his seat and picked up the coffee. "I assume you didn't find anything out at public records."

"Nothing at all, but I have a clerk who is digging back through the archives that were not ruined by the flood. I promised her dinner of her choice if she is able to find anything."

"Damn, why didn't I think of this earlier." Brody slammed his hand down on the table.

"Wha…what?"

"We need to check with immigration. If the woman had a thick Russian accent then she was probably here on a visa."

"Damn, you're right. Do you want me to work on that after we get back from the funeral?" Williams asked.

"No, it won't do any good to do anything until Monday. The powers that be will all be off on the weekend, and you won't get anything but frustrated with the staff who have no authority whatsoever."

"What about the federal boys? Can they pull any diplomatic strings?"

"Give them a call when we get back and see if they can help, or at least get them started on it," Brody said.

For the first time in days, Brody's spirits lifted. He finished his beignets. "Let's head back now."

They walked back to the sedan and drove to the precinct.

†

"I will call the federal agents that are working as part of the task force and get the information we need," Williams disappeared into a vacant office. When he returned to Brody's office he said, "They aren't sure what they can get, but they at least know what we need."

"Thanks." Brody walked to a city map hanging on the wall to his office. He located Lafayette Number One in the Garden District and looked at possible routes. "Have you ever been to this cemetery?"

"Yes, my grandmother was interred there," he said.

"Is there only one entrance?"

"Yes, the one at the front gate."

"So, if TBS comes today he has to pass through there?"

"Yes, unless he climbs a tall fence, which would be too obvious."

"All right, I want you positioned where you can take pictures of everyone entering and leaving the cemetery," Brody instructed.

"Fine. If you don't mind, I will leave now and make sure there is no one already inside the cemetery and then set up my post."

"That's a good idea. Take the sedan and I will ride back with you after the funeral."

"How are you going to get there?"

"I will get a cruiser to drop me off and take the St. Charles Street streetcar."

"That is an unusual route," Williams remarked.

"Our boy is unusual."

"As usual you are right, Brody."

"Of course I am," Brody said with a wink. "Get moving and I'll see you after the service."

Williams picked up the camera and walked out of the office. "Every face," Brody shouted after him.

†

Williams smiled as he walked out of the precinct house and drove to the cemetery. He parked against the curb, legally this time and walked into the cemetery. There was only one person inside, an elderly lady visiting the crypt of her late husband. Williams walked around until he located an open crypt where Dubais would be interred, then walked back to the car. Twenty minutes later he saw the woman leave the cemetery.

At twelve forty-five, Williams saw a hearse, followed by a small train of vehicles, pull up in front of the cemetery. Williams began snapping pictures as the funeral home staff opened up the back of the hearse and several young men serving as pallbearers carried the casket into the cemetery. He made sure he had pictures of each face, male and female, of the people attending the service. He watched as Brody arrived on foot and slipped inside the gate with no more than a quick glance in his direction. Williams chuckled and snapped a picture of Brody.

It was still several minutes before the service was supposed to begin and he watched as Brody followed the casket into the cemetery apparently surveying the small crowd. Williams saw a small group of young men approach before noticing that one seemed to be rushing to catch up with the group. He captured their images and watched for the next mourner to arrive. Several other men and a few older women entered the cemetery, just as the service was to begin.

Talis walked in with the group of men and stood in the back of the small crowd. Although partially sheltered by the corner of a mausoleum he easily made out Detective Brody standing in the crowd. He watched as Brody slowly turned to survey the area. With Brody's eyes so nearly seeing him, Talis felt a chill and decided to cut his visit short.

He carefully turned away and lifted a white handkerchief to his face as he stepped out of the front gate effectively blocking the photograph the young man in the car was taking. *Clever Brody, but not clever enough.* He then walked down the sidewalk, turned a corner and disappeared.

†

The service was brief and Brody followed the group of mourners out of the cemetery. He took the arm of a young man and pulled him aside as they walked through the front gate. Brody flashed his badge and introduced himself.

"How well did you know Thomas and his friends?" he asked the startled young man.

"Very well, I was probably Thomas's oldest friend in the city," the man replied.

"Can I get you to help me for just a few minutes to identify the people at the service?"

"Sure, I'll help if I can."

Brody walked the man over to where Williams was parked. "Williams, this is…umm, sorry, I didn't get your name."

"Carl Berkshire." The man shook Williams's hand.

"My partner took pictures of everyone in attendance, and I hope you can identify them for us," Brody explained.

Carl identified all except one young man who had walked in with Carl's group. "This one I don't know."

"Have you ever seen him before?"

"No, not at all," Carl stated.

"He was the first to leave the service but had a handkerchief blocking his face. I trailed him with the camera in case he turned back around but he never did," Williams said.

"That is probably our boy," Brody said. "Thanks for your help, Mr. Berkshire."

"You're welcome." Carl rushed away to meet the friends who were waiting on him just down the block.

"Which way did he go?" Brody got into the car.

"He turned right at the corner."

"Drive," Brody said when he had his seat belt buckled.

Williams drove the path the man had taken, but there was no one in sight. They made several trips down side streets without luck, and then headed back to the precinct house. "As soon as we get back I want you to find a computer and blow up those pictures as quick as you can and bring them to me."

"Will do."

"I'm getting closer to knowing who you are, you son of a bitch. You better get ready for me," Brody mumbled as Williams parked the car.

†

Talis easily slipped away from the cemetery and hopped a cab. He had the driver drop him off in the Quarter, then he walked down to his garage, got in his car, and drove east from the Quarter. He drove past the channel and onto St. Claude looking for the right spot. When he passed into Holy Cross he knew he was close. Most of the homes were gone and the ones remaining were in horrible states of disrepair from the floodwaters that had wiped whole city blocks clean. The area felt like a ghost town to Talis as he spied two small homes pressed closely together by the rushing floodwaters. He pulled his small car into a driveway between the homes that would conceal his presence and climbed from the car.

He carefully worked his way past the debris and stepped into what had once been a living room to some unknown family. Looking through the broken panes of glass of the front window, Talis could see the river traffic on the Mississippi as it pushed its cargo into port. *This will be perfect.* Remote, considered a dead part of town, and close enough to where he could stage the body close to the river to discover. Talis smiled as he formed the plan in his head and stepped outside to note the address.

He climbed back into his car and drove back to the garage to store it. Monday he would set his plan in motion and soon he would have his perfect ten. He walked back through the Quarter to hit one of the diners for something to eat. He ordered fried pork chops, mashed potatoes with gravy and fresh cooked green beans. He ate heartily, knowing soon he would be in need of all his energy.

†

Williams walked back in to the room and handed Brody an eight-by-ten photograph that showed a good image of the man he felt sure was TBS. Brody smiled and took the photo and pinned it to the crime board. "Soon we will be face-to-face, you and I," he promised.

Chapter Thirteen

"I think I will go for a ride today," Sasha announced after she and Kara finished a late Sunday morning brunch.

"Very well, my love," Kara said. "I have a few files I need to do some work on, so I'll address those while you are gone."

"I'll be back later this afternoon." Sasha bent down to kiss Kara's forehead. "Don't work too hard."

"I won't, I promise, Sasha," Kara answered with a sweet smile.

†

Sasha walked out to the barn to saddle Aries and started down the drive. Sasha needed to think and she had five hundred acres to get lost in as she sorted out her thoughts. Life for her had suddenly become more complicated. Milly's revelation and her request weighed heavily on her mind. If Milly had this much of a connection now, how would that change after Sasha transformed her? Would she feel Milly's every waking moment of emotion?

Sasha was sure even her good friend Marcus, another much older immortal, could not answer that question for her. The situation with Milly was unheard of before. What were Milly's motives in being reborn after her death? Did she intend to come back to reclaim Sasha as her love? Sasha's head spun with all these questions and was getting nowhere in divining answers.

She rode the property for two hours and was no closer to solving any of her problems when she started back down the driveway. One thing was certain, Sasha would have to come up with a solution to block Milly's mind when she and Kara were making love, and vice versa when Milly was experiencing her own private moments. She rode back to the barn and, after giving Aries a rubdown, returned to the house.

†

Kara was still busy at work when Sasha entered the small office. Kara looked up and smiled. "You know what?" Sasha asked.

"What?"

"I think it's time you and I go into town and have some fun,"

"What do you have on your mind?"

"We haven't been to the zoo since they reopened so I thought we could take the riverboat out there and then go for dinner and drinks afterward," Sasha suggested.

"That sounds good to me. Let me finish up here and I'll go shower and get dressed."

"I'll go ahead and get started then."

"Okay, love, I'll see you soon."

†

Sasha climbed the stairs and stripped out of her riding clothes as the shower heated. Her mind needed a distraction from the thoughts of Milly, and TBS. She wondered how both would possibly play out in her future. She stepped into the warm water and had just finished washing her hair when Kara arrived. “Hurry and you can still shower with me,” Sasha called out.

Kara slipped out of her clothes and climbed into the shower behind Sasha. She wrapped her arms around her lover and pressed their bodies close together. Sasha turned in her arms to face Kara and leaned down to kiss her softly, with a slow, sensual kiss.

Kara’s eyes sparkled when the kiss ended. “You shouldn’t kiss me like that if you want to go into town.”

Sasha chuckled softly. “Yes, dear.” She took a washcloth and began washing her body as Kara stepped under the flow of water.

†

After dressing they drove down to Jackson Square to pick up the riverboat for the cruise to the zoo. Sasha and Kara climbed to the top deck and stood together at the railing as the riverboat pulled away from its mooring point. The festive music played loudly as the boat churned on the river and then the voice of the narrator blared across the PA system as he gave the tourists a little bit of New Orleans history.

Kara was not surprised when they made port at the zoo that Sasha walked directly to the big cats’ area. Sasha loved the big cats and always had. There was a pair of black panthers that Sasha had purchased for the zoo a few years back and she went straight to their habitat. "Would you look at that," Sasha said as she stood at the edge of the fence. "Baby makes three," she said with a huge smile.

Kara gazed at the small family lazily playing under a copse of trees. The pair had mated and had a kit that looked to be still very young. "Maybe a month old or so?" she asked.

"Certainly not much more," Sasha said as she watched the male approach across the lot. He fixed Sasha with his yellow green eyes, his muscles rippling across his back and shoulders as he walked toward them. Sasha heard an enthusiastic squeak and looked up to find the young kit running after its father. The male cat sat on his haunches patiently as the young cat playfully chased his father's twitching tail. "You have a beautiful son," she said as she bent down to get a better view of the young cat.

When the kit grew tired of playing, the male led him back to the shade and he sought out his mother's breast for nourishment. Kara watched the expression of joy on Sasha's face as she watched the family rest together in the afternoon heat.

"They make a beautiful family, don't they?"

"Yes, they do," Sasha answered as she turned away from the three pair of eyes fixated on her.

The screeching call of Howler monkeys broke the peaceful silence. "It sounds like someone is stirred up," Kara said. They followed the sound to find two male monkeys verbally sparring from high in the treetops.

"Good lord, they make some racket," Sasha said as they walked past the exhibit onto less vocal animals.

†

It took two hours to complete the circuit of the zoo and when they reached the riverboat landing, the boat was preparing for departure. They rushed on board and walked to the front. A cool wind had come up on the water so Sasha wrapped her arms around Kara and pulled her body close to share warmth as they made the ride back to Canal Street.

"What would you care to eat?" Sasha asked.

"Something hot and spicy," Kara said.

Sasha directed Kara to a small restaurant. When they stepped inside, the pungent smell of seasonings met them with a blast. They ordered cold beer and several pounds of spicy mudbugs and topped off their meals with bowls of steaming gumbo.

"Do you have room for dessert?" Sasha asked.

"I'm stuffed, but I will force myself to split a bread pudding with you," Kara said with a grin.

"You have a deal."

They ate the decadent dessert over cups of rich chicory coffee.

"I'm totally stuffed," Kara said as they walked out to her car.

"How about a stroll around Jackson Square to help our meals settle then," Sasha suggested.

Kara found a parking spot and took Sasha's arm as they walked around the Square, admiring the artwork of local artists and listening to a jazz band that had struck up a song in front of the cathedral. Sasha led Kara to a small bench where they sat until the sun began to set and the artisans packed up their artwork and headed for home.

Sasha had enjoyed an afternoon free of worries and she felt much less stressed as they walked back toward

Kara's car. Until, that is, Kara stopped dead in her tracks in the middle of the sidewalk. "Do you feel that?"

"No, I don't feel anything," Sasha said as she looked at Kara.

"I felt just a momentary twitch. It was as if he had just crossed our path," she said in an effort to explain her feeling.

Talis settled in his flat drinking the first of the six-pack of beer he had just purchased from a small corner store near the Square. He had no idea he had left a mental footprint behind and that was what Kara had experienced. In fact, he had no idea two very dangerous women searched for him at all.

"It's completely gone now," Kara said while they continued the walk back to the car. "Should we take a spin while we are this close?"

"It can't hurt," Sasha said climbing into the passenger seat.

Their trip through the Quarter was fruitless. Neither of them could pick up any signs of TBS, so they turned and drove for home.

"I have a little more work on a file I need to complete," Kara said when they walked back into the house.

"Okay, I'm going to get ready for bed and watch some television upstairs while you finish," Sasha said.

Kara stepped into the office and Sasha climbed the stairs. She changed into sleeping clothes and climbed beneath the covers to watch a show on the History channel. Sasha's eyes grew heavy and she was fast asleep when Kara joined her an hour later. Kara smiled at her sleeping lover and quietly slipped into bed beside her.

†

Monday was Milly's big day. Today she would officially become a college student and she was extremely excited when she returned home from high school to prepare for her night classes. Sasha watched her run into the house to change clothes and then dash back to her car to drive into town. It was only four and her class did not start until six, but Milly did not want to be late. Sasha smiled and waved as she watched the excited teen drive away.

Milly had been so excited to start class that she forgot to eat a snack before leaving home. She arrived on campus with more than an hour to wait and decided to pick up a sandwich for dinner at a small deli directly across from the English building. She could read the first chapter of her English book while she waited.

†

A taxi dropped Talis at the university late in the afternoon. He had a hunch his perfect ten would be starting classes tonight with the beginning of the new session and he would continue his surveillance until he had all the details in place. He was sitting in the shade of an old oak tree when he saw her drive in, and park in the commuter lot. She lifted a book bag and slung it over her shoulder as she walked toward the heart of campus.

Talis rose to his feet and tucked a textbook under his left arm as he leaned on a cane positioned in his right hand. He walked with a noticeable limp and after giving her time to settle in her seat, he followed her into the busy shop. He smiled when he saw her sitting alone, nibbling on a sandwich with a book opened in front of her.

He walked through the line and selected a ham and cheese sandwich and a bottle of water that he placed on a serving tray. After paying for his dinner, Talis picked up the tray in his left hand and began walking slowly toward her. As he neared her table, he allowed the heavy book to slide from underneath his arm and crash loudly to the floor.

Milly jumped in her seat seemingly startled by the loud noised and lowered her book. A handsome young man had dropped a book and was floundering as he was precariously balancing a tray in one hand and a cane in the other.

"Wait, let me help you." Milly placed her book on the table and stood.

The young man looked up with gleaming dark eyes. "Thanks for the help."

"No problem." Milly knelt down and picked up the book. "Microbiology, that's some pretty heavy stuff," she said with a grin.

"Yes, it is." He looked around the area.

"Why don't you join me?" Milly suggested.

"You sure you wouldn't mind?"

"No, not at all, this place is pretty packed."

Milly placed his book on the table and returned to her seat.

"Thank you for your kindness," he said as he reached his hand out. "My name is Talis."

"You're welcome, my name is Milly."

"That's a very pretty name." A charming smile filled his face. "Are you a new student?"

"I start my first classes tonight. What about you?"

"I'm trying to finish medical school," Talis said. "I took a year off after my football injury and now I am trying to get back into study mode."

Milly watched the grimace on his face as he sat down at the table.

"Are you taking strictly night classes?" he asked.

"Yes, I am getting an early jump on college. I don't graduate from high school for two months yet."

"So you are smart and beautiful."

Milly blushed.

"I'm sorry, I didn't mean to embarrass you."

"That's all right," Milly said trying to cover her blush with her book.

Talis unwrapped his sandwich and Milly saw him stealing glances at her as he ate.

Milly quickly finished her sandwich and, though she was still early for class, excused herself from the table. The way the man looked at her made her feel uneasy. "It was a pleasure to meet you, but I must get off to my class," Milly said as she stood.

"Thank you again for your kindness. Good luck with your class and I hope to see you around," Talis said.

"Goodnight," Milly said and walked quickly out the door.

She has such beautiful blue eyes that sparkle when she smiles. Talis was certain that she was untouched and naïve to the ways between man and woman.

Talis enjoyed a leisurely meal and then after dark had fallen completely he went outside to sit beneath the oak as he waited for Milly to return to her car. At a little past ten, he watched as Milly climbed into her car and drove from the lot.

"This is going to be so much fun," he said to himself as he walked to the bus stop and took a bus back to the Quarter. He assumed she was taking Monday, Wednesday, and Friday courses, but would go to the campus again tomorrow night, just in case he was wrong. If all went well, he hoped to have Number Ten in his possession by Friday night.

†

Kara had drifted off to sleep earlier, but Sasha lay awake in the darkness until she heard Milly's car come down the driveway and she knew she was home. She listened for Milly's steps on the front porch and when the front door closed behind her, Sasha knew all was well and closed her eyes.

†

"Have we gotten anything back from immigration yet?" Brody asked Williams.

"Not yet, boss, they are still running down a list of about one hundred Russian women named Anastasia. There were no hits directly to New Orleans, so it is taking some time."

Brody stood and walked to the crime board and picked up a pen. On the long sheet of paper, he wrote the name Anastasia and underneath that, he wrote the word Lust. "What else have we learned recently?"

"He is a bold son of a bitch to come to the funeral," Williams said.

"And arrogant enough to call me directly," Brody said as he added bold and arrogant to the growing list. "Watches," Brody said as he wrote the word on the paper.

He walked back to his desk and sat down wearily in his chair.

"Damn, you would think with all today's technology, tracking an immigrant down would be easy," Brody added.

"How do you think this woman is involved?"

"I am not sure I can explain that yet," Brody said. "I just know she is crucial, to solving this case."

"I'm going to head out now, unless you need me."

"No, you go on ahead. I think we have hit a brick wall for tonight."

"I'm going to walk around the Quarter for a bit before I head home," Williams said. "To clear my head and who knows, maybe I will pass our boy on the street."

"Just be very careful," Brody warned. "TBS has probably seen you with me on more than one occasion and this is one clever son of a bitch."

"Will do, boss. Goodnight."

†

Talis was returning from campus. Just as he assumed, she was not attending classes on Tuesday night. She would be there tomorrow, he was certain. He felt so good about his plan he was suddenly filled with energy and decided to walk home. The long walk would do him good.

†

Williams had walked down Bourbon and stopped at the Cat's Meow for a cold beer. He felt like there was something vitally important to the case right out of his reach, but the harder he thought about what it could be the more boggled his mind became. Frustrated, he took the full bottle of Abita and left the bar. He would walk the rest of the way home and maybe the cool night air would help to clear his head.

The sidewalk was virtually empty as he walked toward Canal. He thought it was strange that there was no more foot traffic on the streets. He was still pondering that thought when a dark figure approached a block ahead. The man stopped under a faintly lit streetlight and looked up for a brief moment before stepping from the curb to make a left turn onto Canal. A moment was all it took for Williams to recognize a familiar face. He picked up his speed and ran to the corner. He watched the man as he casually strolled down the sidewalk; Williams rushed to close the distance between them.

Talis's fears of being recognized sent a chill through his veins when he heard the footsteps behind him. He took a right turn at the next corner, crossing over Canal and headed for a darker section of town.

Talis watched as Williams wove his way through the sudden mass of people on Canal Street as he tried to follow him. When he stepped into a dark alley Talis struck him across his forehead and watched as he fell to the hard concrete of the sidewalk.

Talis then reached inside the man's jacket to pull out the his ID. Just as he had thought, he recognized the face as Officer Williams. Talis dropped the badge and ID onto his chest and reached down to take a cell phone from a holster on his waist. Talis walked back to the corner of Canal and saw that he was on Liberty Street.

With a devious smile, he flipped open the cell phone and scrolled until he found Brody's cell number. He pushed the send button and waited for Brody to answer.

Brody felt his phone vibrate just as he was about to step into his car. He pulled it out and saw that Williams was calling him.

"What's up, Williams?" Brody asked as he climbed in behind the wheel.

"Sorry, Detective, but this isn't your little boy toy," Talis said.

Ice water coursed through Brody's veins when he heard the familiar voice of TBS. He knew that if he was calling from Williams's cell phone, it wasn't a good sign.

"Where is Williams?" Brody demanded.

"Oh don't fret, Detective, he'll be just fine once he gets over a major headache," Talis said. "He got too close, so I had to convince him to back off."

"Where is he?" Brody repeated.

"You'll find him at the corner of Canal and Liberty," Talis said. "You should do a better job of teaching that boy before he gets seriously injured." Talis hung up.

"Bastard," Brody shouted. He called dispatch on his cell. "We have an officer down who needs assistance at Canal and Liberty." He threw his car in gear, and with lights and sirens, headed for Canal.

Talis closed the phone and dropped it back onto Williams's chest. He was starting to groan as he came to and Talis knelt beside him. "You need to back off, little man," he sneered, then stood and walked away. Talis ran down a dark street, his heart racing wildly in his chest. "This is getting to be so much fun," he said with a laugh.

Williams looked into TBS's face, but his vision was so blurred he could not make it out clearly. He felt the warm rush of blood running down his face, and then his head fell back onto the sidewalk.

A marked unit was already on the scene when Brody's car slid to a stop at the corner. He could hear the wail of sirens approach as he ran to Williams's aid. The uniformed officer had Williams sitting upright, holding a pressure pack on a nasty gash above his eyebrow.

Williams looked up, found Brody standing there, and said, "I am sorry, boss, I know I should have called for backup."

"For God's sake don't worry about that, I am glad you are still alive," he told the man honestly. "Can you tell me what happened?"

"I stopped in for a beer and was walking home when I saw him standing under a streetlight. I was positive it was him, so I started following him to get a better look." Williams grimaced in pain. "When I turned this corner he hit me with something that felt like a Mack truck, and my world went black."

"There is a bloody two-by-four right behind you, Detective," the uniformed officer said.

"Yep, that would definitely give you one hell of a headache," Brody said as he turned to look at the bloody board.

The ambulance arrived and prepared Williams for transport. "I'll meet you at Tulane Medical Center in just a few minutes," Brody said as they took him away in a screaming ambulance.

"Have crime scene add that board to our growing list of evidence on this bastard," Brody instructed the officer. "He just added a few more charges to his list," Brody grumbled as he walked back to his car.

†

Brody drove to Tulane Medical Center and sat in the parking lot as he called Crawford to give him an update.

"I'm glad Williams is going to be all right, but he could have gotten his fool self killed," Crawford said.

"He's well aware of that fact, Chief," Brody said. "He just wanted a closer look to see if he could identify the perp. In hindsight, he knows he should've called for backup and I think he's learned that lesson the painful way."

"Okay, tell him to call if he needs anything. I'm sure the doctor will put him off work for a few days," Crawford said. "Try to make it home soon and get somc rest. You sound exhausted."

"I will, boss, once I get Williams home safely," Brody promised.

Chapter Fourteen

Talis was waiting in the deli Wednesday night for Milly. He hoped she would come again before her class as he took a seat by the front door and waited. His smile grew when he saw her walk in and she caught his eye. "Hello again, will you join me tonight?" he asked.

"Sure, just let me grab some food," Milly said.

When she returned to the table and took a seat he asked, "So how did your first night of classes go?"

"It was fantastic," Milly said, with genuine excitement. "So much different from high school," she added.

"I hope you feel that same way all through your college experience. So many people get burnt out so easily today."

"That won't be me, I can't wait to start full time," Milly said confidently.

"Just don't forget to have some fun along the way," Talis said. "I have to get a move on. See you Friday?"

"Sure, take care Talis," Milly watched him limp painfully from the building.

†

Talis walked out of sight and then sat and waited for Milly to finish her classes. Five minutes past ten, she walked to the parking lot and slipped into her car for the drive home. For a moment, Talis considered following her to see where she lived, but decided instead to stick to his plan. He would drive out to Holy Cross to make sure the house was still vacant and then go tomorrow to set up the supplies he would need.

The drive to Holy Cross was even more daunting at night. Shadows danced in front of his headlights as he drove down the streets until he reached his location. Even the homeless would not move in to the area, rumored haunted by the locals. Many of the people who lived here believed their faith would protect them from harm, but Holy Cross was one of the worst hit areas during the storm. Those that survived dared not move back into their neighborhood.

Satisfied that he would have the seclusion to carry out his plan, Talis drove back to his garage and parked the car. He walked back to his flat and lay on the bed admiring the growing collection of his victims. Earlier he had pinned up a Polaroid of Milly. Soon you will join the others. His body twitched with excitement. He got up from the bed and made a list of the items he would need to purchase tomorrow.

Talis sat at his small kitchen table and made a list of the items he would need to purchase the next day. His heart pounded with excitement as each hour passed. “It won’t be much longer,” he said as he turned off the light and climbed into bed.

†

Brody stopped by to check on Williams. "How are you feeling?"

"Much better, thanks. The doctor said I can come back to work tomorrow."

"I'll spare you the full lecture on being careful. I think TBS has taught you a valuable lesson, one I hope you won't repeat."

"It was stupid of me, I know, Brody. I promise I'll never put myself in that position again," he said.

"Good, I think you have a long career ahead of you, as long as you keep your skull away from target practice," Brody teased.

"Trust me I plan on keeping my head down next time."

"I'll see you back at work tomorrow then," Brody said as he stood to leave.

"Do we have anything new yet?"

"No, but I can feel him moving, preparing to strike again."

"Hopefully, we'll get a break soon, before he can kill again."

"I hope so, I surely hope so," Brody said as he walked to the door. "See you tomorrow."

†

Brody drove back to the precinct house and sat staring at the crime board. He was reviewing the list of known souvenirs and an idea came to him. Brody picked up the telephone and called the front desk. "Sarge, aren't all driver's license records maintained in Baton Rouge?" he asked.

"Yes, they are, Brody why do you ask?"

"I am grasping at straws here. Can you call them up and ask them to poll their computers for anyone named Anastasia in the New Orleans area?"

"You are looking at a long shot, Brody, but I will give them a call and see what they can come up with."

"Thanks. I am heading out for the night. If you hear anything will you call my cell?"

"Sure thing, Brody, go get some rest."

†

Brody's dreams filled with the image of the man in the cemetery photograph. He dreamed he was about to capture the man and when he approached, TBS would move just out of his arm's reach at the last moment. The frustration of his failed attempts made Brody thrash between the covers and when his alarm went off the next morning, Brody felt exhausted and mentally drained.

He stopped on his way into the precinct house for breakfast, but the food did little good in relieving the exhaustion he was feeling. Crawford took a long look at Brody when he walked into the office.

"Did you have a bad night, Brody?"

"I chased that bastard all night long in my dreams and each time I got close enough to touch him, he would slip out of my grasp," Brody growled as he faced the crime board.

"The mayor called this morning to remind us that Fat Tuesday is just a few weeks away and that we do not need a serial killer spoiling Mardi Gras."

"Did he actually think we needed a reminder?" Brody snapped.

"Who knows with that idiot? I assured him we were doing everything possible to track the bastard down."

Brody ran his fingers through his thick hair as his frown increased.

"You look like crap. Go home and get some rest and come back later in the day," Crawford instructed. "You are no good to us here in this condition."

Brody attempted to argue with Crawford, but he knew the chief was correct. His mind was so muddled he would do more damage than good to the case. "Okay, boss, I'll be back in the early evening."

"I'll call if we get any breaks," Crawford promised.

"Have Williams do a follow-up call with immigration and the Bureau of Motor Vehicles, when he comes in please."

"Got it, now get out of here," Crawford said sternly.

†

Unlike Brody, Talis woke up invigorated from the night's sleep. After eating breakfast, he walked down to the garage to retrieve his car. He would start his day's journey by leaving the city and driving to an adult toy store between New Orleans and Baton Rouge to buy some supplies on his list. Then he would return to New Orleans to purchase the remainder of the needed items to put his plan in place. He cheerfully drove out of town as Brody cursed the morning traffic.

†

Williams bounced into the office a few minutes later and found Crawford at Brody's desk, writing notes.

"Where's Brody, Chief?"

"I sent him home to get some rest, but he left several assignments for you," Crawford stated before he handed a list to Williams. "How are you feeling?"

"I feel great, thanks," Williams said. "I want to assure you, Chief, that I won't let my guard down like that again."

"You can't afford to, Williams. By all rights you should have been killed, but for some reason TBS enjoys toying with Brody."

"Good thing he does or I wouldn't be here."

"Exactly, and Brody does not need to worry about your safety with everything else he has on his mind," Crawford said.

"I got it, Chief."

"Good, just make sure it doesn't happen again."

"It won't, I promise."

†

Brody arrived home and carefully stripped out of his clothing. He pulled the shades on his bedroom window and dropped the temperature on his air conditioner. His head was throbbing, so he popped two migraine tablets and climbed onto the bed. He placed his cell phone on the bedside charger and prayed it would not ring unless they had captured TBS. He would be horribly disappointed, but at least the nightmare would be over.

Exhaustion overwhelmed Brody and he felt his mind drawn into sleep almost as quickly as his head touched the pillow.

†

Sasha sat at the piano as she thought about her dilemma with Milly. She would have to talk with Kara and bring her current on all the events surrounding her and Milly. Sasha was afraid the longer she postponed the conversation, the more difficult it would become, and Kara deserved her honesty. Still, she was concerned by how Kara would perceive Milly's revelation. She did not want the delay in sharing information to make Kara feel more suspicious than needed. Never before had she given Kara any reason to doubt her love for her, and she wouldn't start now. She had promised to fulfill Milly's request at a later date and time and Sasha would stand by that decision.

†

Milly sat in study hall, her last class of the day. She had been working on a short writing assignment for her English class that was due the next evening, but she found it difficult to concentrate. Every time she put her pen to paper, she thought of Sasha. Especially how much she enjoyed spending time with her alone. It had been a horrible decision for Milly to kiss Sasha, and she knew it seconds after it happened, but for just a moment, it felt heavenly. No matter what she said, Sasha did respond to her kiss and she had enjoyed it too. Milly sat with a smile on her face until the bell rang. She picked up her books and walked to her shiny new car for the ride home. She was barely halfway through her writing assignment and would have to buckle down to finish it when she made it home.

†

Brody awoke and called into the precinct house. The chief had already gone for the evening, but Williams was still on duty. “Any news?” he asked Williams.

“No, not yet, but we are promised some answers by tomorrow. Immigration has reduced the number down to a handful and maybe, just maybe, we’ll get lucky with the DMV. How are you feeling?”

“Much better, thanks, but since there is not much happening, I think I’ll stay home tonight and start out fresh in the morning.”

“That sounds like an excellent idea,” Williams said. “Should I meet you here by eight?”

“Eight would be good.” Brody hung up.

Chapter Fifteen

Kara and Sasha drove into town just after midnight to tour the Bourbon Street area. Sasha felt several twitches, but nothing that had the pull of TBS until they widened the search out to Esplanade.

"Something feels stronger, further east," Sasha told Kara. "Drive out to the Lower Ninth Ward."

Kara took a winding path following Sasha's directions, which brought them to the edge of the Lower Ninth. "Turn south and drive toward the river."

Kara took a right turn as they drove through desolate streets. The night was pitch-black and the lack of power to the area only added to the feeling of gloom. Sasha guided them into the area known as Holy Cross.

"This place looks like a ghost town," Kara said.

The houses that were still standing tilted precariously on their frames. Other lots were filled with mounds of debris from the homes that had previously occupied the area. Even the air seemed reluctant to move in this part of town. The night was deathly still and quiet until a blast from a tugboat sounded as he guided a barge down the Mississippi into the port.

"He has definitely been in this area recently," Sasha said. "I can feel his footprint plainly, but I cannot narrow down an exact location."

"Why would he be in this area? Maybe he used to live here or knew someone who did," Kara suggested.

"I don't know, but he clearly isn't here now."

"Let's make one more pass through the Quarter, if you don't mind," Kara suggested.

"I want to try something a bit different," Sasha said. "Drop me off at the end of Bourbon and I'll walk the street, since we cannot drive down it and then meet you at Canal."

Kara pulled over and Sasha moved to leave the car. "Be careful."

"I will. Make a few circuits around the Quarter while you are waiting on me to see if you pick anything up," Sasha said.

"Okay, see you in about twenty minutes then."

†

Sasha watched Kara pull away from the curb and began her walk down the darkest end of Bourbon. She passed the all-night diners and the gay side of Bourbon, winding her way through a thick crowd. She sensed a faint tingling as she walked down the street, but could not determine whom the signal was coming from in the mass of people.

†

Talis strolled down Bourbon, mingling with the crowd. He felt a strange sensation as he walked, as if someone was following him. He turned to look behind him. Talis searched the faces on the busy street and when he looked across the street to the opposite sidewalk he saw the tall, dark-haired woman who had been at the university with Number Ten. She did not look like the typical New Orleans party crowd and she was no tourist, making him curious as to why she would be on the street this late. He was still pondering this thought when their eyes made contact for just a brief second. Her lavender eyes seemed to pierce right through to his wickedness, leaving him shivering with cold.

Talis turned away from her stare quickly and entered a club, exiting the back door from the storeroom. He had to force himself to walk and not break into a run as he weaved his way toward home. His heart was pounding in his chest as he closed the door to his flat behind him. That was no mere woman who had locked eyes with him tonight and his sweat had a faint tinge of fear. Talis rushed to the shower to wash it from his body.

†

Sasha searched the crowd and saw a tall, dark-haired man looking back at her. The moment their eyes met and she locked onto him Sasha knew she was looking into the dark eyes of TBS. She could feel the evil resonating through him as he glared back at her. For a second, she felt a hint of recognition in his mind, as if he had seen her previously and Sasha wondered where it could have been. An inebriated man stumbling down the sidewalk slammed into her, causing her to lose contact with TBS while she untangled her body from the drunk. When she stood, he was gone from her line of sight.

Sasha searched desperately for the footprint, but TBS had slipped away into the dark night. Sasha walked down the block and took a left, but felt no more of the sensation she had felt earlier. She knew what his face looked like and he knew hers, so if they met again, Sasha knew exactly who to go after without hesitation.

When she reached Canal, she saw Kara driving toward her. She climbed inside the car and Kara could see the excitement on her face. "You saw him, didn't you?"

"Yes, we locked eyes for just one brief moment, but I know what he looks like," Sasha said. "If a drunk had not knocked into me, I could have possibly followed him further, but tonight he slipped away."

"I could feel our hearts race and I knew something had happened."

"I think we are going to have to track him on foot, if we are to catch him," Sasha stated.

"Okay, so tomorrow night we both go looking for him," Kara said as she pulled from the curb and made a U-turn back toward the river.

"When we get home, I want you to enter my mind and see what I saw, so you will know exactly who we are looking for."

"Okay, my love," Kara said with a warm smile.

†

Milly heard Kara's sports car coming down the drive. They must be returning from their search for TBS she thought as she stretched in her bed. She listened for the familiar bang of the garage door and knew they had arrived home safely one more night. Milly had been up late, putting the finishing touches on her English assignment when they left, and she would have loved to join them on their search. Maybe later this weekend she would ask Sasha to let her ride with them as they scoured the streets looking for TBS. Her answer would more than likely be a resounding "No," but it certainly wouldn't hurt to ask.

†

Talis's dreams were filled with visions of Sasha. Maybe when he finished with Number Ten he would look her up. She was definitely a formidable woman, emitting a power that excited him and terrified him at the same time. He was sure she would be a worthy candidate and was dreaming of taking her in his arms when his world went blank.

†

Brody awoke before the alarm went off and walked into the kitchen for coffee. The extra sleep and food had done wonders for his body and his ability to think straight. He felt deep in his bones that TBS would make some move today and he prayed he would be ready to act when that time came. He knew without a doubt TBS would contact him today, he just wasn't sure how or when it would be done.

He prepared for work and stopped off for breakfast. Brody reached the precinct house a little before eight. Williams and the chief were both there already, closely studying a fax.

"What's happening?"

"We just received a fax from Baton Rouge," Crawford said. "There are three women with registered licenses in New Orleans with the name of Anastasia that could be possibilities."

"Better make that two. This one was born in the fifties and I doubt she would interest our boy."

"What addresses are listed on the other two?" Brody asked.

"One is in Kenner and the other is in Chalmette," Crawford said.

"Let's roll then." Brody tossed the keys to Williams and took the papers from the chief.

†

They drove to Chalmette first to find the home at the listed address obliterated by the storm. They canvassed the surrounding area and found a few people that knew of her and her family. "They left for Houston after the storm and we haven't seen them since," said an old man sitting outside a barbershop. "Shame, though, their family had been residents here for so many years." He shook his head sadly.

"Thanks for the information," Williams said as he placed a comforting hand on his shoulder. "They are probably better off in Texas right now anyhow," he added.

"Very true, young man," he said as he watched Williams walk to the sedan.

"Strike one," he said upon entering the car and shifted into drive.

They had slightly better luck in Kenner. At least the home at the address was still standing after the storm. Williams knocked on the door and an elderly woman came to the door.

Williams showed her his badge and introduced them to the woman.

"I am Sandra Jones," she said. "Please come in."

"Mrs. Jones," Brody started, "we are looking for a woman named Anastasia Stoli who used to live at this address."

"Yes, I remember her, a Russian woman with a thick accent," she said. "I bought this place from her five years ago."

"Do you know where she went after she left here?" Brody prodded.

"She bought herself a nice flat on St. Peters, I think it was," Mrs. Jones said. "Can I offer you men some coffee? I was just about to pour myself a cup."

"Go ahead and we'll drink one with you, Mrs. Jones."

She stood and made her way to the kitchen.

The three men waited for her patiently and when she entered the room, Williams jumped up to carry the tray for her. He poured them each a cup and took his seat on the sofa.

"Mrs. Jones, we are interested in a man Anastasia may have been living with. Do you know if she had a boyfriend at the time she lived here?"

"I don't recall that she had a man in her life. I don't think from the way she had this place decorated that anyone lived with her," she said. "Not male anyhow," she said with a giggle. "All the rooms were painted a different shade of pink. Mind you, I like pink, but I felt I was living in a bottle of Pepto-Bismol," she joked.

They all laughed along with her. "What you have done to the place is a drastic improvement," Williams said.

"Why thank you, young man," she said with a brilliant smile to him. "It is good to still see manners in some of today's youth."

Brody noticed that Williams blushed slightly at the woman's statement. He was very good with people and had a knack for getting information out of them easily.

"Thank you for the wonderful coffee and your assistance, Mrs. Jones," Brody said. "You have been very helpful."

"I'm always glad to help out when I can," she said as she started to rise and follow them to the door.

"Stay seated, we will see ourselves out," Williams said.

"Have a good day, gentlemen."

"You too, Mrs. Jones," Brody said.

"Let's swing by your friend at the tax collector's office and see if she can provide us with an address," Crawford said.

†

Talis buzzed with excitement and he could not stay within the confines of his flat any longer. Everything was in place for tonight so he decided he would eat lunch and then make his way out to the campus to lay in wait for Number Ten. When he looked up into the late-morning sky, he saw the dark clouds forming and smelled the salt on the air. "Just hold off a few more hours," he said as he tossed his book bag over his shoulder and swung the cane merrily as he walked down to the Brewery for some mudbugs and a cold beer. He looked across Jackson Square as he consumed his meal and smiled at all the people milling about. He felt very powerful as he looked down upon them, almost like a Greek god looking down from the heavens. Talis knew then that he had ascended and was above all mere mortals and he would take their lives at his leisure while no one from this earth could stop him.

Talis left the Brewery, rode the trolley for part of the distance, and then walked the remaining blocks on foot. He had his props arranged, and would take up his place on campus, eager to set his plan in motion.

†

Williams came running out of the building waving a sheet of paper and jumped in behind the wheel. "This is our lucky day," Williams nearly shouted with excitement. "Anastasia Stoli does in fact have a flat on St. Peters."

"Take us there," Crawford said. He took the paper from Williams and called a judge to obtain a search warrant to enter and search the premises. Crawford radioed dispatch and had them send a squad car to the courthouse to pick up the warrant and rush it over to them at the address on St. Peters.

When they arrived at the address, the street was buzzing with activity. The wait for the warrant seemed to last an eternity for Brody as they sat and looked up at the small flat. "I have a really good feeling about this, Chief," he said, his cheeks flushed with excitement.

"I sure hope this turns out," he answered.

They stepped from the sedan as the squad car approached. Crawford took the warrant from the uniformed officer and looked it over carefully. He would be damned if he would let TBS off on a technicality if the warrant did not read precisely. He smiled to Brody after reviewing it for a second time. "Let's go get this bastard."

The uniformed officers carried a small hand-held battering ram up the stairs ahead of them.

Crawford nodded and Brody knocked loudly on the door. "Police, open up," he yelled. They waited several seconds and heard no movement inside.

"Take it down," Brody instructed them and with a swift swing of the battering ram, the door lock was shattered.

They rushed into the flat with guns drawn and found it to be empty. Empty, but lived in, Brody was thinking as he heard Williams call out from the bedroom.

"Bingo," he shouted. "Brody, we have hit the jackpot."

Brody and Crawford rushed to the bedroom, leaving one uniformed officer at the front door. "Stay on your toes," Brody warned him.

Brody walked into the room and immediately saw what had excited Williams so much. Over half of the large wall in the master bedroom was covered with souvenirs TBS had taken from his victims. Tacked up on the wall were drivers' licenses, newspaper clippings, and photos of all of his previous victims. He had placed them in a very organized manner and the first thing Brody noted was that Lynn Frost had indeed been his first. The next thing he noticed made his blood turn cold. Next to the last article on Thomas Dubais, the obituary, there was a picture of a pretty, young blonde. Above her head, carefully printed on the wall was Number Ten.

Chapter Sixteen

"So he has another already?" Williams asked when he turned to look at Brody.

"I don't know, but he certainly has her selected."

Brody walked back through the flat to a small table. He pulled out an ink pen and used the tip to move several envelopes around the table. Beneath the various junk mail sent to "Resident," there was a utility bill addressed to a "Talis Barker."

"That is an odd name," Brody said as Crawford walked over to the table.

Crawford looked at the envelope and told the uniform officer to call back to the precinct house and get them started finding everything they could about Talis Barker.

"Yes sir," the officer said and went into another room to make the call.

"We have definitely found his lair," Brody said. "But it feels like he will be gone for a while."

"How can you know that?" Williams asked out of genuine curiosity.

"I can't. It's just a gut feeling I have that our boy is out on the street already waiting to initiate his next move."

Brody wrapped his arm protectively around Williams's shoulder. "I want you to stay here on the street to watch the flat until we can get another detective here to keep up the surveillance. He knows what you look like, so we can't leave you here for long."

"What are the two of you going to do?" Williams asked.

"We are going back to the precinct house to start pulling information on our suspect. Get there as quick as you can after your replacement arrives; we need everyone available working on this case."

"I'll be there as quick as I can," Williams promised.

Brody and the chief climbed into the squad car. "Get us to the house," Crawford said.

Brody radioed dispatch to send a pair of detectives out to the flat to replace Williams and then turned to smile at Crawford. "We are getting closer to him," he said.

"Don't count your chickens before the eggs hatch," Crawford warned. "We're still a long way from having him in custody."

Brody nodded his head in agreement. As soon as they cleared the block, the officer hit lights and sirens and raced them back to the precinct house. "Talk to me, Sarge," Brody said when they entered the back door. "What do you have so far?"

"Talis Barker, twenty-six, born and raised in Houma. He was a fourth year medical student at Tulane before he mysteriously quit medical school a little over two years ago." Sarge shuffled through the papers in his hands. "It looks a shame that he dropped out, too."

"Why is that?"

"He was the top of his class of over four hundred," Sarge said. "He can't be your ordinary slouch to be at the head of that list."

"So what happened to our boy to turn from brilliant medical student to a malicious serial killer?"

"That answer you're going to have to find out on your own," Sarge teased. "I would have no clue why someone with such a bright future would throw it all away."

Sarge handed Brody the printouts and turned to leave the room. "Sarge," Brody said to stop him.

"Yes, Brody?"

"Call immigration and find out the whereabouts of an Anastasia Stoli," he requested.

"You got it, Brody. You have got to nail his ass soon," Sarge said then left the office.

"Are you thinking a jilted lover?" Crawford asked.

"That, or she was his first victim and we haven't found her body. I think had she been his first though, she would have been immortalized in his shrine."

"That's true and I see you were right about Lynn Frost as his first. Maybe her death was accidental and when he realized he had gotten away with her death he felt challenged to see if he could do it again."

"After the first few, he must have felt like he was invincible," Brody said.

"That's usually the case and the murders grow closer together as his need grows stronger," Crawford added.

"So why the near month-long break?"

"I think he realized his arrogance had left him exposed and he fled out of fear until his face was less prominent in the public's mind."

Sarge walked back in and handed Brody an enlarged image of Barker's driver's license. "Do we know if he or the woman owned a vehicle?" Brody asked.

"He has a late model import registered in his name. I have already sent the description and plate out across the radio, so if he is out for a drive we might just give him a surprise."

"Good work, Sarge. Do you have any news from immigration yet?"

"Nope, not yet," he said. "I will let you know as soon as they call."

Williams rushed into the office. "What else do we know?"

Crawford brought him up to speed as Brody walked to the crime board and posted Barker's picture. He added Barker's and Anastasia's names to his list. Then he turned to Crawford. "Where was he in medical school?"

"At Tulane," Crawford said, looking at the printout to confirm.

"So, if he had spent four years there already, he would have an intimate knowledge of the campus, correct?"

"At least the medical school part of campus," Crawford said.

"I think that is where we need to focus," Brody said. "We need to pull the task force in and distribute his photograph and have the men flood the campus of the medical school with specific instruction not to approach but to keep him in sight until we can surround him."

"That's not a bad idea," Crawford said.

"I'll start calling in the members of the task force for a meeting. Is three soon enough?" Williams asked.

"It will probably take that long to get everyone in," Brody said. "It's already past two."

"Let me get rolling then," Williams said and went to a vacant office.

He passed Sarge in the doorway. "Anastasia Stoli returned to Russia the first part of July, according to immigration," he reported to Brody.

Brody looked at Crawford. "Jilted lover then?"

"More than likely," he said. Crawford walked over to the crime board and looked at the photograph of Lynn Frost and the DMV photo of Anastasia Stoli. "They do look similar. Maybe he was looking for a replacement for his lost love."

†

Talis walked across the campus to the medical school portion of the grounds. He located one of the Internet cafés frequented by college students and found a vacant station. He searched the Internet until he found the email address he wanted and made note of it as he began to compose his message.

In the subject line of the email he typed TBS in extra-large letters. He would hate to have several days pass before the email was opened. Maybe he would also call to prompt them, as he was sure Brody stayed swamped trying to solve the case. Talis composed his email and pressed the send button then signed off the computer. He left the café and walked further into the medical school to locate a phone booth. He picked up the receiver and dialed 911. When the operator answered, Talis said, "Have Brody check for emails."

"Excuse me?" she said.

"I said, have Detective Brody check for emails," he repeated, loudly this time, and hung up.

The operator called directly to the precinct house and asked for Detective Brody.

"Brody," he said when his phone rang.

"This is 911 Operator 6254, Detective, and I just received a call with a message for you to check for emails."

"Do you have any idea where the caller was when he called?" Brody asked.

"I couldn't get an exact trace, but somewhere near Tulane Medical Center," she said.

"Thank you," Brody said and hung up. "I'm really beginning to hate this bastard."

"What now?" Crawford asked.

"He sent a message through 911 for me to check for emails," Brody said.

"The only public email listed on the Internet is the main mailbox for the precinct house," Crawford said. "I will call them and have them forward it to your email."

Brody grumbled as he spun in his chair and turned on the computer sitting at the end of his desk. "If he only knew how bad I hated these things," he grumbled to Crawford.

"You need to get with the times, Brody," the chief teased.

Brody ignored his remark and opened his email server. "Nothing yet," he groaned as he scanned down the unopened mail. He sat back on his chair and looked up at a smiling Crawford. "What?" he asked.

"I can't believe someone as fearless as you is intimidated by technology."

"It's not intimidation, I just don't like the damned things."

"If you would take the time to learn how to use it properly, you would find that it can be an invaluable tool," the chief said.

"That would be nice if we could ask all criminals to take a week off, so I can learn how to use a damned computer," Brody jeered.

"That's not a bad idea," Crawford teased.

The computer chimed to tell them Brody had a new email. He clicked the mouse on the file and opened the note from TBS.

Dear Brody,

Once again, it is time to play. I have found my next prey and if the timing is right, she will be mine this night. She is definitely a perfect ten—young, sweet, and so innocent. I would tell you to look far to the east to find her, but you probably don't believe me anyhow. So, this is just to let you know the game is back on and to wish you Happy Hunting!

TBS

"Far to the east," Brody read. "Do you think he is trying to trick us into believing that he is not on the Tulane campus?"

"He was obviously there to send the email to you," Crawford said.

"That is true, but could he be deceiving us?"

"That is always a possibility and a gamble we will have to take. Where in the east do you think he could be referring to?"

"Loyola is in the east part of town and UNO has an east campus as well."

"We have a limited number of men on the task force, so how do you want to split them up?" Crawford asked.

"Half at Tulane Medical Center and half at LU," Brody said. "I think those are our two best shots."

Williams returned to the office. "Everyone will be here by three."

"Take this photograph and run copies for everyone on the task force," Brody said as he handed Williams the picture.

Brody looked at Crawford. "Will you brief the rest of the task force and get the assignments set up?"

"Of course I will. What are you going to be up to?"

"Williams and I are going to take another look at his flat and see if there is any clue we are missing, and then we will join the task force at Tulane."

"I will lead the group at LU then," Crawford said.

"Good, I feel better already," Brody said with a grin. "If we cannot catch him in the act, at least we may be able to follow him back to his flat and arrest him there."

"Good luck, Brody."

"You too. I hope we get this bastard before the night is out."

†

Sasha sat out on the front porch of Sugarland and watched the growing mass of clouds move toward New Orleans. The last thing the city needed was more rain. It never took much to flood the city streets and Sasha was afraid the clouds overhead were destined to bring in heavy thunderstorms. Milly would need to be very careful driving through the city tonight, and Sasha would be sure to warn her before she left for classes. She would also call Kara and give her the same warning, as she was sure the rain would begin before Kara left for home.

Sasha stood to walk inside, and as she reached for the doorknob, she heard the first raindrops begin to pelt the metal roof. She went inside and picked up the phone to call Kara.

"Hello, love," Kara said.

"I just wanted to warn you that you have nasty thunderstorms headed your way, so be careful on your drive home."

"That is so sweet of you, Sasha. I will be extra careful on the streets and try to bypass as much of the flooding as I can."

"Do you have any idea what time you are leaving tonight, so I know when to expect you?"

"I will leave here no later than five, so I should be home around five thirty," Kara responded.

"I will have some dinner cooking by then."

"Mmm what are you planning to cook?"

"I was thinking of chicken and rice with some Mexican corn bread," Sasha answered.

"That sounds good."

"I will see you in a few hours then," Sasha said and hung up the phone.

Sasha busied herself in the kitchen preparing the chicken as the rain continued to lash at the windows. She was standing at the kitchen sink when she looked up at the sound of Milly's car approaching.

Be very careful tonight when you go to class. The streets will probably be flooded and you know how the drivers in New Orleans drive, she projected to warn Milly.

I plan on leaving early, so I will have plenty of time to take it slow if need be, Milly returned.

Good, I don't want you stranded in the middle of the storm.

Me either, Milly answered.

Sasha dropped the pieces of chicken into the boiling water and proceeded to season the mixture and add some butter to keep the meat moist. She had already boiled tea and had it steeping on the counter. She would add sugar to the pitcher, pour the tea into it, and place it in the fridge to cool as she waited for the chicken to boil. Later, she would pull out the cooked chicken to allow it to cool before she picked the meat from the bones and dropped it back into the seasoned broth. When it was closer to time for Kara to be home, she would add rice to the broth, and place the corn bread in the oven to bake.

Sasha took a bottle of wine and poured a glass to enjoy as the food cooked. She sat on the counter and looked out the window as large puddles of water began to form in the rain-soaked yard. It would be a nasty night out for everyone.

†

Talis left the Internet café and walked toward the south side of campus as the wind blew in dark clouds and rain began to fall. He walked into a library with large glass windows that gave him an excellent view of that part of the campus to begin his vigil. He checked his watch to find it was just past four. In another hour, he would move down to the deli to wait for Number Ten. He was almost positive that she would arrive early due to the weather. He stared out the window as rivulets of water slid down the smooth surface. Anastasia had always loved the rain. He remembered several nights when they had lain in bed watching the lightning streak down from the sky and listening to the rain pelt the windows. Those had always been such tender moments between them, before his world turned dark. He longed to return to that time in his life. As much as he tried, he could not understand why she had chosen to leave him.

†

"Is there anything in particular we should be looking for?" Williams asked.

"I don't know, but we may have overlooked something on our first visit that may give us an idea what he is up to," Brody said. "Look for receipts, notes, anything that may tell us where he's been lately or what he has bought."

Brody waved at the two detectives sitting in a dark sedan outside the flat as they walked toward the stairs. Rain was beginning to fall. "Great, just what we need," he complained as they ducked into the entrance to the flat. "If he hasn't been back here all afternoon, he is either entrenched at a critical spot or in transit somewhere."

Williams slipped a pair of latex gloves onto his hands. "If he is in transit, he will probably be on foot or using some other mode of public transit. The keys to his car are in the middle desk drawer," he said as he took the keys and dangled them for Brody. "There is also a padlock key on the keychain. Maybe he stores his car in a nearby garage."

"That seems to be a popular thing for the people who own these flats," Brody said. "Take the padlock key off the chain and we will take a look around after we finish here."

Williams removed the key and slipped it inside his pocket as Brody walked into the kitchen area. He opened the refrigerator and found it nearly empty. "He doesn't eat at home much."

Brody saw slips of paper sticking out between two canisters and he reached to pull them out. He found a receipt for an army cot and another for adult accessories dated the previous day. "Do you see an army cot anywhere?" he asked Williams.

"No, no sign of one here, why, what did you find?"

"A receipt for one yesterday," Brody said. "That tells us that he is shifting again."

"How do you mean?"

"With the exception of Frost, who was killed in a hotel room, and Dubais, in the park, all his other victims were killed in their own homes," Brody explained. "If he felt a need to purchase a cot, his new victim either lives in a dorm or at home, where he wouldn't have the privacy afforded him to carry out his plan."

"So he is going to kidnap her and take her someplace?" Williams asked.

"That is what I'm assuming. He is also escalating by reverting to kidnapping versus taking a willing victim. This cannot be good."

Brody returned to the bedroom from the kitchen and looked at Williams. "Take that key and walk two blocks in each direction. If you find a lock that fits and it opens to a garage, check the car for the cot or any other evidence that may give us a lead."

"I am on it," Williams said.

Brody frowned as he looked at his watch. "Make it quick, we are running out of time."

"I'll be back here as quick as I can."

Williams left the room as Brody walked back over to the wall holding the TBS shrine. He stared at the picture of Milly. "I wish you could tell me where you are," he said.

Chapter Seventeen

Talis picked up his book bag and cane before walking to the elevator that carried him back to the ground floor. He crossed a small courtyard to the deli where he would wait for Number Ten to arrive. He bought a sandwich and a bottle of water before finding a seat that would give him a good view of the door and sat down to wait.

†

Milly left home at half past four, figuring that would give her plenty of time to reach campus prior to her class at six. The parking lot was crowded, but she finally located a spot and took out her umbrella to ward off the rain. She reached into her car and picked up her book bag before walking toward the deli. The weather was miserable and chilled her to the bone. *A cup of hot soup and a sandwich would go a long way in improving my mood.*

†

Talis smiled and waved when he saw Milly walk into the deli. Milly smiled back at him as she walked down the line and bought a bowl of soup, half a sandwich, and bottle of water. She walked over to where Talis was sitting. "Beautiful weather, isn't it?"

"If you are a duck maybe," he answered. "How are you tonight?"

"I'm okay, and you?"

"I would be better if this weather wasn't making my leg ache so bad. These cool rainy nights are miserable."

"I can imagine," Milly said.

"You have almost finished your first week of college. How do you like it?"

"I love it so far," Milly said with an excited smile.

"Have you decided on a major yet?" he asked.

"Not definitely. I am leaning toward art history, but who knows?" Milly said with a shrug.

"Are you an artist?"

"I do some painting from time to time," Milly said.

"That is great," he said. "I struggle to draw a straight line."

"I really haven't applied myself to my painting, but it's in my genes," Milly said with a smirk.

"What about you? How are your classes going?"

"Pretty well," he said. "I forgot how easy it is to procrastinate with studying, so I have to retrain myself."

"It is easy to get out of the habit," Milly agreed.

Milly finished her meal and stood to leave the table. "I will see you Monday," she said.

"Have a good weekend," Talis said.

"Thanks, you too," she said.

Talis watched her leave the deli and then walked to the campus bookstore where he purchased a sketchpad and some charcoal pencils. He wrapped them well inside a plastic bag and tucked them into his book bag. He stepped outside of the bookstore and picked up an umbrella, left by one of the shoppers inside the store. “Sorry, my friend, but I need this for the moment,” Talis said.

He walked past the deli and out into the parking lot where he located Milly’s car. He checked the doors and found them locked up tight. He surveyed the area and found a small covered bus stop within sight of her car. He would spend a few hours inside the deli drinking coffee and as the time approached for Number Ten to go home, he would return to the bus stop.

†

Williams did not need much time to locate the garage, but the car tucked inside provided no other information that would be useful to their case. He grinned to himself as he reached inside the driver’s side and pulled the latch to release the hood. Williams opened the hood and removed the sparkplug wires, tucking them into his back pocket. “Just in case you slip by us and have any ideas to make a run of it,” he said to the empty garage. He locked the padlock behind him and hurried back to the flat.

Brody turned when he heard Williams enter. “Did you find anything?”

“Nothing useful, but I borrowed these,” he said with a grin as he held up the wires. “I’d hate for him to try to run on us.”

“Good thinking,” Brody said.

“Have you found out anything more?”

“I feel like we are missing something so obvious,” Brody said, sounding frustrated as he stared at the picture of Milly. “Wait just a damned minute. Come here, Williams.”

Williams walked quickly to where Brody was standing. "Are your eyes good enough to read the title from the book she is holding?"

Williams squinted at the photo. It wasn't a good quality picture, but when he pulled out a flashlight, he could make out the word "English." He grinned at Brody. "It is an English book," he said.

"Holy shit, we have the wrong part of campus under surveillance," he said. "He won't be on the medical campus at all. We need to find out where the fine arts buildings are."

"We can stop at campus security for a map," Williams said.

"Good thinking. I will call Crawford to alert him so he can change positions at LU," Brody said. "Let's get out to TU as quick as we can."

Brody and Williams left the flat and rushed back to the sedan. The rain was really coming down and the drive that would normally have taken twenty minutes, took nearly an hour. Williams had to take several detours to make it past roads that were impassable due to floodwaters. By the time they reached campus and located the security department it was nearly nine.

†

Talis had just returned to the bus stop when he saw a group of students rushing toward the parking lot. *Classes must have ended early because of the weather.* He watched for Number Ten. When he saw her approaching, he stepped out into the rain and walked toward her. He was soaked by the time he reached her car.

Milly did not hear him approach and was startled when she looked up to find him standing so close.

"Damn, Talis, you scared me," she cried.

"I'm sorry, but you are my only hope."

"What's the matter?" she asked, noticing he was drenched and dripping wet.

"My class got out early, but when I got to my car I found I had locked my keys inside," he said. "Could I possibly ask for a ride? I have a spare set at my flat, but I cannot walk in this weather and the bus has stopped running for my area."

Milly looked at him, the rain rushing down his cheeks. She really felt sorry for him and knew from their previous conversation that he was already in pain. It was against her better judgment, but she agreed to give Talis the ride he requested.

"Okay, hop in," she said.

"Thank you so much," he said as he moved around to the passenger side of the car.

He climbed in and placed his cane and book bag on the floorboard, unzipping his bag as Milly buckled in. When he straightened up, he fastened his seat belt and looked over at Milly.

"I can't tell you how much I appreciate this," he said.

"This is no weather to be walking in, unless you are a duck," Milly teased as she put the car in reverse and backed out of the parking spot.

†

Brody and Williams had just pulled into the parking lot when Milly drove by their car. Had the weather not been so volatile, and if Brody had looked to his right, he would have seen Milly drive by with the TBS killer in her passenger seat. Instead, he cursed the weather and opened the door as Milly drove out of the parking lot.

†

Talis took her down several streets until they were on St. Charles. "Pull over and park here, and I will be right back," he said when she reached a darkened section of the street.

Milly felt a short burst of relief to know that they had arrived at his home and her kind deed would be over soon and she could drive for home. She looked at her clock and saw it was growing closer to ten. She did not pay attention to what Talis was doing, which allowed him to reach into the book bag and remove a cloth he had soaking in ether. He moved quickly to place the cloth over her nose and mouth and held her firmly until her struggle ended and she was no longer conscious. He removed the cloth from her face and placed it back in the book bag.

Talis removed a pair of handcuffs and unfastened her seat belt. He snapped a metal cuff around each wrist, opened his door, and pulled her into the passenger seat. He fastened the seat belt around her limp figure and dashed around to the driver's seat. He moved the seat back and climbed in behind the wheel, a smile growing on his face. This is almost too easy he thought as he put the car in gear and continued to drive east in the pouring rain.

†

Sasha had timed dinner perfectly. Kara was pulling into the garage as she took the corn bread from the oven and coated the top with butter. She poured glasses of tea and lit two small candles as Kara walked into the house.

"Hey baby," Sasha said as Kara walked into the kitchen.

"That smells delicious," she embraced Sasha and kissed her softly.

"Have a seat and I will serve up some dinner."

Sasha loaded up two plates with chicken and rice and then placed large slices of corn bread on the plates. She set them on the table then walked to the refrigerator for slices of tomato and onion to eat with the meal.

"This is the perfect meal for this nasty weather."

"Was it a difficult drive home?"

"I had to take a few side streets to avoid some flooded areas," Kara said. "It was really coming down hard in town."

"I hope Milly will be careful driving in this mess."

"I am sure she will be just fine," Kara said, hiding a bout of jealousy in her voice.

Sensing the tension in Kara's voice, Sasha decided to change the subject. "You know, I am not a half-bad cook."

"This is a great meal. Are we going into the Quarter tonight?"

"Let's wait and see what the weather does," Sasha said. "Hopefully all this rain will keep him inside tonight."

"Good, that will give us time for a nice hot bath then."

"Plenty of time," Sasha said.

They finished the meal and Kara cleaned off the dishes while Sasha put the food away. They went upstairs to begin drawing a bath as they stripped out of their clothes. Sasha lit candles around the bathtub after she poured bubble bath in the water and then turned off the lights. The house was quiet except for the gentle falling of the rain on the metal roof.

Kara climbed into the tub and Sasha climbed in behind her. She rested her head against Sasha's chest as she allowed the water to drain the tension from her body. Sasha's hands disappeared beneath the bubbles as she wrapped her arms around her lover.

"This feels good, doesn't it?"

"Yes, it is so relaxing," she said.

Sasha allowed her head to rest against the edge of the tub as she stared up at the ceiling, watching the shadows created by the candle flames dancing on the ceiling; Kara was lost in the flames. They rested quietly, enjoying the peaceful time together until the water started to cool.

"Are you ready to dry off?" Sasha asked.

"I guess we better, before we start to prune up," Kara teased.

They dried off and Sasha picked up a bottle of lotion as they walked from the bathroom. "Lie down on your stomach," she instructed Kara.

Kara gladly stretched out on the bed as Sasha straddled her and sat softly on her hips. She poured lotion into her hands, rubbing them together to warm the lotion before she began to massage it into Kara's shoulders.

"Oh, baby, that feels so good," she purred as Sasha's hands worked deeply into her muscles.

Sasha coated her arms and shoulders then worked down Kara's back, slowly kneading the tension from her knotted muscles.

"You almost have me drooling."

"I think I have sprung a leak."

"Yes, I think you have, my love. What should we do about that?" Kara asked.

"I don't know, but I bet we can think of something," Sasha said as she moved her wetness over Kara's ass so she could feel her excitement.

"I love the feel of you on my body," Kara purred.

"So how about being in your body?"

"Oh hell, yes."

"Roll over onto your back and put a pillow under your hips and I will be right back."

Sasha left the bed and Kara rolled over and placed a pillow under her hips, feeling her body grow wet with anticipation. Sasha felt her clit throbbing as she stepped into the harness, securing the straps around her waist. She slipped a dildo onto the mount, and felt the blissful pressure on her clit as the toy dangled between her legs as she walked back to the bed. She climbed onto the bed between Kara's spread thighs, and smiled as she ran her thumb along the outside of her lips to find her clit swollen with excitement.

"Someone else has sprung a leak too, I see," Sasha said as she circled her clit with her thumb.

"You get me so excited, Sasha," Kara groaned.

Sasha placed the tip of the dildo at her entrance and leaned forward to cup Kara's breasts in her hands, kneading them as the dildo penetrated her lips. Sasha's hips remained still as her hands kneaded and teased Kara's breasts while her desire continued to grow. Sasha's right hand moved down to cover Kara's mound as her thumb rubbed across her clit.

"Are you ready to be fucked?"

"Oh yes, baby," Kara crooned.

Sasha could tell by the burning in her body that it was time for another dose of serum and she would use that desire to give Kara all the pleasure she could stand. The serum they drank every few days helped prevent the physical craving for blood and calmed her lust.

She began moving her hips into Kara as she coated the dildo in her wetness and Kara began thrusting her hips to match Sasha's movements.

"Fuck me, Sasha," Kara begged.

Sasha slid her hands down to Kara's ankles and lifted her legs, opening them wide to enable her thrusts to bury the toy deep inside Kara. Her passion was growing uncontrollably as her hips pounded into Kara, as Kara clutched the sheets in her hands. Sasha blinded with need, used Kara's vocalizations to guide the tempo of her thrusts, sliding fully into her with each stroke.

"Yes, yes, yes, Sasha, fuck me hard, baby," Kara groaned as she released her first orgasm.

Sasha withdrew the dildo and growled, "Roll over and grab onto the headboard."

Kara rolled over quickly and rose up on her knees as Sasha penetrated her with one fluid stroke and then leaned forward to cover Kara's hands on the headboard as they locked eyes in the mirror. Sasha took her roughly, her hips slapping into Kara's ass as they cried out with pleasure together while Kara arched her hips back to meet Sasha's thrusts.

"Come with me, Sasha," Kara begged as her eyes glassed over with pleasure.

Sasha could see the pulse in Kara's neck beating wildly as their bodies moved together and the rush of her blood filled Sasha's ears. She felt her fangs extending and Sasha fought the temptation to sink them deep into Kara's neck as they released together and collapsed onto the bed. Instead, she bent her head forward and licked the side of Kara's neck, feeling the pounding of her heart on her tongue.

Sasha carefully removed the dildo from deep inside Kara then rolled over onto her back, still breathing hard. "I didn't hurt you did I?"

"Dear heavens, no," Kara said. "That felt fantastic."

"Good," Sasha said, trying to control her breathing.

"Are you tired?"

"No, I just need a moment to catch my breath," Sasha replied.

Kara smiled. "I can give you that," she said as she straddled Sasha's hips and guided the dildo with her hand, filling her body completely. The tip of the dildo caressed her G spot when she bent forward to lean over Sasha's body.

"Damn this feels good," she said as she rocked her hips back and forth, stimulating her G spot as Sasha's fingers rolled her nipples.

"Feels great," Sasha moaned as each of Kara's movements pressed the harness mount most pleasurably across her clit. Sasha could feel her excitement soaking the sheets as Kara softly rode her body.

Kara rocked back and forth slowly as her body worked, building a climax. The first two she had were so intense; the next would take longer to build, but she knew it would also feel incredible when it arrived. Sasha quivered as her body peaked and she cried out as she came with Kara still riding her body gently.

Sasha's orgasm stirred deep within Kara who picked up speed until her body convulsed violently and she collapsed onto Sasha's chest, gasping for breath. When she had the energy to move, Kara removed the dildo from her body and rolled onto her back.

Sasha climbed from the bed and walked into the bathroom to remove the harness, placing it on the bathroom counter. She turned to walk back to the bed when she doubled over with pain. She felt a strong feeling of distress from Milly that nearly dropped her to her knees. Sasha grabbed the counter for support and breathed deeply until the pain subsided. She sat on the toilet and tried to reach Milly through projection, but reached only blank space. She looked up at the clock. Milly should still be in class so the distress puzzled Sasha. She would continue to attempt contact with Milly until it was time for her to be home and if she could not reach her, she would drive to town to find her.

Sasha's body was soaked with sweat from the exertion and the feeling of fright she had received from Milly. "I am going to shower off quickly," she said to Kara.

"Okay, baby, I will keep the bed warm," Kara said as she snuggled deep under the covers.

Sasha rinsed the sweat from her body and washed her hair while she continued to try to contact Milly. Her frustration grew and when she dried off, she dressed before walking over to the bed. Kara was looking up at her with sleepy eyes.

"Milly isn't home yet, so I am going to drive into town to see if I can find her," Sasha said. "I will try her cell and if everything is okay, I will make a run through the Quarter and come home."

"Do you want me to go with you?"

"No, baby, you look so comfortable. Stay in bed. If Milly makes it home, give me a call." Sasha leaned down and kissed Kara. "If you can stay awake," she teased.

"I love you, Sasha."

"I love you too. I will be back as soon as I can."

"Be careful, my love," Kara said as Sasha bounded down the stairs.

Sasha stepped off the porch as another wave of nausea struck and she once more doubled over in pain. She tried to contact Milly again. "Damn, why aren't you answering?"

†

Brody stormed across the parking lot with Williams in tow. “We fucking missed him, I just know we have,” he stated. “Damn, why didn’t I think to look at the books earlier?” he asked, second-guessing his action and not expecting an answer.

Williams remained quiet while Brody ranted. He sat behind the wheel of the car and when Brody relaxed he asked, “Where to?”

“Back to the precinct house, we need to regroup and develop a plan.”

Chapter Eighteen

Kara lay awake in bed after Sasha left and worried about how closely connected Sasha and Milly were becoming. She felt ridiculous for being jealous of a child, but Kara could not stop thinking that Sasha was slipping away from her.

†

Talis drove the car through the abandoned streets of the Lower Ninth Ward until he came to the outer limits of Holy Cross. He searched for the landmarks he needed to lead him to the correct house. The ether would have a limited period of sedation and he hoped to have Number Ten inside and properly restrained before she began to rouse. He could easily overwhelm her if she woke up, but he wanted to have the element of surprise when she woke up restrained. He carefully parked the small car between the two houses to conceal it from anyone driving by the area. Slipping a flashlight in his back pocket he walked around to the passenger door and picked up Milly. He carried her into the small building and laid her softly on the cot as he returned to the car for his book bag.

He snapped another set of handcuffs to the rail of the bed above her head and clicked the other around the cuffs attached to her wrists. He took a pair of candles from the bag and lit them to illuminate the dark room. The moon had risen, shadowed by the dark clouds passing in front of it as the storm continued to rage. He picked up the small folding chair, sat it next to the bed, to wait for her to stir.

†

James walked across the yard to meet Sasha. He had seen her double over in pain on the front porch.

"Are you all right?"

"I will be, James. Have you heard anything from Milly?"

"No, I haven't and I am worried. She should have been home a long time ago. I am going out to look for her," he said.

"Me too, if you want to ride with me."

"Pick me up at the house," James said and rushed back across the yard.

Sasha walked to her truck and drove to the front of the guesthouse.

James climbed inside her truck, a pistol in hand.

Sasha saw the gleaming pistol resting in his lap. "I pray we won't need that."

"Me too, but we have it, just in case."

Sasha put the truck in gear and they drove for town. She drove slowly so they could watch both sides of the road in case Milly had driven off the road in the heavy rain. There were no signs of a car leaving the road and when they reached the bridge, Sasha turned to James. "Let's start at the school and see if Milly had car trouble. With a brand-new car, I doubt she would, but you never know."

"And if she is not there? What do we do then?" James asked.

"Then, I guess we start searching the streets for any sign of her car," Sasha said. "Keep your fingers crossed."

Sasha drove onto campus, to the area she knew Milly would have parked, and there were no cars left in the flooded lot. A campus security guard pulled up beside her truck and rolled down his window.

"Is everything all right with you, ma'am?" he asked.

"No, it's not. We are looking for our daughter who is taking some night classes here. She hasn't made it home yet and we are worried about her," Sasha explained.

"They let out the late classes early because of the weather. There hasn't been a car in this lot for over two hours."

"Thank you, sir." Sasha rolled her window up. "Have you tried her cell phone?" she asked.

"I tried earlier from the house, but got no answer," James said.

Sasha took her cell phone from a holster on her belt, dialed Milly's number, and waited for an answer.

†

As Talis carried their book bags into the small house, he heard a vibrating sound coming from Number Ten's book bag. He reached inside and located a cell phone. He looked at the screen to see the name "Sasha." He smiled as he flipped the phone open.

Sasha's heart raced when she heard her call being picked up from the opposite end. Her excitement quickly turned to fear, though, when she heard the male voice from the other end.

"Hello Sasha," Talis purred.

"Who is this?" Sasha demanded.

"I am a friend of hers," Talis answered.

"Where is Milly?"

"She is a bit indisposed at the moment." Talis chuckled.

"I want to talk to her," Sasha growled.

"She is asleep right now. I will be sure to have her call when she wakes up."

"You harm one hair on her and I will make you regret the day you were born," Sasha warned.

"No need to sound so mean. I haven't harmed her and she will be calling my name out in pleasure before the weekend is out."

"Not if I get to you first," Sasha threatened.

"Well, happy hunting then. The police haven't been able to find me so maybe you will be luckier than they are." Talis chuckled softly. "Just out of curiosity, are you the one she brought with her to campus when she registered?" he asked.

"Yes, I was with her," Sasha answered, her anger rising quickly.

"You are quite beautiful and I hope I will be seeing you soon."

"Why don't we trade and you take me and release Milly?"

"You would like that, wouldn't you?" he asked.

"Unless you are scared of a grown woman and prefer to take children instead," she said to provoke him.

"You will have your turn, I promise, but first I will have the young one so sweet and pure. I will have her call you," he repeated and closed the phone.

"You bastard," Sasha growled when he ended the call. She looked worriedly at James. "Milly has been taken by a man and I am afraid it is TBS."

"Oh dear God, not my baby girl! Sasha, we have got to find her," he implored.

"I need to call Kara."

Sasha dialed the number to the house.

"Hello," Kara said sleepily.

"Kara, this is Sasha. TBS has taken Milly."

"Oh no, Sasha, how do you know?"

"I talked to him on Milly's cell phone."

"What can I do?"

"I am going to drop James off at the base of the bridge. I want you to pick him up and drive through the western part of town to see if you can pick up any sign and I will take the eastern half."

"James is with you?"

"Yes, he was worried about Milly too, and rode to town with me to check the school."

"I will be there in fifteen minutes," Kara said.

"Be careful and let me know if you find anything," Sasha requested.

"You be careful too, Sasha. I can sense how angry you are."

"I intend to rip him apart, when I find him."

"No, darling, he needs to be arrested and studied before he gets executed."

"We have to find him before he lays a hand on Milly then."

"We will, my love," Kara assured her. "Keep in touch with me."

Sasha drove to the bridge and dropped James off with her umbrella. "Don't worry, James, we will find her and then I'll make him pay dearly," Sasha promised.

"Let's just get her back, Sasha. I don't want you to get into any trouble."

"I won't, James," Sasha said as she watched him climb from the cab of her truck.

†

Milly began to regain consciousness. She tried to move, but found her limbs placed in restraints. She could not move her arms, but she felt like she was physically intact. She felt her heart racing in her chest and willed her body to stave off the panic that threatened to run rampant. Whatever situation she had gotten herself into was not a good one, she needed to keep her head and remain calm if she had any hopes of surviving.

Milly refused to open her eyes just yet. She knew that when she did, the reality of the situation she was in would come roaring to life. Instead, she reached out with her mind, searching for Sasha.

Sasha, my love, are you there? Milly projected.

Yes, Milly I can feel you. Do you know where you are? Sasha asked.

No, I haven't opened my eyes yet to let him know I am awake.

Good, let's keep it that way for a few more minutes. What is the last thing you remember? Sasha asked.

He said he had locked his keys in his car and asked that I take him to his apartment to get a spare set, Milly said.

Good, then what?

I pulled over to the curb to let him out and he reached into his bag and covered my mouth and nose with a damp cloth.

Probably ether.

All I could tell you is that it was a sweet rush and then I went blank. I think I have handcuffs on, Milly said.

Do you have any idea where you might be?

Not yet, maybe once I open my eyes I can tell something.

Can you hear him at all?

Yes, I can hear him breathing, so he must be close.

Okay, in just a moment I want you to open your eyes and tell me what you can of where you are, but first you must promise me something.

What Sasha?

That you won't try anything dangerous, I will find you.

I know you will, Sasha.

Promise me.

I promise I'll remain calm until you are here to rescue me.

Okay, if you are ready, open your eyes and tell me what you see.

Talis saw her eyes begin to flutter and knew she would be awake soon. He leaned closer to the cot in anticipation of seeing her eyes when they opened, and she found herself held captive.

Milly opened her eyes and after a few seconds, they focused and she saw Talis sitting beside the bed, staring at her, his dark eyes shining with excitement.

I am in a small house, dark except for a few candles. I cannot see much, but the house seems to be damaged and unlived in for some time.

Where is he?

He is sitting right next to the bed, waiting for me to awake.

Keep your mind open, so I will know when I am getting close. Kara and your father are also hunting for you.

"There are those pretty blue eyes," Talis said.

"What are you doing? Why do you have me handcuffed, Talis?" she asked.

"Because I did not want you to panic and try something foolish when you awoke," he explained.

"Why have you brought me here? And where am I?"

"You are safe. I wanted for us to become closer," he said with wickedness in his eyes. "But first, I want you to do something for me."

"What?"

"I want you to sketch me."

"I don't have any supplies for that."

"Don't worry, I have brought them along."

"I will do my best, Talis, but I am really not that good," she said. "I can't do it while I am lying down either."

"I know, I just want you to understand who is in control here," he claimed. "If you disappoint me, I will not hesitate to restrain you again and make your life very painful. Do you understand?"

"Yes, Talis, I do."

"Good, I knew you were smart when I met you," he gloated.

He wants me to sketch a picture of him, Milly said.

Good, that will give me time to find you. Keep him talking as long as you can, but do not provoke him, Milly.

Okay, hurry Sasha. He has a terrifying look in his eyes.

I am doing my best, Sasha promised.

Sasha breathed a short sigh of relief and decided to update Kara.

She is alive and well so far, Sasha projected to Kara.

Great, does she have any idea where she is?

She thinks she is in an abandoned building, but she doesn't know where. I can sense her, but she is far off. Can you feel her at all?

No, not in the least, Kara said.

She must be on the east side. Start working your way to the east and let me know if you pick up her location.

Okay, my love, I will.

Sasha's knuckles were white from her hands gripping the steering wheel so hard. The rage built inside her. She would love to tear him apart, but she knew Kara was right, that he needed to be studied before the state executed him to learn more about why he'd become a serial killer. But if he harmed Milly, he was a dead man and no one would stop her from giving him a very painful death.

†

Talis took the sketchpad and charcoal pencils from his bag and placed them on the chair. "I am going to take the handcuffs off, but don't forget my warning," he said.

Milly nodded her agreement as he moved toward the bed.

Talis used the key to unlock the cuffs and then sat back onto the chair.

Milly rubbed her aching wrists and slowly sat up on the cot. She was in a small house, mostly all one big room, but there did appear to be stairs leading to a second floor. Even now, she still had no more information of where she was.

She leaned her back against the wall for support. Talis reached out his hand and she took the sketchpad and pencils from him. She flipped open the pad and looked up at him.

"So you are the TBS killer?"

"Yes, I am," he answered smugly.

"Why, Talis? You are such a handsome man and you have your medical career ahead of you," Milly said.

"No, I gave that up when she came along," Talis said.

"Who is she?" Milly asked as she began to brush the charcoal across the blank page.

"Her name was Anastasia and I would, and did, do almost anything for her."

Milly could feel the sadness in his voice as he said her name. "What happened to her?"

"She got bored with me and went home to Russia," Talis said.

"Without you?" Milly instantly regretted asking the question. She could feel the rage in his body grow as he thought of how she had abandoned him.

"Yes, just like that," he said as he snapped his fingers. "She woke up one morning and packed her bags and left."

"That sounds pretty heartless," Milly said. "How could she leave you like that?"

"It was not hard at all for her, but she devastated me."

"I'm so sorry, Talis."

"I don't want or need your pity," Talis said angrily.

"That is not what I meant at all," Milly said boldly. "It is not pity to feel the hurt of losing someone you love so much."

"I'm sorry, I didn't mean to snap at you," he said.

Milly looked up at him and smiled. "Turn your face toward the candle, please."

Talis returned her smile and she could feel the anger fade as his smile returned.

Milly really did feel sorry for him. He seemed such a nice man when they met. She could still feel the softness in his voice, but she had also seen and felt his rage. He was such a conflicted soul. She knew his mind must feel torn apart by his warring emotions.

"So you were clever to trick me by feigning an injury," she said.

He grinned at her. "When I was in school, I tutored a football player named Lute. We became good friends and in one horrible moment his professional career was torn away from him when a cheap hit destroyed his knees."

Milly could feel his compassion for Lute and anger for what had happened to his friend. "Where is Lute now?" she asked.

"Down in the bayou, hunting, fishing, and harvesting shrimp for a living on his family's boat," Talis said as he softened again. "I spent a few weeks with him not long ago and he seemed content with the life fate had given him."

"So, even though he didn't play professionally, he is doing something he loves?"

"That is one way of looking at it," Talis said. "He is a mountain of a man, but still bears the scars and pain of his injuries."

"It sounds like you are very close," Milly said.

"He is the best friend I ever had," Talis admitted.

Milly studied the strong angles of his face and the sensual curve of his jawline as her fingers brushed across the page.

†

Brody sat at his desk, the tension so tight in his body he felt like he could snap in two. "I know the bastard has taken her, so why hasn't he called or made contact yet?" he asked Crawford.

"I don't know," Crawford admitted. "Everything is so different with this one. She is much younger, probably a commuter student, so he can't take her home, which means he has her stored someplace, since we know he never takes them to his home." Crawford shook his head. "I just don't know."

"Have there been any reports of a missing persons tonight, Williams?" Brody asked.

"I will go check with Sarge," Williams said and left the room.

†

James and Kara were getting nowhere in their search. "Do you think we should notify the authorities that Milly is missing?" James asked.

"Normally, they won't take a missing person's report until the person is gone for forty-eight hours, but if we told them she was possibly taken by TBS maybe that would get their attention," Kara said. She handed James her cell phone and said, "Call Sasha and see what she thinks."

"I don't see what it can hurt at this point," Sasha said when she answered his call. "Have Kara take you to the precinct house to make a report."

"Okay, thanks Sasha." He handed the phone to Kara and said, "Sasha said to take me to the precinct house to file a report."

"Good, we are only a few blocks away," Kara said as she drove faster down the narrow streets.

†

Williams walked up to the front desk just as James and Kara were walking in. "May I help you?" he asked.

"We would like to report a missing person," Kara said.

"Who is missing?" he asked.

"My eighteen-year-old daughter," James said.

"Is she a blonde and a college student?" he asked.

"Yes, she just started night classes at TU," James said. "How would you know that?"

"I got this one, Sarge," Williams said. He turned to Kara and James. "Follow me, please."

They followed him down a short hall and into an office with two men sitting at a desk studying a report. Kara recognized Detective Brody immediately. Both men looked up when they entered the room.

"Ms. Stewart, it is good to see you again," Brody said when he recognized Kara. "To what do we owe the pleasure?"

"This is my property caretaker, James, and his daughter, Milly, has not returned home from TU tonight, so we came to make a missing person's report," Kara said.

"Oh, dear God," James cried as he felt his knees weaken. His eyes were drawn to the crime board by a picture and when he stepped closer, he saw the photograph was of Milly. He looked in horror at the other pictures on the board and collapsed.

Williams rushed to his side and helped him to his feet.

"Please take him to interrogation room one," Brody said.

"Why don't we all walk that way," Crawford suggested.

Kara saw the photograph of Milly on the crime board and her look to Brody confirmed what they already knew. TBS had chosen Milly as his next victim.

The group entered the interrogation room and sat around a small table. "What can you tell us about Milly's whereabouts?" Brody asked. "Please forgive my bad manners, this is Chief of Detectives Crawford and Officer Williams," Brody said when he realized he had not introduced them.

"Milly takes two classes at TU and the last one ends at ten," Kara said. "She is usually home no later than ten thirty, but tonight she never made it home."

"Let me ask the obvious? Did you check at the university?" Crawford asked.

"Yes, Sasha and I went there first," James, said. "The security guard said the late classes had ended early because of the weather and he had not seen Milly."

"Where is Sasha?" Brody asked.

"She is still out searching for Milly," Kara said.

Brody looked at Kara and nodded his head. *If any woman was safe on the streets of New Orleans it would be Sasha.* There was some strange power about her that Brody had never been able to figure out. He knew Sasha had a connection to the disappearance of the Bellfontaine brothers, but he had no proof. If she had disposed of them as retribution for their treatment of Kara then she had done him and the city a service that would not be any further investigated.

"We had men at TU and LU tonight, so they must have slipped past them," Crawford said.

"You have got to find my baby girl," James pleaded.

"We are doing everything we can at this point," Brody assured him. "We know who he is and where he lives now. It's just a matter of tracking him down."

"What is the make and model of your daughter's car?" Williams asked. "If you have a license plate number that would help too," he added and handed James a notepad. "I will get an APB out on the vehicle."

†

Sasha followed the road east and with each passing block, Milly's signal grew stronger. She pulled up to a stop sign and looked across at what had once been the Lower Ninth Ward. The rain had begun to slack off, but the dismal, dark neighborhoods had an eerie feel to them. She felt a pull from Milly and instinctively turned right to drive toward Holy Cross.

Her heart raced and her rage brewed as she felt herself drawing closer to Milly and her captor.

I am getting closer she projected to Milly.

Yes, my love, I can feel you.

Kara sat and listened while Brody and his men tried to put the information together to find out where TBS had taken Milly. She listened intently until it dawned on her that Sasha somehow had a connection with Milly or else she would not be able to share projections with Milly. Sasha had not mentioned anything about a connection with Milly, which made Kara suspicious of other things Sasha may have not shared with her regarding Milly. Kara pushed the thoughts aside. This is not the time to let jealousy stand in your way, she told herself. There will be a time and a place for that conversation and she would have her answers soon.

Chapter Nineteen

"Talis, what makes you want to hurt people?" Milly asked.

Talis whipped his head around to stare at her. "I don't hurt them," he said. "Quite the opposite, actually, I give them great pleasure before I take their power from them."

"What is their power?"

"Inside each of us is a well of power. Sometimes we don't realize it is there, but everyone has it," he explained. "Some people have tremendous powers and those are the ones that call to me. Their powers are strongest when they are experiencing pleasure and when I wrap my hands around their throats I can feel the power surging into my body, making me stronger."

"Did my powers call to you?" she asked.

"Yes, yours are very strong, and I knew from the time I laid eyes on you, I needed to have you," he said.

"What makes mine strong?"

"Unless I am wrong about you, you are still a virgin," Talis said. "You will realize those powers when you and I are together."

Milly shuddered at the thought of having sex with Talis. There was only one lover for her and he was definitely not the one she would choose.

"So you intend to take my power from me."

"Yes, I need yours to make mine stronger."

"Why do you need to be stronger?" Milly asked.

"To make her come back," Talis said, as if that answer should have been obvious to Milly.

"Anastasia?"

"Yes, together we would rule the nights in New Orleans again," he spoke confidently. "No one would dare deny us pleasure once we are together again."

"Why do you want me to draw you?"

"I need your sketch to add to my shrine," he said. "I want to place it above all of you, in appreciation of your sacrifices."

Milly was unsure if she should feel more pity or fear of Talis. His obsession with Anastasia had definitely caused him to walk a fine edge between insanity and reality. The more they talked of Anastasia, the clearer it became that Talis was precariously perched on the edge of insanity.

†

When Sasha crossed Esplanade, she knew immediately where she was going. Earlier in the week, when she and Kara had driven out to Holy Cross, Sasha remembered feeling TBS there and now she knew why he was there. He would have gone to Holy Cross to choose one of the abandoned homes to use with his next victim. It was all beginning to make sense to her. He could not take her to his place and Milly lived at home with her parents, so he had to find an alternative if he was going to select Milly as his next victim. Sasha drove as quickly as she could through the Lower Ninth Ward.

She stopped at a stop sign and looked ahead of her for any signs of TBS and Milly. She could not detect any lights in the area, but she knew from the strength of Milly's presence, she was here somewhere in one of the homes.

Kara, I know where she is, Sasha projected to her lover.

Where? Kara asked.

He has taken her to Holy Cross, I don't know exactly where yet, but I'm sure she is here.

Find her, Sasha, and I'll bring Detective Brody and reinforcements, Kara said.

Just look for my truck. I'll go and make Milly safe from him.

Do not harm him, Sasha. The authorities know we are involved now, Kara said.

Yes, my dear. He will still be alive when you get here.

Kara pretended that her cell phone vibrated. She stood and walked a short distance away to take the imaginary call.

"You what? That is fantastic news. Yes, I'll bring them in a hurry," she said and closed the phone.

The four men apparently puzzled by her excitement, were staring at her.

"Sasha has found where they are," she said.

"Where are they?" Brody asked.

"She doesn't have a specific address, but they are in Holy Cross."

"That would be the far east, he was referring to," Crawford said.

"What does that mean?" James asked.

"Never mind, we can explain later. Right now, we need to find them. Tell Sasha not to act, to wait on us to arrive," Brody said.

Kara picked up her cell phone to dial Sasha's number. *Don't answer. Brody wants you to wait until we get there to act,* she projected.

No way. I am going in as soon as I find them.

I know, but please be careful, Kara said.

Always, Sasha projected back.

"There is no answer. She must have turned her phone off or she's not in her truck," Kara said apologetically.

"What is she driving?" Brody asked.

"A black extended cab, Silverado," Kara answered.

"Okay, let's go," Brody said as he ushered them down the hallway. "Williams, I want you to get on the radio and send several units down to the Holy Cross area to search for Sasha's truck. No lights, though. We don't alert TBS."

Williams nodded in agreement with Brody.

"Tell them to radio us with the address and to sit tight until we arrive," Brody instructed.

"Got it," Williams said as they dashed for Brody's car.

†

Sasha, is that you getting close? I thought I just saw headlights, Milly said.

I can't be too far away I can hear your heartbeat. Just be patient, I will be there soon.

Sasha turned off her headlights. She drove down one of the main streets and carefully searched down side streets, looking for any evidence of Milly or her car.

Nothing. Not even a breeze seemed to move in the neighborhood. There were no abandoned animals crossing the streets and there was no sound to the night. The area was completely still, as if death had arrived and frozen it in time.

Just ahead, Sasha saw the flicker of candlelight coming from a window in a small house on her right. She cautiously crept past the house and saw Milly's car tucked away between the two buildings. She turned into the next driveway and quietly slipped out of her truck, closing the door carefully to prevent making any noise.

Moving stealthily through the dark night Sasha reached the front porch of the house where Milly was captive. The walls of the house were askew and Sasha worried that a stiff wind would be strong enough to bring the building to the ground. Thankfully, the air was calm as she stepped onto the porch. She peered through a crack in the front door and saw Milly in the candlelit room. She was perched on a folding cot with her back resting against the wall. In her lap was a sketchbook. Milly appeared to be drawing a picture of the man sitting across from her. TBS was sitting on a folding chair, three feet from Milly. She did not appear restrained any longer. Sasha scanned the room for any signs of a weapon. Finding none, she reached out to Milly.

I am here and can see you. Are there any weapons that you are aware of? Sasha asked.

Not that I have seen, Milly answered.

Good. I am going to crash the door in just a moment and I want you to run to me as quickly as you can.

Yes, Sasha, Milly answered.

Sasha's first action would be to get Milly out of the room safely and then she would detain TBS until the authorities arrived. She took a deep breath before she stepped forward. Reaching for the doorknob, a floorboard made a loud, creaking noise. *It's now or never.* She crashed through the door and into the room.

†

Talis was turning away from Milly when Sasha entered the room. He made a run for his backpack as Milly lurched from the cot and ran into Sasha's arms.

Sasha could feel Milly's body quivering with fright as she clung to her.

"Are you all right?" Sasha asked.

"Yes, I'm okay, he did not hurt me, Sasha," Milly said.

"Ah, Sasha," Talis said. "What a good Russian name." He grinned as he reached into the bag and pulled out a knife.

"My truck is parked outside. Go now and wait there for the police to arrive," Sasha instructed.

"I don't want to leave you," Milly said.

"Go now," she said in a firm voice leaving no doubt that she wanted Milly to leave immediately. "I will be with you soon."

Milly followed her instructions and quickly left the room and ran into the night.

"I was hoping we would meet again, but under much different circumstances," Talis said as Milly ran from the room. "You have spoiled my plan, so now I'll be forced to make you my Number Ten."

"Oh please, do try to do that," Sasha said as her rage flared in her eyes.

Talis flinched and paused in his advance of Sasha.

Sasha saw him cringe at the look he was receiving from her. "What's the matter, are you scared of a grown woman?" she taunted.

Talis rushed Sasha wielding the knife in his right hand, slashing it through the air.

Sasha met his approach and easily trapped his wrist in her hand, paralyzing his arm. He struggled to free himself from her grasp, but her immortal power easily restrained him. "I bet you can't do this," Sasha said as she raised her left arm and forced him to slice open her forearm. "Watch fool," she said as she lifted her arm before his face.

Sasha could see the fright on Talis's face as he stared at the wound he had just made on her arm began to instantly heal, and then there was nothing more than a fading scratch mark. She smiled as Talis's face covered with the realization he was dealing with someone much more dangerous than a mere mortal.

Sasha wrenched his wrist and Talis cried out in pain as the knife fell from his hand. She did not break his wrist, but she knew it would hurt for days to come. Sasha kicked the knife away and reached out to grab him by the throat knowing she could easily crush it. She had promised Kara that she would not kill him and that, and only that, would keep him alive this night.

Talis felt the hard wood of the wall against his back and felt himself lifted off the floor. His eyes grew wide with shock and terror. He felt his feet leave the solid floor and he kicked wildly looking for something solid to release some of the pressure she was placing on his throat. He could not speak and breathing was becoming increasingly difficult. Sasha's rage was nearing an uncontrollable point and when she glared at him, Talis could see the fangs that had descended.

He struggled to be free of the monster that held him in her clutches, but his every movement was unsuccessful in gaining his release. He was now her victim and he feared those fangs would rip his neck open in an instant.

"You know I can read your mind, hear your thoughts, and smell your fear." Sasha said. "You disgust me." She dropped him back to the floor.

"You are a fucking monster." He yelped as his feet hit the floor as his hands wrapping around his bruised throat.

The crazed woman wheeled back around and had him by the throat again in less than a second. She slammed him back against the wall and moved in very close as she spoke between clenched teeth. "If I had not made a promise, this is what I would do to you," she said.

Talis suddenly felt like he was dreaming as he witnessed Sasha's fangs ripping his neck open while she painfully broke his arms and legs. The vision was so vivid he soiled himself in his terror, and he stopped struggling against her.

"Now you see what you have to look forward to if somehow you are ever set free. I will hunt you down and make you painfully pay for all you have done to the people of my city." She eased her grip on his throat and he swallowed hard. "Do we have a clear understanding?"

"Yes, we do." Talis was unable to look her in the face.

"Good. In a way, I do wish you would get off, just so I could take care of you myself." Talis could feel his body trembling in fear as her words rang true in his ears.

†

Outside, Milly saw two squad cars approach, one from each direction and sit in visual range of the house. Then a dark sedan pulled up and her father and Kara got out of the backseat. She quickly climbed out of Sasha's truck and ran into her father's arms.

Witnessing that Milly was free and safe Brody pulled his gun. He nodded to Crawford and Williams. "Let's go get this son of a bitch."

Williams ran around to the back of the house as Brody and Crawford bracketed the front door. Brody reached for the doorknob and pushed the door open as he and Crawford rushed in from the front and Williams appeared from the back. All three men looked at Sasha with a death grip on the TBS killer. For a moment, Brody thought he saw the killer's feet dangling from the floor. *That's impossible.* Even though Sasha was a tall woman, she could not possibly possess the strength to lift a man his size off the floor with one hand.

"Relax, Sasha, we are here now," Brody said calmly.

Sasha turned to look at Brody with a feral fire burning in her eyes. She released her grip on TBS and stepped away from the killer.

Brody and Crawford held TBS at gunpoint as Williams holstered his gun and rushed in to cuff their killer.

"Read him his rights please, Williams," Brody said when Williams had snapped the cuffs around his wrists.

"With pleasure, boss," Williams said.

Brody listened as Williams read Talis his rights and then stepped across the room. He pulled out his ink pen and flipped the sketchbook over onto its back. The face of Talis

Barker smiled up at him. Milly had drawn a very accurate sketch of him and Brody was curious to find out why.

†

Sasha walked outside with Crawford to check on Milly.

"He is in custody now," Crawford softly said to Milly. "He won't be able to hurt anyone else."

Sasha watched as Brody stepped out of the house and walked toward the small crowd.

Wrapped in her father's arms Sasha felt Milly shivering as he approached. "Chief, would you take these folks down to the precinct house and we will meet you there in a few minutes?"

"Sure thing, Brody," he said.

"I will follow you in my truck," Sasha said.

"What about my car?" Milly asked.

"I'm sorry, but we will have to impound it for a while until we can gather all the evidence from it," Crawford said. "You and your dad can go with me."

Milly frowned.

"I'll ride with you, Sasha," Kara said, then walked with Sasha to her truck.

Crawford pulled away from the house with Milly and James tucked safely inside, soon followed by Sasha and Kara.

"I'm so glad everyone is safe," Kara said. "You were fantastic, Sasha."

"Thanks, I am just glad the worst part is over and Milly will be fine."

"It was incredible how you were able to track her down."

"That is something we need to talk about, but not right now," Sasha said.

"I agree."

†

Brody watched them drive away and then called in the two marked units. "Get crime scene techs on the way and you stay and guard the place until they are finished," he told one of the uniformed men. "The other unit will take us in to book Barker, and then I will send him back to relieve you," he explained.

Brody walked back inside and took Talis by the right elbow as he and Williams escorted him to the squad car. Brody placed Talis in the backseat and climbed in beside him as Williams walked around to the other side. Once seated the officer pulled onto the street and drove away.

"Finally, we shall dance, you and I," Brody said to Talis, repeating a statement he had made often in the last few weeks. "I can't believe a woman was able to capture you," he said in disbelief.

Talis turned to look at Brody, staring him directly in the eyes. "That is no ordinary woman," he said. "She is a freaking monster."

"That is very ironic coming from someone who has brutally murdered nine people," Brody said.

"What I did was nothing in comparison of what she has planned for me," Talis said.

"You look like you are in good shape to me," Williams said. "Maybe a few bruises, but nothing any worse."

"You just don't understand, man," Talis said and shook his head from side to side.

Brody knew Talis was partially right, Sasha was no ordinary woman, but as long as she was working on his side, he would let it remain at that. In this day and age, the police force needed help from any source they could get, and he wasn't going to turn away any assistance. He just wished one thing. He wished he could figure out how Sasha had tracked him down. They had all the clues, and yet, she was the first to find them. Brody pondered that thought all the way back to the precinct house allowing Barker to stew in his own misery.

Chapter Twenty

After arriving at the precinct house everyone was ushered into interrogation room one. A few minutes later Sarge brought in a pot of fresh coffee and some beignets. "It's going to be a long night," he said to the group. "If I can get you anything, just ask for Sarge," he said with a twinkling smile.

"Excuse me for a minute," Crawford said when he heard Brody enter the building.

"What is going to happen now?" Milly asked.

"They will interview you and ask you to give a sworn statement on the events that have taken place since you met Talis Barker," Kara said. "You need to be as thorough as possible and give them all of the information you can think of," she added. "Remember, he will go on trial for not only kidnapping and assaulting you, but for the murder of nine other people."

"What will happen to Talis now?" Milly asked.

"I imagine he is being booked in right now and once he is photographed and fingerprinted he will be taken into an interrogation room much like this one to be interviewed.

Afterward, he will be placed in a holding cell until his first arraignment tomorrow morning."

"What is that like?" Milly asked.

"They will take him into a room with a video link to the courthouse and he will stand in front of the camera to face the judge to hear the charges against him and to determine if bond will be set. He may even be asked to give a plea on his innocence or guilt," Kara explained.

"Will I have to go to court to testify?" Milly asked.

"If he pleads not guilty and the case goes to court yes," Kara answered.

"Does that scare you?" Sasha asked.

"I guess it does, a little," Milly answered.

She seems so innocent at times. "It is not difficult, you just tell the truth of what occurred," she said. "You have nothing to hide or be ashamed of."

Milly nodded her head and sipped a hot cup of coffee, while they waited. A few minutes later, Crawford returned to the room. "Milly, I need to take a statement from you now, if you are ready," he said kindly.

"I'm ready," Milly said.

"Come with me then and we will get started," he said as he ushered her from the room.

"This may take a while, James, if you want to call and let Marie know she is safe," Sasha said.

"Here, you can use my cell and we will step out to give you some privacy," Kara said.

Sasha and Kara stepped outside just in time to see Talis led into an interrogation room. Brody saw them in the hallway and nodded to them. He walked over to them and asked, "Is Milly okay?"

"Yes, I think she will be fine," Sasha answered.

"Are you about to begin your interrogation with Barker?" Kara asked.

"Yes, we are. He has denied wanting a lawyer, so we will begin in just a few minutes."

"Could we look on for a little while?" Kara asked.

"I don't think that would be a problem, however, I don't think it wise for her father to be there," he said.

"You go ahead and I will stay with James," Sasha said.

†

Kara followed Brody into a small room with a speaker and a wall consisting of two-way mirror glass and took a seat next to the wall. From there she could see and hear what was going on in the interrogation room. Brody got her seated and left the room. A moment later, Kara watched him enter the room where Barker and Officer Williams were sitting at a table. He was still handcuffed, but in the front this time.

Kara listened as Brody explained the process to Barker and the charges he was facing to make sure he understood exactly the charges brought against him. Kara noted a tape recorder on the table that was running and felt sure there was a video camera operating to record the conversation as well.

She listened for over an hour as he explained to Brody how he had met and fell in love with Anastasia. It was easy to see how deeply obsessed with her he had become from listening to him. Brody prompted him with several questions, allowing Barker to describe each of the killings he had perpetrated. He took great joy in describing his sexual performance and after the third victim, Kara had heard enough. She turned off the speaker then walked back to where James and Sasha were waiting.

†

It was nearly four in the morning and Sasha could tell James was exhausted from the ordeal. "Kara, would you drive James home and let him get some rest? I will wait for Milly and bring her home as soon as I can."

James lifted his head and began to protest. "Sasha is right, James, there is nothing you can do here, so we might as well go home," Kara said.

"Thanks," Sasha whispered when she hugged Kara. "I will be home as soon as possible."

"Just be careful," Kara said. "I know you must be getting tired too."

"I will be just fine," Sasha said with a smile.

She walked with James and Kara to the back door and watched them cross the parking lot to climb into Kara's car. She waved at them and stepped back inside the building to wait for Milly. She poured herself another cup of coffee and sat at the table. She used her mind to search for Barker and when she entered his mind, she could hear what he was saying.

Talis was describing to Brody how he had drugged Number Eight and taken her to the cemetery. Sasha could feel the quiver of excitement running through him as he described each detail of his plan. *You are one sick bastard* she projected to Barker.

Barker's hands went to his head as he cried out in fear. "Make her go away," he pleaded, "just make her go away."

I will be with you checking in on you from time to time, Sasha told him and then left his mind.

"There is no woman here," Brody said.

"Not here, here," Barker said as he pointed to his head. "That freaking monster woman is in my head."

"Who, Barker, you are not making sense?" Brody asked.

"Never mind, she's gone," he said. Talis took a long drink of water and continued his story.

Sasha then peeked into Milly's mind to see how she was doing and found her busy writing her statement. She sat back in her seat to wait and felt her eyes begin to grow heavy. Sasha leaned forward and placed her arms on the table to rest her head then drifted off to sleep.

†

At nearly six in the morning, Crawford led Milly back into the room. Sasha was still rubbing the sleep from her eyes after her nap when they walked in. "Are you all done?" she asked.

"I think so. We have the contact numbers if we need any other information, but what Milly was able to give us is priceless," Crawford said. "She is a really special young woman," he added and watched Milly smile.

"Thank you," Milly said. "I hope you'll keep me posted on what is happening with him."

"Yes, we'll be in touch with you often to let you know how the case is progressing," he said.

"May I take her home now?" Sasha asked.

"After one more stop," Crawford said as he pulled out his wallet and handed Sasha a twenty. "This young lady deserves a hearty breakfast after all she has gone through the last twelve hours or so," he said.

"How about it, are you up for some breakfast?" Sasha asked.

"I thought you would never ask," Milly said as she hugged Sasha close.

"Let's get out of here and get some food into you before I take us home," Sasha said.

"Waiting on you," Milly said and walked to the door.

"Thank you for all that you and your men have done, Chief," Sasha said.

"You two deserve all the credit," Crawford said.

"I know you'll bring him to justice for what he has done."

"Yes, you can bet we will," Crawford stated.

Sasha shook his hand and then led Milly out of the building. "One of the diners down in the Quarter?" she asked.

"That's about all that is open that is decent at this time of the morning," Milly said.

"Now how would you know that?" Sasha teased.

"That's what I have heard," Milly said with a chuckle.

"Well, let's go see if it is true."

†

She and Milly climbed into her truck and they drove to the Quarter. She was lucky to find a parking spot within a block and they walked to the diner where they shared a huge breakfast. When they had finished, they walked back to the truck and Milly stopped Sasha.

"I never said thank you for saving my life tonight," she said.

"You never have to thank me. I would have died if anything would have happened to you," Sasha said.

Milly leaned into Sasha, brushing her lips with a soft kiss. This time Sasha was not startled and pulled Milly in closer for a deep, sensual kiss that lasted for several minutes.

When Sasha broke the kiss, she saw tears flowing down Milly's cheeks and tenderly wiped them away. "I am happy that no harm came to you," she said as she hugged Milly close.

A speechless Milly smiled at Sasha, who opened the door for her before walking around to the driver's side of the truck.

Sasha drove for home and smiled when she saw Milly's head begin to nod. She pulled up in front of the guesthouse porch and carried Milly inside the small house. James was waiting in the kitchen. He took Milly from Sasha's arms and carried her to her bedroom. "I'll see you all later," she whispered and walked out to her truck.

She drove to the garage and parked. The burning in the pit of her stomach reminded Sasha that she was way past due for a dose of serum. She went to the kitchen and pulled a vial from the refrigerator and downed it before walking into the bedroom. Kara was deeply asleep. Sasha quietly removed her clothes and crept into the bed to snuggle into Kara's warmth and fell fast asleep.

Chapter Twenty-one

When Sasha woke up to an empty bed hours later, she still had the taste of the kiss she had shared with Milly on her lips. Sasha knew she should probably feel guilty for kissing Milly, but it felt so natural to be kissing her. Still, Sasha was worried what her future would hold. Would she continue to live with Kara, whom she loved deeply, or would she allow the relationship with Milly to rekindle? She buried her face in her pillow in despair. No matter which way she chose, one of the women she loved would be hurt.

†

Kara had woken earlier and gone downstairs for coffee and to read through the morning paper as she waited for Sasha to wake. Of course, the headlines were filled with the news that after a long investigation the TBS killer was in police custody. Thankfully, there was no mention of Milly or their involvement with the events of last night. Kara hoped that, at least for a short while, New Orleans's citizens could release a collective sigh and relax until the next major event would take place.

Milly was still on her mind as she walked into the kitchen to get another cup of coffee. She felt Sasha stirring in the bed upstairs and poured a second cup for her lover. She would not wait for Sasha to broach the subject of her connection with Milly. If Sasha wanted to be with Milly, Kara intended to know now before she felt any further humiliation. With her anger rising, Kara climbed the steps to their bedroom.

"Good morning," she said as she handed the cup to Sasha. "I hope you slept well."

"Thanks, I slept pretty well and you?" Sasha asked in return.

"I slept well, thank you," Kara said as she sat on the edge of the bed. "We cannot put this conversation off any longer, Sasha."

"Which one?" Sasha asked coyly, which irritated Kara even more.

"About the connection you have formed with Milly and why you have not shared this information with me before now," Kara said.

"I haven't shared it with you before now because I have not come to grips with it myself," Sasha said defensively. "Milly confronted me one afternoon with a request of what she most deeply desired for her eighteenth birthday."

"Which was what?"

"Milly is not just an eighteen-year-old woman, Kara," Sasha started to explain.

"What is it you are trying to say, Sasha?"

"What I am saying is that when Milly was born, Milly Vansant was reborn with her."

"She was reincarnated into little Milly?" Kara asked.

"Don't ask me how it is possible, but, yes, Milly has all the memories and experiences of Milly Vansant."

Kara sat with her eyes wide on the edge of the bed. *How could this be*?

"I was stunned to find out about it too, as you can imagine, but it is true. She knows things that only Milly Vansant would have known," Sasha said.

Kara lifted the coffee cup to her lips with a trembling hand.

"So what is it that she wants?" Kara steeled herself for Sasha's answer.

"Milly wants me to transform her into an immortal once again."

"How can you even think of agreeing to that?" Kara said as her rage boiled over. "She is still just a child and you and I have a life together."

Sasha could feel the racing of Kara's heart as her anger and jealousy grew.

"That is what I thought too, at least at first. I agreed to transform Milly only when she turned twenty-one and had a chance to live as a mortal adult for a few years."

"So you have already made your mind up without discussing this with me at all?" Kara shouted. "Do I truly mean that little to you, Sasha?"

Sasha recoiled from the lashing of emotions Kara had just struck her with. It was impossible for Kara to understand how she felt about the situation. Sasha was doubtful of her own understanding of what had taken place between the three of them. "You mean the world to me, Kara, and you know it," Sasha struck back.

"I thought I did, until I saw you two kissing out in the yard," Kara stammered.

So she did witness the kiss we shared the night they returned from the university. Sasha watched Kara's tears begin to fall.

"That was never meant to happen," Sasha said. "Milly's excitement about starting college just got the better of her."

"You didn't seem to mind and it took a while before you ended the kiss," Kara snarled.

Sasha let out a deep sigh. "I know you won't understand this because you have never been in the situation, but I forgot who and where I was for that moment," she said. "For just one brief moment, Milly was back in my life."

"You are right, I don't understand it, and I don't intend to sit here and listen to this garbage." Kara stormed out of the room.

Sasha sat in speechless shock as she heard the front porch door slam and the sound of Kara's sports car driving quickly away.

"Well, that certainly did not go well at all."

†

Kara raced down the driveway blinded by her tears. When she reached the hard road, she turned away from town. She needed to do some serious thinking about her future and the long country roads south of Sugarland would give her the opportunity to drive and think without having to dodge other drivers.

Her hands hurt from the tense grip she had on the steering wheel. She had barely driven a mile before she pulled over to the side of the road. She took her hands off the wheel and closed her eyes, willing her heart to stop racing in her chest as she breathed deeply.

"How could you do this to us, Sasha?"

When Kara regained control of her emotions, she lowered the convertible top to allow the wind to whip through her hair as she drove. She had no clue where she was going, but felt she had to put many miles between her and Sasha.

†

Kara's exit really worried Sasha. She'd never seen Kara that angry before and would never have guessed she would react so jealously toward Milly. Sasha did realize her mistake in not discussing the issue with Kara sooner, but there was nothing she could change about that now. That damage—Sasha prayed—was not beyond repair.

As the afternoon began to fade and Kara had not returned home, Sasha left the empty house and drove to town. As she had always done in the past, Sasha went to the cemetery where her parents and grandmother were to sit and sort out her thoughts. Being in their company always brought comfort to Sasha, and at present, any form of comfort would help to ease her conflicted soul.

†

Milly woke for a second time when Sasha drove off. She could sense the horrible tension between Kara and Sasha and it didn't take Milly long to determine that somehow she was in the middle of their conflict. Her heart reached out to Sasha. She had not meant to cause such pain to Sasha by returning to life, but felt her return had caused great misery. Milly pulled the covers back over her head and cried herself back to sleep.

†

Kara drove until the sun started to set and her rage had burned itself out. Other than not being truthful about Milly's reincarnation, Sasha really had not done anything to warrant being so cruel to her. At first, Kara's jealousy blinded her to Sasha's dilemma. The first great love of her life was asking her to give her the gift she had bestowed upon Sasha, the same gift that Sasha had ultimately given to Kara after Milly's death. Kara felt the shame of jealousy and selfishness burn into her soul.

When her rage and jealousy subsided, Kara realized that Sasha could not deny Milly's request. Her fear that Milly had come back to claim Sasha stayed first and foremost in her mind, but Kara would have to trust Sasha to make the right decision.

Kara stopped to fill her car and then turned back toward home to find Sasha and set things right.

†

Sitting amongst her family had given Sasha the peacefulness she was searching for. Even though they could not provide her with the answers to her future, the time spent with them helped Sasha think more clearly.

The sun was setting as she walked back to her truck. She reached into her pocket and pulled out her cell phone to dial up an old friend.

"Hello Marcus, this is Sasha," she said when he answered the phone.

"Girl, it has been a long time since you have called. How are you?" he asked in his wildly campy voice.

"I need someone to talk to," Sasha said. "May I take you to dinner?"

"You most certainly cannot, but you can come to my place for dinner," he teased. "Where are you?"

"I am just now leaving the cemetery."

"Visiting or planting?" he asked.

"Just visiting with the family."

"Well, come on over. I am about to boil some mudbugs and I have cold beer in the fridge."

"I'll be there soon," Sasha said and ended the call.

She already felt better. Marcus had a way of lifting her spirits when it seemed no one else could. She looked forward to visiting with him.

When Sasha pulled up to his house, Marcus flung the front door open and said, "Gimme a hug, beautiful."

Sasha smiled and wrapped her arms around the petite man who so easily made her smile. She followed him into his kitchen and sat on a barstool at the counter to watch him cook.

"So what is on that beautiful mind of yours?" he asked. "I can tell by the tone of your voice this isn't just purely a social call."

"I have run across a situation and I need your advice."

"Do tell, honey, you have got my full attention," Marcus said as he dropped the crawfish into boiling water.

"Milly has come back and I don't know what to do," Sasha stated bluntly.

"What do you mean, 'has come back'? She has been gone for years," Marcus said, confused.

"My Milly was reincarnated in little Milly when she was born."

"You are kidding me, right?"

"No, my friend, I would not joke about this," Sasha said.

"Holy shit, girl, I've never heard of that before."

"Me either, but Milly has asked me to transform her to an immortal," Sasha said.

"Well, you can't blame her for that," Marcus said. "Our life is so much better than mortal life." He cocked his head at Sasha. "So what's the issue? Is it Kara?"

"Yes, I just told her today and she stormed out of the house," Sasha said.

"I can see that happening. From her standpoint, your first love has come back to rip you from her arms," he said. "She has a right to be angry, especially if you have kept this news from her for a while, as I suppose you have from the guilty look on your face."

"Damn, Marcus, I haven't come to grips with it myself," Sasha said.

"Girl, this definitely calls for a beer or two or more." He walked to the refrigerator and pulled out two beers. "So what are your intentions toward Milly?" he asked, point-blank, as he handed her a beer.

"I don't know, Marcus. I love Kara deeply, but I think you know it was nothing like the love Milly and I shared."

"The first bond you have is always the deepest. I still have regrets for ever leaving my first," he said, "but I was young, wild, and stupid back then."

Sasha sighed and propped her chin on her hand.

"You are absolutely sure it is Milly?"

"Yes, Marcus, she knows things that only my Milly would know."

"That is the damnedest thing I have ever heard. You must have something good for her to come back from the dead for, honey," he said, making Sasha blush.

"Marcus, you are such a wicked fiend."

"I know, darling, but you love me," he said as he stirred the pot. He looked at Sasha and saw that she was truly conflicted over what to do in her situation. "Have you and Milly done the deed?"

"No Marcus, we have done nothing other than kiss twice," Sasha said.

"How did it feel?"

"If felt completely natural," she admitted. "Milly always had a way of stirring me with a soft kiss."

"Does Kara make you feel that way?"

Sasha hesitated for a moment. "Yes, but it is very different, and I am not sure I can explain."

Marcus moved about his kitchen, taking down large platters for their meal and placing them on the small bar where Sasha sat. "So what do you plan on doing?" he asked as he dipped ears of corn, red potatoes, and crawfish from the boiling water for their meal.

"I am not really sure," Sasha said. "I know I must make good on my agreement to transform Milly, but when is the issue. I feel like I need to move more quickly now."

"What has urged that decision?"

"Milly was taken by the TBS killer yesterday," Sasha said. "I was only able to find her through projecting with her and rescued her before he could harm her."

"Well, I'll be damned," he said. "I knew there had to be more to the story than what the paper reported. Is Milly all right?"

"Yes, I think she will be fine, but I worry about her safety now."

"I can understand that. You realize you're connected to her forever again if you transform her, right? Are you ready for that?" he asked.

"I just don't know."

"What do you think Kara's view of all this is?"

"She is so angry with me right now, I don't know if she has a view yet."

Marcus chuckled as he picked up an ear of corn. “I can guarantee she has a view, but it may not be one you want to hear,” he warned.

†

Sasha and Marcus finished the meal and then took fresh beers out to the balcony to watch the barges pass by on their way into port. Marcus could sense Sasha’s despair. “I think the best thing for now is to go home and talk with Kara once she has calmed down, find out what her view is,” he said. “Kara is crucial to your future, no matter which avenue you choose, and you have no choice but to discuss your feelings candidly with her. You owe that to her.”

“I know you are right, but I know Kara is going to pressure me for a decision, and I am not ready for that,” Sasha said.

“Then you need to tell her that and stick to your guns until you are ready to make a decision,” Marcus said. “Kara has no other choice, unless she wants to leave right off the bat,” he added.

Sasha had not really given thought to that prospect. What would she do if Kara packed up and moved into town, or worse, moved back to Atlanta? Sasha listened to the chimes of the cathedral ring eleven and then drained the bottle of beer. “I guess I had better help you clean up and start for home,” she said.

“Girl, I can handle a few dishes. You go home and keep in touch to let me know what’s going on,” he said. “If you need anything, just call.”

Sasha stood and wrapped the small man in her arms. “Thank you for being such a good friend, Marcus.”

“You know I love you, Sasha, and there isn’t anything I won’t do for you,” he answered.

"I know," Sasha said as she released him.

"Good luck and call me soon," Marcus said as he walked her to the door.

"I will," Sasha promised.

She drove through town and stopped at the end of the driveway. She took a deep breath and drove into the garage and parked next to Kara's car. Sasha was not looking forward to the conversation waiting for her inside, and the dread of what was to come weighed on her shoulders like the weight of the world.

Chapter Twenty-two

Sasha was shocked when she opened the front door and stepped inside to see Kara and Milly in the parlor. She was dreading a confrontation with Kara and was completely surprised to see the two of them waiting for her return.

"Welcome home, baby," Kara said.

"Thanks. What is going on?" Sasha asked.

"Milly and I were waiting for you to return home so we could talk."

"Do you really think this is the time?"

"Yes, we think it is," Milly said. "Kara and I have been talking for the last two hours and we have some ideas to share with you."

"Why do I feel like I am outnumbered here?" Sasha asked as she hung her jacket behind the door.

"Because you are, honey," Kara said. "Be brave and come sit with us."

Sasha walked over to the couch to sit across from Kara and Milly. *What a lovely pair of women, and what a devious pair as well.* They smiled at her.

"So, what is going on?"

"Milly came over to talk to me when I returned from my drive, and we have discussed a few things we wanted to share with you," Kara said. "Milly told me of her request for you to transform her. She has also assured me that she has no intent to interfere in our relationship."

"Is that what you were so worried about earlier today?" Sasha asked.

"I am very hurt that you kept this information from me," Kara said. "I was also hurt by the kiss the two of you shared out in the yard, but Milly has confirmed that it was her emotions getting the best of her. I admit that I am still angry with you, but I am beginning to understand the dilemma you are in."

"I realize, in hindsight, I was wrong to not discuss this with you earlier, but I still don't understand what all is happening myself."

Milly turned directly to Sasha. "I know you are deeply in love with Kara and it makes me happy to know that you are in love," Milly said. "I don't know how or why I was chosen to be reincarnated, but I do know that our time has passed."

Hearing those words reminded Sasha of the day of Milly's death and the pain of her heartache rushed back at her. She had lost Milly once, could she survive losing her again?

"So what are your plans?" Sasha asked Milly.

"I hope that you will transform me as I have asked. I want to finish college and maybe I will return to Europe," Milly said.

It was Sasha's turn to feel the pain of selfishness. "Europe is so far away."

"That is true, but that decision is still several years ahead of us."

"In the meantime," Kara said. "We have decided that you should take Milly to Paris for graduation as we had planned, but you and Milly go alone. If the two of you agree the time is right for her transformation, it will happen there, between the two of you as it was the first time."

"I still don't know if it is a good time for that," Sasha said.

"Do I need to remind you how close we were to losing her to TBS?" Kara said. "If she had her immortal skills, that incident would have never occurred."

"Yes, I have thought about that too."

"I will be ready when you think the time is right," Milly assured Sasha. "If you remain adamant that I wait a few years, then I'll be satisfied with your decision."

Sasha knew Milly was being truthful. "We can start working on plans to travel to Paris then," Sasha said.

"Very well, Sasha." Milly stretched and suppressed a yawn. "I am still exhausted, so if you ladies will excuse me, I am going home to bed."

"Sweet dreams, Milly," Kara said as she stood to hug her goodnight.

"Come over some time after lunch tomorrow and we can begin making plans."

"Thank you, Sasha." Milly embraced her warmly.

"Good night." Sasha and Kara walked Milly to the door.

Sasha closed the door behind her and leaned into it. "I am sorry for making you feel so much distress," she said.

"I should have shown you more trust," Kara admitted. "I allowed my jealousy and anger to get the better of me."

The grandfather clock struck one as Sasha took Kara into her arms. "I think we both have had a very stressful few days. Why don't we head up to bed as well," Sasha suggested.

"Waiting on you," Kara teased as she turned away from Sasha's embrace.

Sasha smiled and followed Kara up the stairs. All was well at Sugarland once more. No matter what would happen over the next few months or years, Sasha was content with the love of two very special women.

Sasha and Kara undressed and crept between the crisp sheets. Then wrapped in one another's arms they dreamt the dreams of eternity.

About the Author

Ali Spooner

Ali Spooner, a native of Florida, currently lives and works in Memphis, TN. As an "Indie" author, Ali has been writing for many years as a hobby, and with the assistance of the Affinity team has taken her love of storytelling to a new level.

Ali's characters range from cowgirls and psychics, to a healthy dose of supernatural beings. She has written stand-alone titles and series. Ali is an avid reader and her other hobbies include photography, outdoor activities, and watching college sports.

Other Books from Affinity eBook Press

Requiem for Vukovar by Angela Koenig Requiem for Vukovar continues the Refraction series and the exploits of Jeri O'Donnell and her partner, Kelly Corcoran. In an epic siege largely ignored by the wider world, Kelly, who was prepared to give up comforts and certainties when she became part of Jeri's nomadic life, encounters more than physical danger. Her ability to maintain her core integrity is assaulted by the inevitable ugliness of war. For Jeri, the true battle is confronting her attraction to violence as she struggles against losing herself in the exhilaration of combat.

Against All Odds by JM Dragon From award winning and bestselling author JM Dragon, with significant updates by, Erin O'Reilly comes an original tale of romance where everything seems to be stacked against two women whose destinies bring them together. Life however takes a twisted path setting both Steph and Louise in directions they never thought possible. Will love win out against all odds or will love be forever lost?

The Settlement by Ali Spooner The outpouring of love and friendship toward Cadin helps her on her path to healing and learning to trust her heart to love once again. Join bestselling author Ali Spooner on this sensational journey that ends with a heartwarming romance.

Once Upon a Time by Alane Hotchkin Raven only wanted to escape the blows that life had dealt her. She longed to be on the open sea and free. When she came upon a beautiful young girl sitting alone in the middle of a meadow, little did she know that her destiny would be changed forever. Will they become the pawns of the ancient vision or will both paths lead to the same port of destiny? Find out it in this exciting high seas adventure that will capture your imagination.

Asset Management by Annette Mori Follow the twists and turns to the explosive conclusion. Not everything is black and white. There are many shades of gray and sometimes it's difficult to decipher who is good and who is evil. No one is all virtue or all malevolence, but sometimes love helps us rise above.

Do Dreams Come True? by JM Dragon How do two people who really shouldn't get on end up in a relationship? Find out in this deliciously ordinary romance.

Return to Me by Erin O'Reilly Will Salvation bring just that to Ellie, allowing her to find peace and happiness again, or will it have her questioning all that she believes in? A wonderful romance cloaked within an intriguing mystery.

Arc Over Time by Jen Silver This wonderful romantic continuation with the characters from *Starting Over* ties up loose ends. But the question is—does everyone have a happy ending? A must read.

The Presence by Charlene Neal Can Rebecca and Kayleigh overcome ghosts from the past and their own insecurities, or will a presence from the past tear them apart?

A Walk Away by Lacey Schmidt Sometimes chance brings you to the right person to help you resolve some of your baggage, and you learn to like yourself a little more. Kat and Rand are smart enough to recognize this chance in each other, but they also find that there is a catch to every opportunity—walking toward something is always walking away from something else.

Possessing Morgan by Erica Lawson The investigation has barely begun when Andrea becomes the target of a nearly fatal hit-and-run. But was it really aimed at her? Can she and Morgan find the common ground they need to solve the case and stop the attacks, or are the gaps just too wide to bridge?

Twenty-three Miles by Renee MacKenzie This is a story about community, and how it comes together in dangerous and devastating times. When you don't know who to trust, you better have friends who will rally around you. Will Talia and Shay find the answers they need to the mystery of the murders on the parkway, or will justice be elusive? Will they survive their quest for the truth?

Reece's Star by TJ Vertigo Under Faith's guiding, loving hand, will Reece successfully traverse the rocky road of emotion and embrace the positive changes in her life? Or will she panic and be unable to control that Animal part of herself? Will she take that next step to declare herself fully capable of love and devotion? This third installment in the popular series that began with *Private Dancer* continues the passionate and often hilarious romance of Reece and Faith as they both grow in love and in trust.

Confined Spaces by Renee MacKenzie Corporate politics, complicated romance, and long distances conspire to keep Andie and Kara all boxed in. Can love triumph despite the Confined Spaces?

Twenty-three Miles by Renee MacKenzie Will Talia and Shay find the answers they need to the mystery of the murders on the parkway, or will justice be elusive? Will they survive their quest for the truth?

Cowgirl Up by Ali Spooner Ride along with the MC2, for boot scootin', butt kickin', dirt eatin', rodeo adventures, with a love story thrown into the mix.

If I Were a Boy by Erin O'Reilly Will Katie and Helen be able to make a life together work or succumb to doubts and the pressures of family? This story will fill you with the thrill of passion and the tenderness of love.

The Chronicles of Ratha: Book 2 A Lion Among the Lambs by Erica Lawson Can Jordana believe in herself like her Noorthi sisters do? Only then can she fulfill her destiny as The Chosen One. Follow the colorful cast of characters in this action-packed adventure sequel as they traverse the galaxy. Of course, nothing ever goes smoothly when Jordana is involved.

Terminal Event by Ali Spooner Will the killer be caught or continue to evade authorities? Can Tally and Blair's budding romance survive the possibility? Read this intense murder mystery romance and find out.

Love Forever, Live Forever by Annette Mori Fate intervenes and puts Nicky directly back into the path of her first love, Sara, and the corresponding events send her into a tailspin. Now she must decide—who will be the person she ends up living with and loving forever?

The One by JM Dragon *2015 GCLS Winner for Romance, Intrigue, and Adventure. The One* is a romance with everything, love, intrigue, misunderstandings with a happy conclusion—the only question—who gets the girl?

Reflected Passion by Erica Lawson Through a mirror, Françoise embraces life anew, while for Dale it is a powerful awakening, forcing her to discover not only her sensual nature, but the inner strength she possesses.

Flight by Renee Mackenzie Some lives will be lost and others changed forever when the sisters' lives intersect. Will they be consumed by the wreckage, or will they be able to pick themselves up and take flight?

E-Books, Print, Free e-books

Visit our website for more publications available online.

www.affinityebooks.com

Published by Affinity E-Book Press NZ LTD
Canterbury, New Zealand

Registered Company 2517228

www.ingramcontent.com/pod-product-compliance
Lightning Source LLC
Chambersburg PA
CBHW051244260626
47162CB00002B/596

* 9 7 8 0 9 0 8 3 5 1 1 2 1 *